MYSTERIES *of* MARTHA'S VINEYARD

MYSTERIES *of* MARTHA'S VINEYARD

Maiden
of the
Mist

NANCY MEHL

Guideposts
New York

Mysteries of Martha's Vineyard is a trademark of Guideposts.

Published by Guideposts Books & Inspirational Media
110 William Street
New York, NY 10038
Guideposts.org

Cover and interior design by Müllerhaus
Cover illustration by Greg Copeland, represented by Deborah Wolfe, LTD.
Typeset by Aptara, Inc.

Printed and bound in the United States of America
10 9 8 7 6 5 4 3 2

Maiden
of the
Mist

CHAPTER ONE

Priscilla Grant strolled down the wooden walkway with her cousins, Joan, Trudy, and Gail. Martha's Vineyard was bustling with locals and tourists in town for the annual Fall for the Arts Festival. Shops and galleries were full of creations from local artists. Paintings, crafts, needlework, carvings—there was something for everyone.

Priscilla was still trying to process the recent revelation that mild, practical, quiet Joan had been hiding a secret talent. Her interest in flowers and gardens was well-known to everyone, but her ability to transfer her passion to canvas was a surprise. When she finally admitted it and showed her work to her cousins and sister, they were all impressed with her still-life rendering of the flowers she loved. Trudy had insisted that Joan show her paintings during the festival. At first Joan had refused, but after some gentle but firm goading, she'd grudgingly agreed. A local store that sold artwork and crafts by local artists, the Art Attack, had accepted four of Joan's paintings to show.

After stopping for some coffee, the women had stepped out into a beautiful evening in Tisbury, Massachusetts. Although the air was a little chilly and a light wind whisked around them, a jacket was sufficient. Everyone seemed to be enjoying the festival. Priscilla loved quiet, comforting times spent in her cottage on Misty Harbor, but she also enjoyed the excitement and energy of the tourists who surrounded them. As winter approached, the number of visitors would decrease and the town would become peaceful again. But for now, businesses were doing well, and the enthusiasm was infectious.

She couldn't help but compare her life here to the one she'd lived less than a year ago in Wheatfield, Kansas. Although she'd loved their family farm, when her husband, Gary, died, the quiet wasn't comforting. It was stifling. After inheriting her aunt's cottage and lighthouse on the Vineyard, Priscilla had packed up and moved. Changing direction at age fifty-eight wasn't easy, but she was so grateful she'd taken the plunge. Although she missed Gary and the life they'd shared, she'd found a new one here. Different. Exciting. Wonderful.

When Priscilla and the others entered the Art Attack, they found it packed with people. It didn't take them long to find Joan's pictures, three of them all lined up together.

"I was told they were going to display all four paintings," Joan said under her breath.

Joan was a no-nonsense woman, logical and practical. Seeing her nervous about this recently discovered talent revealed a new side of her. Joan's brown eyes flicked around the shop as if trying to locate the missing painting.

"I wouldn't worry about it," Gail said. "Looks like they just ran out of space. Most artists only have one or two items on exhibit, Joan. You should be proud."

"Aren't they lovely?"

Aleeta Armbruster, the owner of the Art Attack, stood behind them, smiling at the paintings. Her lithe figure was covered by a clingy black dress accented with silver jewelry and a shiny silver ribbon braided through her long white hair. Priscilla suddenly felt dumpy in her black slacks and light blue sweater. Without thinking, she reached up and touched her hair, hoping the wind hadn't messed it up.

"We've had so many people ask about them, Joan," Aleeta said. "I think you could easily build a clientele if you wanted."

Joan blushed. "I . . . I don't know. It sounds like a lot of work. I don't think I want to do that."

"Up to you, dear, but they're really popular." Someone called Aleeta's name. "Excuse me," she said, rushing off to another part of the shop.

"They really are beautiful," Priscilla told Joan. Each painting portrayed a different kind of flower. One showed a bunch of wildflowers in a blue-and-white jar. The next one displayed purple irises lying on a white lace tablecloth. The third featured yellow roses in a clear vase with an orange-and-green butterfly perched on its edge.

"Which one isn't here?" Gail asked.

"The lilies of the valley," Joan answered.

"I think Gail is right," Trudy said. "Aleeta just ran out of space. She seems really busy right now, but maybe you could ask her about it later."

Priscilla was about to agree when someone bumped her from behind. She had to grab Joan's arm to keep from stumbling. She turned around to find a teenage boy with large brown eyes and shaggy dark hair staring at her.

"Sorry, lady," he said. His three friends snorted and shoved him as if they found his apology funny. He looked embarrassed, and the teens walked quickly away.

"Those boys are always causing trouble in town," Trudy said, her soft blonde curls bouncing as she shook her head. "They created a lot of mayhem last year on Halloween. The boy who ran into you is a sad case, though. I'll tell you about him later."

Priscilla nodded. Over Trudy's shoulder she noticed a woman and a man looking her way. They appeared to be talking about her. The woman was thin with dyed red hair, a sharp face, and black eyebrows that looked as if someone had drawn them on in the dark. The man was balding, portly, and had a florid face. Dressed nicely, he looked more like a businessman than a tourist or a local out to enjoy the festival.

Priscilla turned away. Were they really looking at her, or was she being paranoid? She tried to focus on the other artistic displays. A painting next to one of Joan's caught her eye immediately.

"Oh my," she said, grabbing Trudy's arm and pulling her over to look at it. "That's my lighthouse."

"You're right," Trudy said. "How cool!"

The painting was done in shades of blue, gray, and gold. It was night, and the lighthouse beacon cut through the black sky, highlighting the dark ocean with a bright, piercing beam.

"Look at that," Priscilla said, pointing to a single figure standing on the edge of the cliff outside her cottage. It was a woman in a glowing blue dress. Her head was turned away as she gazed at the sea. Long black hair flowed down her back. Priscilla stared at the title typed on a card below the painting. *The Weeping Woman.* She turned to Trudy. "Who is the Weeping Woman?"

"I've heard of her, but I can't remember the details." Trudy frowned. "Who's the artist?"

"Veela Tharmas Davirney," Priscilla read. "What an odd name." She opened her purse and took out a piece of paper then quickly wrote down the name.

Gail came over to them. "I need to get going. Work in the morning." Priscilla really liked the dentist Gail worked for as a hygienist and was happy to have found a good replacement for her dentist back in Kansas.

"Sure," Trudy said. "Come on, Priscilla."

Priscilla desperately wanted to ask Aleeta about the lighthouse painting, but she was deep in conversation with someone interested in buying a large seascape on the other side of the shop. Priscilla decided to come back tomorrow and see what she could find out. Who had painted her lighthouse, and who was this Weeping Woman?

She tried to put it out of her mind as they prepared to leave. She was almost to the door when someone stepped right in front of her. Priscilla had noticed the woman at church, but she couldn't remember her name. Priscilla smiled at her. "Hello, nice to see you."

The woman didn't respond, just scowled at her. "Is Captain O'Bannon here?" she asked, her voice nasally and unpleasant. She wasn't unattractive. Short, with a tight figure and nicely coiffed blonde hair piled on top of her head. Her makeup was a little over-done, making her look older than she probably was. She clutched a large red tote bag, which she kept in front of her as if it offered some kind of physical protection.

"I...I'm sorry. I have no idea," Priscilla said, confused by her question. "I haven't seen him."

The woman stared at Priscilla for a few seconds, making her feel decidedly uncomfortable. Finally, the strange woman turned on her heel and strode quickly away.

"What in the world was that about?" Priscilla whispered to Joan, who stood next to her.

"Let's get outside, and I'll tell you."

When they stepped outside onto the boardwalk, Joan pulled Priscilla aside. "That woman is Eleanor Gufstead."

"Oh, that's right. I've seen her at church, but I couldn't recall her name. I hope she didn't notice."

"Well, she certainly knows *your* name."

Trudy and Gail joined them.

"We should have told you about her before," Trudy said, "but we assumed she'd given up."

Priscilla frowned at her. "Given up on what?"

Gail rolled her eyes. "Gerald O'Bannon."

"I don't understand."

Joan sighed. "Eleanor has had her sights set on the captain for a while."

Priscilla's mouth dropped open. "What does that have to do with me? He's not interested in me. We're just friends."

Trudy shrugged. "I guess Eleanor thinks there's something going on between the two of you."

"Well, I can guarantee it's not true. For crying out loud." Priscilla took off walking toward their car. Of all the silly things. Why did this woman think she had an interest in Gerald O'Bannon? It was ridiculous. She was still grieving for Gary. The very idea...

"Hey," Joan said, catching up to Priscilla, "don't be upset. Eleanor's just a lonely woman. She lost her husband ten years ago, and she's been trying to find a replacement ever since. Don't be offended."

"I...I'm not offended. It's just—"

"I know. You still feel married to Gary. You'll probably feel that way for quite a while. Trust me, I understand. Allan has been gone a long time, but I still feel connected to him."

Priscilla turned to see all three women looking at her, compassion on each face. For some reason, it made tears wash into her eyes. "I'm sorry. Let's just forget it, okay? I need to get home, and so does Gail."

The women walked silently to the car and got inside. By the time Priscilla dropped everyone off and arrived home, it was dark. Her dog, Jake, was sitting by the door, ready to go out. Priscilla put a leash on him, and they walked around outside until he finished his business.

As Priscilla headed back to the house, Jake suddenly began to bark. Before she could stop him, he pulled the leash out of her hand and ran toward the cliff where a woman shrouded in mist and dressed in a glowing blue dress stood, looking out to the sea.

Just before he reached her, the woman stepped off the cliff and disappeared.

CHAPTER TWO

After securing a flashlight from the house and frantically searching the cliffs below, Priscilla finally concluded she'd imagined the entire thing. There was no one there—no broken body lying below. Although she didn't consider herself very susceptible to suggestion, there just wasn't any other possibility. The painting she'd seen had put an image in her mind, and somehow she'd transferred it to something she'd imagined on the cliff. The mist from the ocean had a way of creating shapes, just like clouds.

As for Jake, he loved to bark at seagulls. He'd probably spotted one she hadn't.

Although Priscilla knew she was trying hard to explain away what she'd seen, she didn't believe in ghosts, and there was no evidence that a human being had been on the cliff. What else could it be?

The next morning, Priscilla and Jake walked back to the place where she thought she'd seen the woman. Then they walked down the long, weather-beaten wooden stairs that led to the beach. Priscilla wasn't sure what she expected to see, but everything looked perfectly normal. Nothing out of place, and certainly no woman's body lying on the rocks below the cliff.

"You're losing it, Priscilla," she told herself.

Even though she'd chalked her late-night visitation up to her imagination, she still wanted to know more about that painting. Tonight she was supposed to meet her cousins at the Little House Café for Taco Night. Should she tell them what happened or keep it to herself? She wasn't sure.

She and Jake walked up the stairs and back to the house. Even though he had barked last night, he seemed perfectly calm today. Many times when he thought someone had been on the property, he would run around, sniffing at any new smells left behind. Today he didn't seem to detect anything out of the norm. Further proof the incident the night before was a vision fueled by the painting she'd seen.

Of course. Ghosts don't leave any scent behind.

"Oh no, Priscilla," she said out loud, chastising herself. "Stop that!" She pushed the ridiculous thought out of her mind. She didn't believe in ghosts. Never had. Never would. She decided not to mention her hallucination to her cousins. It was probably best just to let it go.

She and Jake had just entered the cottage when the phone rang. It was Trudy.

"Priscilla, would you mind getting to the café a little early tonight? I'd like to talk to you before Joan and Gail show up."

"Sure, I guess so. What time?"

"Meet me at five thirty. They're supposed to show up at six."

"I'm not in trouble, am I?"

Trudy laughed. "No, not even a little. I'd like your help with something, and I just need a few minutes to tell you about it."

"Okay. I'll see you then."

Priscilla hung up the phone, wondering what Trudy wanted. First, however, she planned to talk to Aleeta about the painting of the Weeping Woman. Who was she, and why was she depicted standing on Priscilla's property?

Priscilla dressed quickly, fed Jake, and was getting ready to leave when he joined her at the front door. She smiled down at the red-and-white dog, his big brown eyes wide with expectation. "I don't think you'd enjoy going," she told him. "You'd have to sit in the car for a while."

His only reaction was a big smile and a tail that thumped loudly at the prospect of accompanying her to town.

"Okay," she said, laughing. "I'd love the company."

She and Jake got into her SUV and headed for Tisbury. After grabbing a coffee and a cranberry muffin at Candy Lane Confectionery on Beach Road, she drove over to the Art Attack. Aleeta was just unlocking the door as Priscilla walked up onto the porch.

"Well, hello!" Aleeta said. "Back again?"

Priscilla nodded. "I wanted to ask you about a painting I saw here last night."

"Sure. Just point it out." She swung the door open.

Priscilla hurried over to where she'd noticed the picture the night before. But today all four of Joan's paintings were on the wall. *The Weeping Woman* was gone.

"It . . . it was right here," she told Aleeta. "Right next to three of Joan's paintings." She pointed at the depiction of the lilies of the valley. "This one wasn't here."

Aleeta shook her head slowly. "You're mistaken. I put up all four of your cousin's paintings." She waved her hand along the line of paintings and prints. "Everything is just as it was last night."

"But...but that's not true. Why are you saying that?" Priscilla felt a flash of frustration. Surely Aleeta knew better. She had been standing next to Priscilla when they looked at the paintings. Could she really have forgotten?

"I'm really sorry, Priscilla," Aleeta said. "You might be right. I'm not saying you're not. I'm just telling you that I hung all four. In fact, not long after you left, someone asked me about them. Was interested in buying two of the paintings. They were all there then, I'm sure of it." She frowned at Priscilla. "What painting did you see that's not here now?"

Priscilla sighed. She found it hard to believe Aleeta was telling the truth, but maybe with all the different displays, she really hadn't noticed that one painting had been removed. "It was done in blues and grays. A woman in blue, standing on a cliff, looking down at the ocean. Right next to my lighthouse. It was called—"

"*The Weeping Woman*," Aleeta said softly.

"Yes, that's it. So you know the painting."

Aleeta shook her head. "No, dear. I've never seen a painting of the Weeping Woman, but I've heard of her. When we were kids, we used to tell ghost stories about her. Supposedly her husband didn't come back from the sea, so she threw herself off the cliff near your lighthouse." Aleeta shrugged. "That's all I know. I'm sure the details of those stories were far from the truth. If you want to know what really happened, perhaps you should talk to Mildred at the museum. Maybe she can fill you in."

"Okay," Priscilla said slowly. There didn't seem to be a reason to argue with the shop owner. She really didn't seem to know anything about the painting. "If the painting resurfaces, will you please contact me?"

Aleeta nodded. "I will, but I doubt it will show up." She stared at the wall for a moment. "You know what? Maybe it was a mistake. You know, someone who thought their work was supposed to be hung for the festival. Perhaps they realized they were wrong and removed it."

Although her reasoning sounded a little contrived, Priscilla shrugged. "You might be right. Well, I'd better get going. Thanks again for your help."

She hurried out of the store. Wait till the girls heard about this tonight! Was Aleeta telling the truth? Priscilla couldn't be sure. She appeared to be someone with an eye for detail. How could she have possibly missed seeing that painting?

CHAPTER THREE

Priscilla got back in her car. Thankfully, it was cool outside, so Jake was perfectly comfortable waiting. He loved to look out the window at the people who walked by. "Gotta stop by the museum," she told him. "Might be in there for a little while. If you're good, I'll take you out, and we can walk a bit."

Jake's big doggy grin made it seem as if he understood. Priscilla reached over and rubbed his head. "You're a great dog, you know that? I don't know what I'd do without you."

He licked her hand, and she took it to mean the feeling was reciprocated. Priscilla smiled at him. Before driving over to the museum, she made another quick stop and then continued to the East Shore Historical Museum. When she entered, she found the curator, Mildred Pearson, standing behind the front counter, preparing the book used to collect signatures of visitors. She was dressed in what looked like authentic Native American garb.

"Indians?" Priscilla asked as she approached the counter.

Mildred nodded. "I'm dressed as the wife of Hiacoomes, the convert of Thomas Mayhew Jr., the first missionary to Martha's Vineyard. It's quite a story. In the 1600s, Hiacoomes and his family were spared from a terrible fever that spread throughout the island and took many lives. Hiacoomes believed they were spared because they'd been attending church. Mr. Mayhew preached a sermon from Psalm Ninety-One: 'There shall no evil befall thee, neither shall any plague come nigh thy dwelling. For he shall give his angels charge over thee, to keep thee in all thy ways.' Hiacoomes believed Mayhew's God was real and followed him the rest of his life."

"What a great story," Priscilla said, smiling. "Thank you, Mildred. This is the first time I've heard it."

Mildred smiled, obviously pleased that her efforts meant something. She was passionate about the museum and loved bringing history to life for its visitors. Priscilla liked the friendly caretaker. She was very honest and forthright, qualities Priscilla admired.

"Is there something in particular I can do for you today?" Mildred asked. "I have a school group coming in around eleven."

"That's okay. My dog is in the car, so I can't stay long."

Mildred smiled. "I used to have a cat. Martha. I know, not very original. She passed away a couple of years ago. I certainly miss her."

"Maybe you should get another cat."

Mildred didn't say anything, and Priscilla recognized the look in her eyes. The pain of losing a beloved pet. It wasn't easy to get over.

"So what can I do to help you?"

"I have a question. Have you ever heard of the Weeping Woman?"

Mildred's eyebrows arched. "The Weeping Woman? Where did you hear about her?"

"It's a long story," Priscilla said, hoping she wouldn't have to reveal too much. Mildred didn't seem like the type who would appreciate a ghost story. She spent her time in the research and reality of history. Stories about otherworldly entities would probably offend her. Instead of explaining right away, Priscilla held out the bag of crème horns she'd bought at Candy Lane Confectionery during her second stop there this morning. She knew crème horns were Mildred's favorite pastry. "I hope you haven't had breakfast already."

Mildred's expression changed from curiosity to joy. She grinned at Priscilla. "This must be really important if you're willing to ply me with crème horns." Priscilla started to protest, but Mildred laughed and waved her protestations away. "I am more than happy to share my knowledge of the Weeping Woman with you." She pointed at a nearby table with two chairs. "Let's sit, and I'll tell you what I know. How about a cup of coffee?"

Priscilla accepted gladly. Once Mildred had retrieved two cups of coffee from the museum kitchen, she went off to find a book. Then she sat down at the table with Priscilla, who was grateful when Mildred offered her one of the crème horns. Everything from Candy Lane Confectionery was delicious. Candy Lane, the owner of the bakery, was a master baker.

Mildred ate a crème horn and then cleaned her hands with a wipe before touching the book she'd brought to the table. She was very careful with museum property. "We have a good number of diaries and historical accounts written by past residents. This particular book was put together by a woman who considered herself a historian. Her efforts have given us incredible accounts about the early days in the Vineyard. I remember some mentions of the Weeping Woman."

She pulled the cover open and carefully flipped through the pages until she reached the spot she was looking for.

"Here it is," she said, pointing to a particular section of the book. "Here she talks about Jeremiah Hennesey. He was the captain of a fishing boat called the *Lady Olivia*. He took his ship out in October of 1854 and never came back. The boat was never found, and his body was never recovered. According to the writer, his wife, Olivia, stood on the edge of the cliff near your lighthouse every night for over two weeks, crying, praying, and waiting for her husband to come home. Friends tried to convince her to give up, to accept what was clear to most of them: Jeremiah had been lost at sea. Finally, in despair, she flung herself over the edge of the cliff. Just like her husband, her body was never discovered." Mildred looked up at Priscilla. "It must have washed out to sea. Thus the story of the Weeping Woman became a local legend. Residents and visitors alike have claimed they've seen her standing on that cliff in the moonlight, but the mist from the water can make even the most practical among us see ghosts." She gently pushed the book toward Priscilla. "There's actually a picture of the Henneseys."

Priscilla leaned over to stare at the couple. The picture was old and obviously not as sharp and clear as photos in more modern days, but the images were good enough. It looked as if it had been torn from a newspaper and pasted into the book to correspond to the account about the couple. Olivia was a beautiful woman with long black hair braided, looped, and pulled back behind her head. She had large dark eyes and full, bow-shaped lips. Likewise,

Captain Hennesey was extremely attractive. Although the pictures were black-and-white, his hair looked blond, as were his mustache and beard. His eyes were light, maybe blue, and they sparkled with personality. He wore a dark suit that set off his light coloring. Priscilla imagined he was quite a catch back then.

She looked up at Mildred. "I know this sounds absurd, but is there anything there that refers to Olivia wearing blue?"

Mildred flipped through the book's pages. "Here's another entry that mentions she wore blue every day after Jeremiah disappeared because it was his favorite color." She turned back to the original page and pointed at the picture of Captain Hennesey. "The previous account mentions a ring he always wore. A blue sapphire."

Priscilla peered closely at the picture. "It looks huge. Must have been very valuable."

Mildred shrugged. "I'm not an expert on gemstones, but I suspect you're right." She sighed deeply. "The only valuable piece of jewelry we ever had in the museum was a ruby-encrusted gold cross brought to the Vineyard by some of our first settlers. It was displayed in a local church for many years until they moved and acquired a new building. Because of the cross's history, the church kindly donated it to the museum."

"You said you *had* it. It's not here anymore?"

Mildred shook her head. "No. Believe it or not, it was stolen almost four years ago. One of the worst days of my life." She looked at Priscilla, confusion in her eyes. "How could someone steal from a museum? We try to document our history here. That should matter to everyone."

Although Priscilla wouldn't risk saying it, she knew that not everyone shared Mildred's vision for embracing and protecting the past.

"I'm sorry, Mildred. Maybe someday it will come back."

"I doubt it. The police said the rubies were probably removed after it was taken and the gold melted down. What a terrible thing to do to such a wonderful icon." She cleared her throat, obviously still bothered by the theft. "Back to your Weeping Woman wearing blue. Some people refer to her as the Woman in Blue." Mildred stared at Priscilla for a moment before saying, "May I ask why you're interested in Olivia Hennesey?"

"It's...it's nothing. I saw a painting of Olivia standing at the edge of the cliff on my property. I wanted to know more about her. Nothing more."

"I see. Is there anything else I can do for you?"

"No, thank you, Mildred. As always, you've been a big help. I truly appreciate it."

"You're more than welcome. Let me know if you have any more questions." She grinned at Priscilla. "You won't even have to buy me crème horns."

Priscilla laughed. "I'll keep that in mind. Goodbye."

She left the museum with more questions than she'd come with. Now she knew the Weeping Woman was a real person. Could the incident at the cliff have been real? Was someone trying to make her think she was being haunted by the ghostly wife of a long-dead fisherman?

CHAPTER FOUR

Priscilla got to the Little House Café a few minutes before five thirty. After walking Jake around town for a while, she'd taken him home and changed clothes. The small dog was happy and worn out, and he'd immediately settled down on his bed and fallen asleep. He probably wouldn't even notice she'd gone.

Priscilla was looking forward to spending time with her cousins. The Little House was a favorite eating spot for those living on Martha's Vineyard. Its warm, relaxing atmosphere added to its appeal. Gold hobnail candleholders held flickering lights as they adorned the dark wood tables. The walls were tastefully decorated with art that fit the casual yet classy dining room.

Taco Night at the Little House was really popular, and she was grateful she'd found an empty table. Their delicious tacos were nothing like the fast-food tacos she'd been used to in Kansas. They had many other great dishes too. Priscilla loved their fried egg sandwich for breakfast and their red Thai curry chicken kebabs for dinner, and their specialty coffees were incredible. Her favorite dish of all was their muffuletta pressed sandwich. Her mouth watered just thinking about it. But tonight… tacos. Although she hadn't been that hungry when she arrived, thinking about all that good food and being surrounded by the incredible aromas wafting from the kitchen made her stomach growl.

The waitress had just brought the iced latte she'd ordered when Trudy came through the front door. Priscilla waved until her cousin spotted her. As she hurried over, Priscilla smiled. Trudy was usually upbeat and almost always in a hurry wherever she went and whatever she did. It was just her personality. Priscilla was much slower, much more circumspect, but she admired Trudy's enthusiasm for life.

"Thanks for meeting me," Trudy said when she sat down. She waved at the waitress and pointed at Priscilla's latte, indicating she wanted the same thing.

"Sure. What did you want to talk to me about?"

"It's only five more days until Halloween, you know."

"Yes?"

"Well, last year we had some problems. Mischief on the island. Remember the boy who ran into you at the Art Attack? The one I said I'd tell you about later?"

"Yes."

"His friends caused quite a bit of trouble. They TPed some houses, including Mildred Pearson's. Supposedly they were angry because she gave out boxes of raisins instead of candy."

Although Priscilla didn't say anything, she almost didn't blame them. She didn't like raisins herself. Of course, a distaste for wrinkled grapes wasn't an excuse for throwing toilet paper all over someone's yard. A really annoying gesture, as far as Priscilla was concerned.

"I don't think teenagers should be trick-or-treating anyway."

"I don't either," Trudy agreed. "But these boys don't care what anyone thinks. The boy who bumped you is Tony Gonzalez. He's living with his aunt and uncle. His parents were killed in a terrible accident in Colorado, where he's from."

"Oh, how awful," Priscilla said. "Poor thing."

"He's a good kid," Trudy said, "but he's fallen in with this bad crowd. I'm afraid we're in for it again this Halloween, and I hate that they may drag Tony into it." She sighed. "Some parents are worried and don't plan to let their kids go out at all this year."

"Oh my. That hardly seems fair."

"Exactly my thought." Trudy leaned forward in her chair. "We've been talking about an alternative party at the church. I mean, kids can certainly go trick-or-treating if they want to, but they can also come by the church for candy and games. I know a lot of parents on the island might prefer another choice so they don't have to deal with some of the antics of the past."

Trudy attended Grace Community Church in Tisbury, a great church that did a lot for the community. As Priscilla considered Trudy's idea, the waitress came over with Trudy's latte.

"Are you ladies ready to order?" she asked.

"Thanks, but we're expecting a couple of other people," Trudy said. "We'll order when they arrive."

The waitress smiled. "I'll watch for them and come back later."

Priscilla and Trudy thanked her. "They're so nice here," Priscilla said when the waitress walked away.

"Yes, they are. I love this place." Trudy took a sip of her latte. "Now, what do you think about my idea?"

"We used to do something like that at my church in Wheatfield. We called it Hallelujah Night."

"Oh, that's a cute title!"

"We had a lot of fun. Set up different booths for games. Each booth had candy, plus we had snacks. The ladies in the church made cookies, cupcakes…" Priscilla laughed. "It was a great success, but we certainly had those poor kids hyped up on sugar. I'm not sure how much the parents appreciated it."

Trudy grinned. "It's Halloween. I think it's expected." She leaned her cheek on her hand. "Will you help me put something together for our church?"

Priscilla stared at her cousin for a moment, thinking. She really wasn't doing anything else right now. Why not? It might be fun. She smiled. "Okay. I think I'd like that."

"Great! Can you meet me at the church in the morning? We have quite a few volunteers. We just need someone like you to tell us what to do."

"Oh, Trudy. You don't have any plans in place yet?"

"No. I mean, yes. I mean…" She took a deep breath and let it out slowly. "Let me start again. First we wanted to make sure we had enough help to pull this thing off. We have that. And we've floated some ideas, but we just need someone with past experience." She grinned at Priscilla. "We need you!"

"How many volunteers do you have?"

Trudy looked up at the ceiling and mumbled quietly to herself while flicking her fingers. Finally, she met Priscilla's eyes. "At least twenty."

Priscilla nodded, relieved. "Twenty people should be able to pull this off just fine. And people in the church who won't be working the night of the event can donate baked items and candy."

"I'm sure that won't be a problem."

"Then I think we're on our way to a Hallelujah Night."

Trudy laughed. "Good." She held up her latte, and Priscilla, who caught her meaning, clicked her cup to Trudy's. "This will be great. We need to get Candy Lane involved. If she would donate some cupcakes and cookies..."

"That would be awesome," Priscilla finished.

She happened to look up and saw Joan and Gail coming in the front door. She pointed them out to Trudy, who flagged them down. A few minutes later, the women were seated, and the waitress returned to take their orders. Within fifteen minutes, they'd all been served.

"I just love Taco Night at the Little House!" Trudy said, taking a bite of her roasted butternut squash taco. Her blue eyes sparkled with enthusiasm.

"Me too," Priscilla said. She'd chosen the honey-lime glazed chicken taco with roasted corn salsa, avocado cream, pickled jalapeños, and queso blanco. It was absolutely delicious.

Joan and Gail had ordered the crispy fish tacos, which were amazing as well.

"Maybe tonight we could get dessert," Joan said. "If you have time that is, Gail."

"I have plenty of time," Gail replied. "Sara is watching Dad, so I don't have to rush home. He and Sara have plans to eat hummingbird cake and play a rousing game of chess. I don't really enjoy the game, so letting Sara fill that need is a real blessing."

Gail took care of her father, Hugh, who couldn't live alone any longer. He didn't need constant care, but Gail didn't like leaving him by himself too long. Her daughter, Sara, who ran a bookstore in Edgartown, was close to her grandfather. Priscilla was glad to see Gail get a night off for herself.

"Aleeta called me today," Joan said. "It seems someone is really interested in buying a couple of my paintings. The one with the wildflowers and the one of the purple irises."

"Well, I'm not surprised," Gail said. "They are really good. Are you going to build up your inventory?"

"I . . . I don't think so. I mean, I painted them because I . . . well, I just wanted to. I don't think I want to make a business of it. Painting is just something I do for fun."

"There's nothing wrong with that, Joan," Priscilla said then smiled at her cousin. "But if you do any more painting, I would love to have something for the cottage. Your work is so lovely. The colors, the detail."

Joan blushed. "Thank you, Priscilla. That means a lot to me."

"Not sure why you felt you had to hide this from us," Trudy said, frowning at her sister. "Why didn't you trust us?"

"It wasn't that I didn't trust you." Joan stared down at her plate for a moment. "I ... I guess I just wasn't sure they were any good. I was embarrassed."

"But you felt confident enough to show them to Aleeta?" Gail asked. "I don't understand."

Joan nervously cleared her throat. "I guess I was afraid you'd tell me you liked them ... to be kind. But I knew Aleeta would tell me the truth."

Priscilla nodded. "I totally understand that. Several years ago I wrote a poem for our church newsletter back home, but I didn't show it to Gary or Rachel first. The editor of our newsletter was kind of a literary snob. When she told me she liked the poem and was going to publish it, I felt much more confident. I knew my family would tell me they loved it because they wouldn't want to hurt my feelings. But this editor was honest. I've never regretted that decision." She smiled at Joan. "And you shouldn't either."

Joan wrinkled her nose and grinned at Priscilla. "I don't. But thanks for sharing that story. It really helps."

"Good. I'm glad. By the way, I went by the Art Attack before coming here. Your fourth painting is on the wall now, next to your other paintings."

Joan put her taco down. "Really? That's odd. What happened to the other picture? The one of the Weeping Woman?"

Priscilla sighed. "Here's the weird thing. Aleeta says she doesn't remember anything about it. Says she never noticed it. That all four of your paintings were hung at the same time and, as far as she knows, were there all night."

"I don't understand," Trudy said. "We all saw it. And Aleeta was right there with us." She shook her head. "That doesn't make sense."

Priscilla stared at her cousins for several seconds and prayed she was doing the right thing. "Look, there's something I have to tell you. Please don't think I'm crazy."

"We would never think you're crazy," Gail said forcefully. "Why would you worry about something like that?"

"Well, let's see what you say after I tell you that last night... after I got home..." She stopped and cleared her throat.

Trudy put her hand over Priscilla's. "There's nothing you can't share with us, you know."

"Okay." Priscilla took a deep breath and started again. This time her words came out in a tumbled rush. "Last night I saw the Weeping Woman standing on the cliff outside my house... right before she jumped off the edge and disappeared!"

CHAPTER FIVE

The silence after Priscilla's declaration was deafening. She immediately regretted her decision to share what she'd seen with her cousins.

A long-ago family feud had kept them out of Priscilla's life until she moved to Martha's Vineyard. Now they really felt like family. Each cousin was different. Trudy was the most extroverted, Joan was the most introverted, and Gail was the most pragmatic. But somehow they seemed to bring out the best in each other. Priscilla had grown to love and appreciate them. Had she just ruined relationships that she'd grown to treasure?

Gail looked at Priscilla through narrowed eyes, as if trying to decide if she were mentally imbalanced.

"Look," Priscilla said, "I know how insane this sounds. Believe me, I do. But I know what I saw."

"Please don't be offended by this question," Trudy said, "but did you have anything…I mean, maybe a little nip before bed? Something to help you sleep?"

Priscilla's mouth dropped open. "Of course not. I don't drink." She shook her head. "I shouldn't have said anything. Please, just forget it."

"We're not going to forget it," Trudy said. "And of course we believe you." She leaned back in her chair and studied Priscilla.

"Can you describe everything you saw?" she asked finally. "We need to hear the whole story."

"All right. As long as you promise not to have me committed."

"I'm not promising anything," Gail said, "but I want to hear the details too."

Priscilla looked at her with alarm, but she could see the twinkle in Gail's eye, and it relaxed her some.

She slowly began to describe everything she'd seen.

"And Jake barked at . . . her?" Joan asked. "Even chased after her?"

"Yes. But this morning when we walked down to the beach, he didn't seem to pick up any scent. Wasn't the least bit interested. He loves to bark at seagulls. It's possible he saw one last night, although I didn't. You know how it gets out there sometimes. The mist from the ocean makes it hard to see."

Trudy nodded. "But if there weren't any gulls on the cliff last night, it means someone really was out there, Priscilla. Jake wouldn't chase after your hallucination."

"I realize that. It certainly occurred to me, but . . . Well, I've been telling myself that I imagined it. You know, because of the painting."

"I don't believe you're someone who could be so easily manipulated," Joan said. "And of course we know you well enough to know you'd never make up something like this."

"And if you weren't drinking . . . ," Trudy said.

"Oh, for crying out loud," Joan said, "will you stop calling Priscilla a drunk?"

"I'm not," Trudy protested. "I'm just trying to say that I believe she actually saw something."

Priscilla leaned forward so she wouldn't be overheard by other diners. "I went by the museum this morning and talked to Mildred. She told me the real story of the Weeping Woman."

"Tell us," Trudy said breathlessly. It was easy to see the interest in her expression.

"Okay." Priscilla paused for a moment, trying to remember everything she'd learned. "In October of 1854, Jeremiah Hennesey, the captain of a fishing vessel, took off on a fishing trip. He never came back, and his wife, Olivia, watched for him for a couple of weeks, standing on the cliff near my lighthouse, crying. When he didn't return, she became despondent and finally threw herself into the ocean. Her body was never found, and her husband was never seen again. Neither was the ship ever found. Or any wreckage. It's quite a mystery."

Gail frowned at her. "If her body was never found, how does anyone know she jumped off the cliff?"

Priscilla shrugged. "That's a great question. I have no idea. I'm just telling you what Mildred showed me in a journal written by a local woman who lived during that time."

"Maybe someone saw her jump," Gail said.

"It's possible."

"So do you think you saw a ghost?" Joan asked.

"No, of course not," Priscilla said. "I don't believe in ghosts." Her gaze swept over the other women. "You don't believe in them, do you?"

All three of them shook their heads, but only Gail said, "Of course not." She pointed a finger at Priscilla. "If you didn't see a ghost, then you saw a person trying to make you think they were a ghost. The question is . . . why?"

"I also wonder how they knew about the painting I'd just seen." Priscilla watched as each of the women realized how odd the coincidence was.

"That's a little too convenient, isn't it?" Trudy asked, her forehead wrinkled in thought.

"Good point," Joan said. "First the painting, then the event at the lighthouse. Then today the painting goes missing." She shook her head. "I think someone's playing games with you, Priscilla."

"I agree. But why?"

Trudy leaned over and patted Priscilla's shoulder. "I have no idea, but we'll help you find out. Whoever it is must have been at the showing last night. They probably hung the painting and stayed around to make sure you saw it."

"They must be trying to frighten me," Priscilla said.

"It's the only thing that makes sense," Gail said. She shook her head. "If we figure out who did it, we'll be able to find out why."

Priscilla sighed. "I don't remember everyone who was at the Art Attack last night. There were so many people."

Joan pulled a notebook out of her purse. "Let's think about it, ladies. Surely we can recall most of the people who were there."

"How do we know it was someone who was there?" Trudy asked. "Couldn't they have put up the painting and left? Maybe they came back later."

"But Aleeta might have noticed that, wouldn't she?" Priscilla asked. "Wouldn't they have to make the switch rather quickly to avoid detection?"

"Unless she's in on it," Gail said.

"How did she act when you talked to her?" Joan asked. "Did she seem guilty? Act suspiciously?"

"No, not at all. Actually, she was very nice about it." Priscilla shrugged. "She just thought I was wrong. I certainly didn't tell her about seeing a ghost."

Joan took a deep breath and let it out quickly. "Good. I don't want her to think my cousin is . . . you know, in case I want to show something there again sometime." Her eyes widened, and she looked at Priscilla. "I—I'm sorry."

Priscilla arched an eyebrow. "You don't want her to think your cousin is crazy? Is that what you were going to say?"

"No. Well, yes. But I know you're not." Joan sighed. "I'm sorry."

"You did the right thing telling us," Trudy said gently. "Now, let's get back to last night. Was there anyone you noticed at the Art Attack who made you feel . . . uncomfortable?"

Priscilla thought for a moment. "Actually, there was. A couple kept staring at me. The woman was skinny and had rather bright red hair and weird, black, pencil-drawn eyebrows."

"That's Sylvia Peabody," Gail said. "She works for Elmer McBroom, a local insurance agent who covers most of Tisbury. I can't imagine she'd do anything to scare you. I mean, why? She's lived here all her life and doesn't even know you."

"What did the man she was with look like?" Trudy asked.

Priscilla thought for a moment. "He was overweight. Bald. Older. Red face. He was really overdressed. A nice suit and a tie. He looked professional. Not like most tourists who might be visiting the island."

Gail frowned. "Not that there aren't a lot of old, chubby, balding men on Martha's Vineyard, but he doesn't sound familiar."

"Now that you mention it, I did see that guy," Joan said. "At first I thought he was staring at my paintings, but as I watched him, I came to the same conclusion you did, Priscilla. He was watching us. Or you." She shook her head. "I'd never seen him before. Maybe we can ask Sylvia about him." She wrote something in her notebook. "Okay, the first thing we do is check with Sylvia and find out who that man is. What's next?"

"What about that boy who ran into me?" Priscilla asked. "Tony . . . what was his last name again?"

"Gonzalez," Trudy said slowly. "I don't think he'd do anything like this. As I said, basically he's a good kid."

"Oh, Trudy," Gail said, "why do you defend him? He and his friends could be behind it. I'll bet it's some kind of Halloween prank."

Joan snorted. "Seriously, Gail? A Halloween prank? Maybe they could pull off whatever it was Priscilla saw on the cliff, but do you really think any of them could have painted the Weeping Woman? I mean, it was very well executed. These are teenagers."

Gail rolled her eyes. "Teenagers can paint. And besides, maybe they just found the painting on the Internet. Who says they had to paint it?"

Priscilla took a drink of her coffee. The last thing she wanted was to cause division among her cousins. She was beginning to regret bringing up the incident near her lighthouse.

CHAPTER SIX

A ll right, you two," Trudy said sharply. "Keep it civil. We're not going to fight over this. Priscilla came to us for help."

"Sorry, Priscilla," Joan said softly. "I've been a little tense ever since my paintings were hung in public. I'm not used to putting myself out like that."

"You have nothing to worry about," Gail said, taking Joan's hand. "Your paintings are absolutely wonderful. We're all very proud of you."

The corners of Joan's mouth twitched. "Thank you. That means a lot."

Gail released Joan's hand and leaned back in her chair. "So what do we have so far?" she asked.

Joan looked down at her notebook. "I've got Sylvia Peabody—and a note that we need to ask her the identity of the man she was talking to last night. And I have Tony Gonzalez and his friends." She began to write. "Those boys he was with. I noticed Teddy Martin. Who were the other ones?"

"Jason Atwater and Monty Anderson," Trudy said. "Jason and his parents moved here about six months ago. They run that new jewelry store downtown."

Gail quirked an eyebrow. "Didn't they go to Wesley Chapel for a while?"

Trudy nodded. "I think so. I'm not sure their business is going well. We should pray for them."

"We're getting off track," Joan said. "What about Monty?"

"He's the real troublemaker of the bunch," Trudy said. "His father is president of the Island Bank and Trust. A real snob. Monty is a chip off the old block. Rude and disrespectful."

"Trudy, that's not nice," Gail said sharply.

"It might not be nice, but it's true," Joan said. "I'm sure Monty is the leader of that unholy alliance."

Priscilla couldn't help but smile at Joan's description.

"Who else was there last night who might have had something to do with that painting?" Gail asked.

"I don't think we can forget about Aleeta," Priscilla offered.

Joan scribbled in her notebook. "We should have thought of her first." She looked up. "She's always been a rather odd duck." Her eyes widened. "She paints. I just remembered. Some of her work was up in the shop."

"That might move her to the top of our list," Gail said.

"She is the most likely," Trudy said. "I mean, she could have easily moved the paintings and lied about it."

"But why?" Priscilla said, trying to keep the frustration out of her voice. Her cousins were trying to help, but frankly she was starting to feel a little confused. Why would anyone want to scare her? It didn't make sense.

"I don't know," Trudy said slowly. "There's no reason for it."

Gail snapped her fingers. "What if she's trying to stir something up about the Weeping Woman because she thinks it will make that painting more valuable?"

"You mean the painting that she says she knows nothing about?" Joan said. "The painting that has disappeared?"

"Yeah, you're right. But if it shows up again..."

"Gail's right," Trudy said. "We need to watch out for it."

"I don't know. That's pretty weak." Priscilla didn't want to discount any of the cousins' theories, but so far she couldn't find a solid motive behind the ghostly appearance the night before.

"Oh, for crying out loud," Trudy said suddenly. "We're forgetting the most obvious person."

Everyone looked at her. Priscilla had no idea what she was talking about.

"It's Eleanor Gufstead. Has to be."

Priscilla had totally forgotten about her confrontation with the rude woman. "But why would she go to all this trouble?"

"Because she wants you to leave town," Trudy said. "That's got to be it."

"Really? I mean, I'm not dating Gerald. I'm not dating anyone. Eleanor would have to be nuts to do something like this to someone who's not any kind of a threat to her."

"Well, unfortunately, Eleanor might actually qualify for the 'nuts' category," Gail said.

"So you think it's Eleanor." Priscilla turned this over in her mind. "Do you think she's the Weeping Woman?" She shook her head slowly. "She's really going overboard, isn't she? Seems ... weird. Out of balance."

"She's probably not done," Gail said. "You better prepare yourself for more *visits* from your blue, glowing friend."

"Good thing I don't have any more tours planned this month," Priscilla said. "I'm not sure having a ghost show up sets the tone I'm hoping for."

"Teresa doesn't have a tour planned for this Saturday?" Gail asked.

"No. Her mother lives in Nebraska, and she fell and broke her hip. She's fine and Teresa's brother is taking care of her, but Teresa wants to see her. Besides, with the art festival this weekend, she feels most people will be busy with that anyway."

Teresa Claybrook ran a tour company on the island. Every Saturday afternoon she brought a group to Misty Harbor to see Priscilla's lighthouse. Although she hadn't been sure about the experience in the beginning, now Priscilla enjoyed having the bus stop by. The tourists only stayed for twenty minutes, and they were so appreciative of the lighthouse and its history. It had turned out to be a fun event for them—and for Priscilla.

Gail frowned. "Do you think the Weeping Woman will visit tonight?"

Priscilla looked at her in horror. "I certainly hope not."

"Wait a minute," Trudy said. "I don't think she is, but if Sylvia is your ghost, all we need to do is let her know we're on to her. Then she'll knock it off."

Priscilla nodded. "That makes sense. But how would we do that?"

Trudy frowned at Joan. "Didn't you say you needed to make an insurance payment?"

"Yes, but I do that online."

Trudy giggled. "How about paying in person tomorrow? We could, I don't know, drop a little hint?"

"Oh, Trudy. I don't know..."

"If you could do something to make her stop, I'd appreciate it," Priscilla said. "It really is disconcerting." Actually, it was more than disconcerting. It was downright disturbing. The idea that anyone would go to such extremes frightened Priscilla. She'd grown stronger since coming to Martha's Vineyard, but knowing Gary wasn't beside her still made her feel vulnerable. And this *ghost* situation wasn't helping.

Joan sighed. "Okay." She pointed at Trudy. "But you're coming with me. You can deliver the warning, or whatever it is you intend to do. I'm just going to pay my insurance premium."

Trudy laughed. "Fine. I'll pretend to be the bad cousin, and you can be the good cousin."

Priscilla had to bite her lip when she heard Joan mumble, "What do you mean, pretend?" under her breath. Thankfully, Trudy didn't hear her.

"Priscilla, is there any way to do more research on Olivia Hennesey? I'm intrigued by the fact that her husband and his ship completely disappeared, and Olivia's body was never found." Trudy shook her head. "It certainly seems suspicious. I mean, I guess her body could have washed out to sea, but that's quite a coincidence."

"I've been thinking the same thing," Priscilla said, "and I intend to see what I can find out. Of course, I doubt I can discover much after all these years, but it really is an intriguing mystery."

Trudy snapped her fingers. "Oh, I'm so dense. I know who we should talk to. Ed and Myrna Holtman. They run the West Tisbury Ghost Tours."

"Oh, heavens no," Joan said. "They're weird."

"Because they believe in ghosts?" Trudy shook her head. "A lot of people do, Joan."

"Well, *we* don't," Gail snapped.

Trudy sighed deeply. "I'm not advocating a séance. I'm saying they should know more about Olivia Hennesey than anyone else on the island."

"I don't know," Gail said slowly. "I'm not sure their stories are based on fact."

Trudy rolled her eyes. "I really think you should talk to them, Priscilla."

"Where would I find them?" Priscilla wasn't sure she wanted to sit down and talk to people who ran ghost tours, but if they could tell her more about the Weeping Woman, it might be worth it. She was starting to feel a connection to Olivia. After all, she'd ended her life on the edge of Priscilla's cliff—under the gaze of her lighthouse.

"Are you ladies ready to go yet?" Joan asked.

Priscilla quickly finished her taco. "I'm ready," she said as soon as she swallowed her last bite.

The other women nodded their agreement, and Trudy waved at their waitress so they could get their bill. She brought it over, and Trudy grabbed her purse and whipped out her wallet.

"My treat," she said. "We're celebrating the emergence of a great new American artist, Joan Abernathy."

"Oh my goodness, Trudy," Joan sputtered. "I'm hardly a *great* artist. A few pictures of flowers aren't going to shake up the art world."

"We all think they're lovely," Gail said.

"And that's all the recognition I need." Joan smiled. "I'm sorry for acting so squirrelly last night. I really do appreciate your encouragement."

"Good," Priscilla said. "Just remember that we're all being honest. You're very talented."

Gail nodded. "I agree."

"Did you want to go by the Art Attack again this evening?" Trudy asked.

Joan shook her head. "One time was more than enough for me. I'm satisfied. When the festival is over, I'll go back to pick up any of my paintings that haven't sold, but I don't want to see them displayed in public again. Too nerve-racking."

Gail nodded. "Okay. I have another suggestion."

"What's that?" Trudy asked.

"Trudy, you and Joan need to spend the night at Priscilla's. I can't because of Pop. But I think Dan would be fine with it, Trudy. I know you have work in the morning, Joan, but you could figure it out." She waggled her finger at them. "You need to watch for the Weeping Woman."

Joan's face turned pale. "I—I don't know."

"Why not?" Gail demanded. "Why can't you just drive to work from Priscilla's in the morning?"

"Actually, I'm off tomorrow." As soon as the words left her mouth, Joan's eyes widened, and she clamped her lips together. Priscilla got the distinct impression she was sorry she'd shared that information.

"You don't need to come over," Priscilla said. "I'm fine. Really. Besides, I have Jake. No ghost is safe around him."

Although she meant her comment to sound as if she were completely confident, she hadn't managed to keep her voice from trembling a little.

"That's it. We're coming," Trudy said. She took her phone from her purse. Within seconds she was calling her husband. After telling him her plans, she hung up. "He says it's fine. There's some important football game on tonight." She snorted. "He probably won't even notice I'm gone." She took some cash from her purse and slid it into the check folder on the table. "Let's get going."

As the women followed her out, Priscilla wondered what each one was thinking. Trudy was ecstatic. Gail seemed worried. Joan looked scared to death. What in the world was she getting herself and her cousins into?

CHAPTER SEVEN

When Priscilla pulled up in front of her cottage, she was already feeling better about having Joan and Trudy stay over. They'd stopped by their houses on the way so the women could each pack a bag.

Even though Priscilla didn't fear ghosts, wondering if the woman on the cliff would show up again tonight made her nervous. At least having company would take her mind off of ghosts and women who liked Gerald O'Bannon. She still couldn't believe Eleanor Gufstead thought Gerald liked her. It was probably because she was new to the island. Maybe after Eleanor got to know her, she'd realize Priscilla wasn't interested in Gerald—or anyone. Of course, if that really was Eleanor out on the cliff, she had bigger problems than a crush on Gerald. She needed professional help. Pretending to jump off a cliff was a dangerous and crazy way to make a point.

As soon as she got out of her SUV, Priscilla could hear Jake barking from inside the house.

"It's us, Jake!" Trudy called out. Of course, that made him bark even more.

When Priscilla unlocked the door, Jake jumped up on her and then took turns welcoming Trudy and Joan.

"I need to take him out," Priscilla said. "One of you can take your bag to the guest room, and the other can have my room. I'll sleep on the couch."

"Oh, don't be silly," Trudy said. "I'll take the couch. You stay in your own room. Joan can have the spare room."

When Joan started to protest, Trudy held up her hand. "I won't argue about this. You know when I make up my mind, nothing will make me change it."

Joan sighed. "She's telling the truth, Cousin," she said to Priscilla. "Might as well give in."

Priscilla laughed. "All right. My couch is pretty comfortable, so I think you'll be okay, Trudy."

Trudy smiled. "I regularly fall asleep on the couch at home. In fact, I enjoy naps there. Sleeping on your couch won't bother me a bit." She pointed at Jake. "Why don't we come with you when you walk Jake? I'd like to see the place where you saw the Weeping Woman."

"You mean the place where she saw someone pretending to be the Weeping Woman," Joan said.

"Of course." Trudy shook her head. "Boy, it irritates me that someone would go to all this trouble to scare you off the island."

Joan shrugged. "I'm not sure we should immediately jump to that conclusion. No pun intended. Maybe something else is going on."

Priscilla grabbed Jake's leash from the coat rack near the door. "I hate to think there's more than one possibility. Surely there aren't several people who want me gone."

Trudy put her arm around Priscilla's shoulders. "Of course not. We'll figure this out, believe me."

"Thank you. I really appreciate that. Now, let's get this dog outside before he explodes!"

Trudy and Joan laughed and followed Priscilla outside. The sun had slipped below the horizon, and the beam from the lighthouse swung around, slicing through the darkness.

"It never gets old," Trudy said. "There's something magical about lighthouses."

Joan snorted. "It's a light that goes around in a circle, Sis. It's not really all that magical."

"You know what I mean." Trudy pointed toward the cliff. "Is that where you saw her, Priscilla?"

"Yeah. It was later than this, though. Probably closer to nine o'clock."

"You think she's on a time schedule?" Joan asked, grinning.

"No...I don't know." Priscilla shook her head. "Sorry. I've never been haunted before. I'm not sure what to expect."

"You're not being haunted now," Joan said emphatically. "Whoever is behind this is flesh and blood, and we'll catch her."

Something suddenly ran across the edge of the cliff, causing Joan to cry out.

Priscilla laughed. "Oh, Joan, look. It's just a cat."

Sure enough, a large black-and-white cat sat near the cliff, licking its paws and staring at them.

"That cat scared me silly," Joan said. "All because of this stupid story."

"I wonder if he belongs to anyone around here."

"Actually, some friends mentioned that there was a feral cat living out here. I'd forgotten about it."

"Poor thing," Priscilla said.

She had stopped while Jake took care of business. Joan waited with her, but Trudy ran ahead, right up to the edge of the cliff. When the cat saw her, he ran away. Right over the edge of the cliff. Although Priscilla wasn't worried about him, knowing how sure-footed cats were, she wasn't prepared for what happened next.

Trudy turned to look at them for a moment. Then she stepped off the cliff—exactly where the cat had gone. Suddenly, she was gone.

Joan screamed and ran toward the cliff. Priscilla started pulling on Jake's leash, but he'd found something interesting he wanted to sniff in the grass and stiffened his legs, making it almost impossible to drag him away. Priscilla turned toward him. "Jake, come on. Now!"

He looked up at her as if trying to decide if she was really serious. Whatever he saw seemed to convince him, and he abandoned the spot he'd been so interested in. When they reached the cliff, Joan was yelling at someone. A look over the side revealed Trudy standing on a large rock jutting out of the side of the cliff.

"Gertrude Latham Galvin!" Joan shouted through gritted teeth. "How could you do something like that? You scared us to death!"

"Oh, don't be silly, Joan. I was simply showing you how your Weeping Woman vanished the other night. I saw the cat jump onto this ledge and then easily run down the rest of the way. Look."

She pointed out a series of rocks that created a natural set of steps.

"So she jumped onto that rock?" Priscilla said slowly. "Then what? When I left, she pulled herself up or scaled down the rocks to the beach?"

"You bet." Trudy stuck her hands in the crevices created by the rocks above her and easily climbed to the top. She took Joan's arm. "I'm sorry. I guess I should have warned you. I assumed you'd know I wouldn't just throw myself off a cliff. Obviously, I was wrong."

"Just don't ever do anything like that again," Joan said.

Priscilla felt sorry for Trudy's older sister. Even though it was hard to make out details in the dark, thanks to the lighthouse and a full moon, it was clear that Joan had been truly frightened for her sister.

"I won't." Trudy hugged Joan and apologized again.

"Well, at least now I know how my *ghost* got away last night," Priscilla said.

Joan rubbed her arms. "It's getting cold. Let's go inside and have something hot to drink. We'll keep our eyes open to see if your visitor decides to make another appearance."

Before leaving, Priscilla gazed over the cliff again.

Joan took her arm. "The cat will be fine, Priscilla. He's been here awhile, and he seems to be in very good shape. My guess is that someone nearby is feeding him and making sure he's safe."

"I'm glad, but it would be better if he had a home."

"I know, but you already have a dog. I'm not sure you're ready for a dog and a cat. Besides, you have no idea if Jake even likes cats."

"Maybe that's what he barked at last night."

"But that would mean you didn't actually see anyone. And I believe you did. Now let's go in. We don't want to scare away your unearthly friend. I'm hoping she shows up tonight."

Although Priscilla didn't respond, secretly she prayed the Weeping Woman would never materialize again. Her peaceful life had been shattered by this unwelcome presence. Would life ever be the same again on Misty Harbor?

CHAPTER EIGHT

The women headed back to the cottage. Once inside, Priscilla took the leash off of Jake. Then she addressed her cousins. "Decaf tea or hot chocolate?"

Trudy and Joan said, "Hot chocolate!" at precisely the same time, causing them to laugh.

"Gail's not the only chocolate lover," Trudy said. "I'd love a cup of cocoa. Hope you have marshmallows."

"Whipped cream for me," Joan said with a smile.

Priscilla grinned. "I have both."

They went into the quaint kitchen decorated with old tea tins. Joan and Trudy sat down at the small table and watched Priscilla as she pulled out her stainless-steel pan and put it on the stove. She made cocoa the old-fashioned way with cocoa powder, sugar, vanilla, and milk. She tried to keep her hands steady as she measured out the ingredients. Seeing Trudy go over the edge of the cliff had scared her. At the same time, she was grateful. Trudy had made it clear how the person who'd impersonated the Weeping Woman had pulled it off. Even though Priscilla didn't believe in ghosts, the whole experience was creepy. To see the more human side of it put it into terms she could understand. Almost.

She finished the cocoa, went to her pantry to get marshmallows, and then got whipped cream out of the refrigerator. When the cocoa was ready, she handed the cups to Trudy and Joan. "I think we need to go out on the porch if we hope to see a repeat performance tonight," she said. There was a covered waterfront verandah at the front of the cottage. "I know it's chilly, but we can wrap up. It's either that or we hang out around the front windows all evening."

"The porch is fine with me," Trudy said. "Let's grab some blankets."

Priscilla told the sisters to wait and went to the linen closet in the hallway, where she removed two afghans and a beautiful quilt with a nautical theme. She carried them back to the kitchen and put them on the table. "Take the one you want, and we'll go outside."

Trudy picked up the quilt. "This was Aunt Marjorie's. I remember it. It's been a long time since I've seen it."

Priscilla noticed Trudy's eyes grow moist. "Please, Trudy, take it home with you. It doesn't mean as much to me as it obviously does to you."

"I'm not trying to steal your belongings, Cousin," she said in a soft voice.

"Oh, Trudy, I know that. I'm serious. It was here when I moved in. It doesn't mean anything to me."

Joan smiled at her sister. "That's the quilt you helped Aunt Marjorie make, isn't it?"

Trudy nodded. "Yes. She was trying to teach me to quilt. I wasn't very good at it, but she told me it was her favorite quilt in the whole world." She laughed lightly. "Of course, I know now it's not perfect. But it seemed perfect to me back then."

"If there are other things any of you might like, you should tell me," Priscilla said. "You were much closer to Aunt Marjorie than I was."

"There really isn't anything else," Joan said. "She left all three of us quite a few things in her will. I guess she didn't realize how much this quilt meant to Trudy."

"You know, she also promised Gail her ruby ring," Trudy said. "Gail always admired it. But after Aunt Marjorie died, we couldn't find it. In fact, several pieces of jewelry were missing."

"She probably gave them to her friends," Joan said. "You know how she was. She loved to give. I'm sure she just forgot about promising Gail that ring."

Trudy nodded. "I know. I don't think Gail's worried about it, really. Aunt Marjorie was very generous with us. Gail would have loved to have it, though."

"I haven't found any jewelry," Priscilla said. "But if I ever run across that ring, I'll make sure she gets it."

"Thank you, Priscilla," Trudy said. "She'll really appreciate that."

Priscilla gestured toward the afghans. "Do these mean any-thing to either one of you?"

Joan grinned. "Yeah, they mean warmth while we're bundled up outside."

Priscilla laughed. "Let's go then."

The women grabbed their jackets, their hot cocoa, and their blankets. Then they went out to the covered porch. Joan and

Priscilla sat in the rocking chairs while Trudy lowered herself onto the steps and pulled one of the afghans around herself. "I really don't think Eleanor will put on a show if she sees us sitting here," she said.

"With the porch light off, I doubt she'll spot us," Priscilla said quietly. "Anyway, I hope not." She sipped her hot cocoa and let the liquid slip down her throat and warm her insides. Even though it was a little cold, it was a beautiful evening. The full moon looked huge and bathed Misty Harbor in soft moonlight. Thankfully, the shadow of the lighthouse fell on the cottage, keeping it hidden in the dark. It would be difficult for anyone to see them sitting out here.

"So are we assuming this is Eleanor, or do we intend to follow up on any other possibilities?" Priscilla asked.

"I think we should find out who that man was Sylvia Peabody was talking to," Joan said. "He seemed a little too interested in you."

"What about Tony Gonzalez or the other boys?" Priscilla asked Trudy. "Should we actually consider them?"

"I hate to think they could be involved," she said, "but it's so close to Halloween. With their past antics, I think we have to consider them."

"And then there's Aleeta," Joan reminded them. "Still seems odd she didn't notice the paintings had been switched. Maybe she was lying."

"I still think it's Eleanor," Trudy said. "That makes the most sense."

Jake, who lay on the porch next to Priscilla, began growling. All other conversation stopped, and Priscilla felt the hairs on the back of her neck stand up. Another sound wafted through the night air, floating above the sound of waves crashing against the cliff. A high-pitched cry.

Slowly, the figure of a woman began to materialize through the mist surrounding the cliff. She was tall and glowed like she was encased in blue fire. Priscilla's body seemed glued to her seat. Her cousins must have felt the same way because neither one of them moved. Jake began to bark loudly, but Priscilla held on to his leash with every ounce of her strength. Suddenly, Trudy threw off her quilt and jumped off the verandah. She began running toward the ghostly figure. But before she reached the cliff, the woman disappeared.

Somehow that seemed to give Priscilla the ability to move. She stood up. "Come on, Joan," she hollered. Both women rushed toward Trudy. When they reached her, Priscilla gazed at her face, highlighted by silvery moonlight. She looked confused. Priscilla and Joan looked over the edge of the cliff, but no one was there. No one stood on the jutting rock—or anywhere else.

"Where did she go?" Priscilla asked Trudy.

"I . . . I have no idea, but I'll tell you one thing." She turned to look at Priscilla. "That's not Eleanor Gufstead."

"How do you know that?" Joan asked, her voice shaking slightly.

"I know what Eleanor looks like. That wasn't her." Trudy frowned. "Eleanor is short. This woman was tall. And she had . . . black eyes."

"You could see her eyes?" Joan asked.

"She stared at me for just a second before she vanished." Trudy kept shaking her head and repeated, "Not Eleanor Gufstead."

Priscilla peered over the edge one more time, holding tightly to Jake. The last thing she needed was for him to pull them both off the ledge. There was nothing to see besides the cliff face and the rocks and ocean below. "Let's go back to the cottage," she said. "We need to talk."

"Yeah, we do," Trudy said, her eyes wide. "I know I said I didn't believe in ghosts..."

"Oh Trudy, for heaven's sake," Joan said with a deep sigh. "That wasn't a ghost. It was a person, and we're going to figure out exactly who it was."

CHAPTER NINE

Priscilla poured fresh cups of hot cocoa and slid them in front of Trudy and Joan. Then she grabbed her own cup and sat down at the kitchen table. "I still don't know how you could be sure that wasn't Eleanor," she said to Trudy. "Obviously she was wearing a costume."

Trudy shook her head. "A costume that makes you look taller?"

"Of course," Joan said. "She could wear heels. Platform shoes."

"I don't know." Trudy sighed. "Maybe. It's just...well, it didn't seem like Eleanor." She took a sip of her cocoa. She repeated something she'd said earlier on the cliff. "She had black eyes."

"You mean dark eyes?" Priscilla asked. "She could have been wearing contacts. Anyone going to all this trouble might buy colored contacts."

"I don't mean she had dark eyes," Trudy said, her tone defensive. "Where her eyes were supposed to be, there were just...black holes."

"Oh, Trudy. Stop it." Joan stood up and walked over to the window. "You're scaring me."

"I'm not trying to." Trudy looked at Priscilla. "I'd never purposely do anything to frighten you. I'm simply telling you the truth."

Priscilla patted her hand. "I believe you. This is very disturbing, and I'm committed to finding out what's really going on. I love it here, and I don't like having my life invaded in this way."

"I agree." Joan walked over and sat down again. "Frankly, it's beginning to make me really angry. Whoever's behind this...well, it's not funny. It's scary, and it's meant to be."

"Then we'll just have to figure this out," Priscilla said. "Excuse me a minute." She hurried to the bedroom, where she retrieved her purse. She fumbled around until she found her small notebook. Then she took it back to the kitchen. "We need to do some research about the painting," she said as she slipped back into her chair. "Veela Tharmas Davirney. What a crazy name. Have either one of you ever heard anything like it?"

Both women shook their heads.

"Did you copy this down exactly?" Trudy asked, frowning at the name scribbled on the page.

"Yes. I was very careful to get it right."

"It's a really weird name," Trudy said. She pulled her iPhone from her purse, pushed a couple of buttons, and then verbally spelled out the entire name. A voice confirmed the spelling then after a few seconds said, *I'm sorry. I'm not finding anything like that.* She put her phone back in her purse. "If this person existed, I think there'd be something online."

"Not necessarily," Joan said firmly. "Not everyone puts their private personal business on the Internet. I certainly don't."

"You don't have to purposely share your information," Trudy said slowly, as if speaking to a child. "Many things can make your name end up on the Internet. For example, if this person's relative died, she'd be listed as a survivor."

Priscilla sighed. "Also, she could be mentioned as Veela Tharmas. Or Veela Davirney. That makes it even harder to locate her."

Trudy grabbed her phone again, but Priscilla held up her hand like a cop directing traffic. "Why don't you work on that later? Let's stick to our list of suspects. Joan, didn't you start a list back at the restaurant?"

Joan got up and grabbed her purse. She removed her own notebook and brought it over to the table. "We'd just gotten started. I don't have a lot here. We did wonder about the man Sylvia was talking to at the exhibit."

"Hopefully, we'll learn something about him tomorrow when Joan pays her insurance premium," Trudy said.

Priscilla nodded. "Great. And we need to talk to the people who do the ghost tours. I want to see what they know about the Weeping Woman."

"Sure," Trudy said. "What about Eleanor?"

Priscilla frowned at her. "I thought you said it couldn't be her."

Trudy shrugged. "You convinced me. I guess she could be wearing heels." She snapped her fingers. "I'll see if I can find out where she was tonight. I mean, if she was doing something else, we'll know it couldn't be her."

"Why does she glow?"

Priscilla looked at Joan. "What?"

"Why does the Weeping Woman glow?" Joan raised an eyebrow. "I mean, unless you believe she's projecting some kind of spectral energy or something…"

"Of course I don't." Priscilla thought for a moment. "Paint. It's got to be some kind of glowing paint."

"Exactly. We need to check with anyone in Tisbury or Vineyard Haven who sells luminescent paint. Anyone buying a large quantity could be our ghost."

"Oh, Joan," Trudy said, "whoever it is could have ordered it online. It would be nice if they bought it locally, but if I were trying to scare someone, I certainly wouldn't buy my paint from someone in my own town. I'd get it sent to me so no one would know about it."

Joan was quiet for a moment. "Yeah, you're right. Sorry."

Trudy sighed. "No, I'm sorry. We should research every possibility. I guess I'm just a little flustered."

Joan smiled. "Don't worry about it. This has been a really strange evening. We're all a little shaken up."

Priscilla tried to stifle a yawn but couldn't. "I'm getting really tired," she said. "I think we all need to get some sleep. We'll follow up with these ideas tomorrow."

"Sounds good," Joan said. "I'm beat."

"You said you have tomorrow off?" Priscilla said to Joan.

"Yeah. It's my work anniversary day. I have to take it off before the end of the month or lose it."

Trudy laughed. "Wow. You pushed that almost as far as you could. Why didn't you pick the thirty-first?"

"Because this way I get a three-day weekend."

"And you said there's no tour this Saturday?" Trudy asked Priscilla.

"Right. Nothing going on at all this Saturday."

"So that gives us three uninterrupted days to investigate," Joan said.

"Except I'm spending time tomorrow morning with Trudy," Priscilla said, directing her statement to Joan. "We're working on some kind of alternative Halloween party for kids."

"I'll help," Joan offered.

Trudy grinned. "That would be great. Thanks. I know this seems last-minute—well, okay, it *is* last-minute—but we planned it a long time ago. I just...left some of the details until now."

"*Some* of the details?" Joan said. "What else has been left until the last minute?"

"Don't panic. We have lots of volunteers and supplies. Some good ideas. We just need direction. We'll have some teenagers, and I'm afraid most of the games are kind of childish."

Priscilla's mouth dropped open. "I have no idea what kind of games teenagers like."

Trudy winked at her. "That's why Tony is going to meet us there. He's supposed to help with that."

"One of the boys who might be behind the Weeping Woman?" Joan said. "Is that really a good idea?"

"Like I said, I don't think he's involved. If his so-called friends are behind this, letting him meet Priscilla might make him want to tell the truth."

"Boy, I'm not sure that's a good idea," Priscilla said. "What if your idea backfires? If he doesn't like me..."

Trudy stood. "Oh, don't be silly. He'll love you. Everyone does."

Joan finished her cocoa and got up too. "Obviously someone doesn't love her. Whoever is putting on this nightly extravaganza isn't doing it because they think Priscilla's the cat's meow."

"'The cat's meow'?" Trudy said, laughing. "How old are you?" She turned to Priscilla. "If you want Tony to like you, don't say things like *the cat's meow.*"

"You're very funny." Joan rolled her eyes. "I'm going to bed. See you two in the morning."

She headed for the spare bedroom, and Priscilla heard the door close. She stood up and smiled at Trudy. "I'll get you some sheets, a blanket, and a pillow to make up the couch."

"Thanks, Priscilla. Do you mind if I turn on the TV for a few minutes? I'd like to see the news before I go to sleep. I'll keep it low."

"No, of course I don't mind. I want to do something in the kitchen before I go to bed. I won't let the TV bother me if you'll ignore the light on in here for a little while."

"Deal."

Priscilla went to the linen closet and got everything Trudy needed for the couch. Within a few minutes, she'd set up a comfy place to sleep. When she was finished, she went back into the kitchen. She had an affinity for puzzles, and something was pricking her curiosity.

After cleaning up the cups and pan she'd used to make hot cocoa and starting the dishwasher, she sat down with her notebook. She pulled out a few pieces of paper and wrote *Veela Tharmas Davirney* at the top of each sheet. Then she began to spell out other words with the letters in different orders. She had a suspicion that the name was some kind of anagram. Maybe she was being silly, but she couldn't get the idea out of her head.

She worked for about ten minutes, but she couldn't make anything out of it. Perhaps she was just seeing things that weren't really there. Like the woman in the mist. "No," she said softly to herself. "That's not your imagination, Priscilla. And I don't think this is either."

She got up, turned off the kitchen light, and tiptoed into the living room. Trudy was already sound asleep, her mouth open, her gentle snoring making it clear she wasn't watching the news. As Priscilla picked up the remote and clicked off the TV, a man was talking about the weather tomorrow on Martha's Vineyard.

She put the remote down and was on her way to her room when something struck her. She turned around, hurried back to the kitchen, and grabbed her pen.

A couple of minutes later, a chill ran down her back as she stared down at the words *Leave Martha's Vineyard.*

CHAPTER TEN

The next morning Priscilla showed Joan and Trudy what she'd found by readjusting the letters in the name of the artist who supposedly painted *The Weeping Woman*.

Trudy's mouth dropped open. "So whoever painted that did it to send you a message?"

"They must have. Why else would they have gone to the trouble?" Priscilla sighed. "You know, one thing I keep wondering—how did they know what night we would be at the Art Attack?"

"I told some people about it," Joan said quietly. "I'm sorry."

"Sorry?" Priscilla shook her head. "Don't be ridiculous. You had every right to share your success with people." She hesitated a moment. "I don't suppose you remember who you told?"

"Don't even go there," Trudy said sheepishly. "I told everyone I knew about the showing. In fact, I told people I *didn't* know. There's no way to narrow down that list." She smiled at Joan. "I was so proud of you. I shared your showing with everyone I ran into."

"But did you two tell people exactly what night we'd be there?" Priscilla asked.

Trudy shrugged. "Wednesday was the opening night of the festival. Even if I didn't mention it, I doubt it would be hard for anyone to figure out. My guess is they waited until they knew we were there and then switched the paintings. If we hadn't shown up Wednesday, they probably could have carried out their plan whenever they finally got the chance."

"But it still bothers me that they would think no one would be suspicious about them changing the pictures." Priscilla picked up her coffee cup. "I find that hard to believe."

Joan stabbed at the scrambled eggs and bacon on her plate. "This is the first time you've been to one of these festivals," she said. "Pictures and displays are moved around a lot. People buy things, and new exhibits replace them. Trust me, no one would have noticed anything out of the ordinary."

"Still…"

Joan took a sip of coffee. "If Aleeta didn't think something was odd…"

"Then it's likely no one else did either." Although Priscilla hated to admit it, it was unlikely they'd discover the person they were looking for by trying to find out who hung the painting. "And if they walked out of the store with a painting…"

"Everyone would think they bought it," Joan finished for her. She tapped the side of her plate with her fork, obviously deep in thought. Finally she looked up, a frown on her face. "But would they let someone just walk out like that? I mean, wouldn't they be suspicious if someone tried to carry something they hadn't paid for out of the store?"

"That's a good point," Trudy said. "Unless they slid it into a tote bag or something."

"Eleanor Gufstead had a tote bag," Priscilla said.

"That's interesting," Trudy said. "Maybe that's where the painting was hidden."

"Maybe…," Priscilla said slowly. There was no way to prove that Eleanor had anything in her bag that shouldn't be there, so she wasn't sure that this information helped them.

Joan pointed her fork at Priscilla. "After Trudy and I go by the insurance office, I'm going to the Art Attack to ask Aleeta's employees about that painting. We might have had this backward. Instead of asking how the painting got there, let's see if we can figure out how it left the shop. We can compare notes at lunch. How about the inn?"

"That's a great idea," Priscilla said. "Thanks, Joan."

They quickly finished their breakfasts and began getting ready for the day ahead. As Priscilla brushed her teeth, she ran different scenarios through her mind. Even as she considered several possibilities, the reality of her situation still seemed *im*possible. Of course, there were people in Wheatfield she hadn't been close to. Even one woman who really didn't like her. But in all the years she'd lived there, no one had hated her so much they'd gone to this kind of trouble to get rid of her. It not only made her angry, it made her even more determined they wouldn't get their way. The sooner this person figured that out, the sooner they could leave her alone.

After getting dressed, Priscilla grabbed her purse and met her cousins in the living room. She dropped Joan and Trudy off at Joan's house so they could get Trudy's car, and then she drove herself to Grace Community Church.

She'd just walked into the spacious building when a side door opened, and a boy walked into the foyer. Tony Gonzalez. Although he was most certainly a suspect in the appearance of the Weeping Woman, Priscilla's first reaction wasn't suspicion. It was compassion. She felt bad for the boy.

"Hi, Tony," Priscilla said. "I'm Mrs. Grant. Thanks for offering to help us today. I really appreciate it."

"Principal Mayhew said I had to." He looked down at the ground as he spoke.

"Really? I don't understand." She frowned at him. "Why aren't you in school today?"

"Got suspended for fighting," he mumbled. "One week."

"Oh. I'm sorry." Priscilla wasn't quite sure what else to say. She looked out at the gym, which was quickly filling up with volunteers. The youth pastor, Tim Carpenter, seemed to be assigning duties. "Why don't you ask Pastor Tim what you can do to help? Mrs. Galvin had an errand. She should be here soon."

He nodded and headed toward the youth pastor, who seemed a little overwhelmed. After putting her purse in the kitchen, Priscilla was ready to work but wasn't sure what to do. She was glad to see Trudy come through the door to the gym. She hurried over to where Priscilla waited.

"Well, that was a waste of time," Trudy said breathlessly.

"What do you mean?"

"Sylvia wasn't in. I guess she's given her notice and is moving away. Right now she's just working part-time until Elmer finds a replacement. Poor man was so befuddled, he didn't even know how to process Joan's payment. She just left it on Sylvia's desk."

"So we still don't know the identity of the man Sylvia was talking to."

"No. Sorry. Joan dropped me off and went to the Art Attack. Hopefully, she'll dig up something there that will help."

"Trudy, Tony told me he was kicked out of school for fighting. You made it seem like he wasn't the kind of boy to get into trouble like that."

Trudy sighed. "Tony was defending a younger student against bullies."

"And they suspended him for it?"

"Yes. The school policy is no fighting. Period."

"Well, they're right. But still..."

From across the room, Tony noticed Trudy and came over.

"Hi, Tony," Trudy said. "I was just telling my cousin why you were suspended."

"Because fighting isn't the way to solve anything." The sing-song quality of his voice made it clear he was imitating someone else.

"That's right. We can't have kids knocking each other around when they disagree, can we?"

Although Priscilla expected Tony to react with disdain, he didn't. He just shook his head and said, "No," so softly she almost missed it.

Trudy gave Tony a quick hug. He winced as if it hurt to be touched, but he didn't pull away.

"Let's go in here," Trudy said, pointing at a door to their right. "Tony, why don't you come too? I want your advice about something."

Priscilla and Tony followed Trudy into a room set up like an informal waiting room. There was a small couch, a few stuffed chairs, and a coffee table.

"Pastor uses this for counseling sometimes," Trudy said, "but he said we could have it this morning for our planning meeting."

Priscilla sat in one of the chairs. "Is he going to talk with us?"

Trudy shook her head. "No. I told him you were helping and mentioned all the other volunteers. He thinks we're doing fine without him. He did have some flyers made for the event. We can pick them up before we leave." She looked at Tony. "Maybe you and your friends could pass out our flyers."

Priscilla was certain she'd caught a quick look of panic in Tony's eyes. She suspected his friends weren't the kind of people who would want to help.

"Maybe you and I could work together, Tony," Priscilla said. "I love to walk. Between the two of us, I think we could get these flyers out. What do you think?"

The relief on his face was evident. He clearly didn't want to approach his friends with a request to assist the church.

"Tony, why don't you go to Pastor Billings' office? Get the flyers from his secretary, Marsha."

"Sure." He left the room and headed toward the office.

"Thanks for offering to go with him, Priscilla. The school says he needs counseling. They want him to find a way to control his anger. I suggested he talk to Pastor Tim, since he's a trained thera-pist. Thankfully, the school agreed. I think it's helping. He really just needs to get away from these *friends*. They've been bullying kids at school. I've talked to the principal, and the school is look-ing into it. I do wish they'd move a little faster, though."

"Bullying isn't something to take lightly," Priscilla said. "So many young people today are targeted by bullies. Schools need to get involved. Parents don't know everything that's going on when they're not with their kids."

"I know." Trudy sighed. "I don't want it to sound like the prin-cipal isn't taking the situation seriously. He is. He just wants to make sure he knows the truth before he approaches some of the parents. Kids have this dumb code. You're not supposed to rat on a fellow student."

"Or what?"

Trudy shrugged. "I don't think anything too dreadful would really happen, but kids get afraid. Their imaginations are worse than reality."

Priscilla started to respond, but Trudy's cell phone went off. Trudy reached into her pocket and grabbed it.

"Hello?" she said. She listened for a few seconds. "That's great. Thanks. I really appreciate it. Where can we meet you?" She listened to whoever was on the line and then said goodbye. "That was Myrna Holtman. She and Ed can meet us at Candy's around eleven."

Priscilla's shoulders slumped. She'd forgotten about the ghost tour people. "Oh dear. I don't want to fill up on sweets before lunch."

Trudy frowned at her. Priscilla knew that look. She'd seen it from other people who never had to watch their weight.

"Just get coffee," she said simply, like that solved everything.

"Good idea." As if it were easy saying *no* to the various delights at Candy's. Priscilla waved her hand toward the gym. "We need to get busy. Not a lot of time."

Tony came back into the room with a stack of flyers. Priscilla quickly read through one of them. It promised a lot, and there wasn't much time until Halloween. They spent the next forty-five minutes tossing around ideas. Tony made it clear that he didn't think the church needed to find ways to entertain teenagers.

"Why aren't they helping?" he asked. "They should be volunteering. Helping the younger kids."

Priscilla was struck by the wisdom of his opinion, and Trudy quickly agreed with him. By the time they were ready to leave, Priscilla felt they had a pretty good handle on things. Although she was looking forward to the party, a thought kept tugging at her. As they moved closer to Halloween, was the person who'd been harassing her also advancing toward an end goal? And if so, what was it?

CHAPTER ELEVEN

Priscilla and Trudy left the church a little before eleven. First they called Joan, who'd been held up. She promised to meet them at the Colonial Inn as close to noon as possible. That gave Priscilla some time before she and Tony were scheduled to meet and pass out flyers. Trudy wanted to help, but she had a doctor's appointment. Priscilla wasn't worried. She felt she and Tony would be fine on their own.

She and Trudy arrived at Candy Lane Confectionery at eleven on the dot. When they walked in, the few café-style tables were already taken. The shop was full of people laughing and talking. It was a popular place with locals and tourists, and a line had formed at the counter of people picking up desserts and taking them home. At the tables, residents gathered to talk and gossip. Priscilla recognized several regulars.

A couple at one of the tables waved them over. Priscilla was surprised that the Holtmans looked incredibly normal. Ed, who appeared to be in his fifties, was skinny and balding, with large black-framed glasses. Myrna seemed almost motherly, plump and attractive with red curly hair. She had a nice smile, and Priscilla felt drawn to her—something she hadn't expected. They certainly didn't look like people who ran ghost tours.

Ed stood up when they reached the table and stuck out his hand to Priscilla. "So nice to meet you, Ms. Grant." His handshake was firm and his smile sincere.

"I'm happy to meet you too," she replied. "Please call me Priscilla."

"Myrna Holtman," the woman said, also shaking Priscilla's hand. She pointed at the chair next to her. "Have a seat. Have you been here before?"

Priscilla smiled. "Oh yes. I'm particularly fond of Candy's cranberry muffins and chocolate chip cookies."

"You must try her pumpkin muffins," Ed said. "Cream-filled. Absolutely out of this world."

"That sounds good." Priscilla was ready to try something new, and the pumpkin muffin was right up her alley.

Ed went to the counter and ordered pumpkin muffins and coffee for everyone then returned to their table.

"I thought you were just going to get coffee," Trudy whispered.

"That was your idea," she responded quietly.

"So Trudy tells us you're having *ghost* problems," Ed said.

Priscilla nodded. "I'm not sure what's going on. I've seen... Well, I mean, someone..."

Myrna patted Priscilla's arm. "Honey, don't feel uncomfortable. Ed and I lead these tours because we wanted something interesting to do after he retired. The people who used to run the tours were moving away, so we took it over." She lowered her voice and leaned over with a conspiratorial look on her face. "We actually don't even believe in ghosts. Of course, you can't share that with anyone else. We just tell the stories. It's up to our customers to believe them or not."

Priscilla breathed a sigh of relief. Feeling more relaxed, she quickly launched into what had happened Wednesday night. "Look," she said when she finished, "I have no idea what's really going on, but I'm certain someone planted that painting just for me. Then they put on that ridiculous show on the cliff outside my house."

"And last night as well," Trudy interjected.

"We were at the Art Attack Wednesday night," Myrna said, "but we didn't see that painting. I'm sure I would have noticed it."

"What time were you there?" Priscilla said.

"Right when it opened. Aleeta Armbruster is a friend. We helped her set up. There was no painting of Olivia Hennesey. I'm certain of that, Priscilla. We would have remembered it. Especially because of what we do."

"Then whoever put it up must have done it after the exhibit opened."

Myrna nodded. "I believe you're right."

"So you saw the Weeping Woman again last night?" Ed asked.

"Yes." She started to tell them the details of the night before, but the waitress showed up with their food.

Priscilla's muffin looked awesome. There was a dollop of cinnamon-dusted cream on top of the pumpkin-colored pastry. The aroma was so incredible that Priscilla almost forgot what she was talking about.

"Was last night's show the same as the night before?" Myrna asked once the waitress left.

Priscilla tore her eyes away from her muffin and nodded. "Yes." She gestured toward Trudy. "Except I wasn't alone this time. Trudy saw her and so did my cousin Joan."

Myrna looked over at her husband. "You're saying three people saw Olivia?"

Priscilla nodded as she used her fork to cut off a large piece of her muffin. "We chased her to the edge of the cliff, and she disappeared. We looked everywhere, but we couldn't find her."

She noticed that Myrna and Ed had grown quiet, and they hadn't even touched their muffins.

"Look, please understand me," Priscilla said. "I don't believe this was a ghost. It's a real person. Someone who might be trying to get me off my property." She frowned at Trudy, who was obviously enjoying her muffin. The look of ecstasy on her face was starting to bug Priscilla. She wanted a chance to enjoy the tasty dessert herself. She sighed loudly. "Trudy, why don't you tell them what you saw last night?"

Her cousin, who had just stuffed a large piece of muffin in her mouth, gave Priscilla a dirty look. Ignoring her, Priscilla took a bite of her own muffin. It was everything she thought it would be. It tasted like incredible pumpkin pie with rich cream inside. She tried to pay attention to Trudy, who was attempting to talk as she swallowed.

"Yump. Issa jummed ober climm. Bah nah ghoms."

"Excuse me?" Myrna said.

A spot of red colored each of Trudy's cheeks. She swallowed and cleared her throat. "I'm sorry. I was agreeing with Priscilla.

Someone really does seem to be trying to frighten her. Last night we all saw this supposed *ghost*. There's a rock that juts out right under the top of the cliff. I jumped onto it myself, and it looked as if I'd suddenly vanished. I believe that's what happened to our fake Olivia last night. Whoever it was knew about that rock, and they also knew how to get down the cliff without being seen. It really looked like she disappeared completely after her little show."

Ed nodded. "I see. I believe the reason you asked to meet with us is that you wanted to know more about the Weeping Woman."

Trudy put her hand on Priscilla's arm. "I need to make a trip to the ladies' room. I'll be right back."

Priscilla nodded at her, and Trudy got up and left.

"May I ask why the Weeping Woman isn't on your tour?" Priscilla asked the Holtmans.

Ed laughed lightly. "It isn't because we didn't want to include her. Your aunt wouldn't allow us on your property. She didn't believe in ghosts and thought our tours were silly. And that's okay. We were disappointed but certainly not upset. We understood."

"So she knew about Olivia?" Priscilla said.

Ed nodded. "Your aunt loved history, but to her, the story of Olivia and Jeremiah Hennesey was just fiction. A ghost story. She never gave it any credence."

Well, that might explain why her cousins had been clueless about the Weeping Woman. "But couldn't you talk about Olivia at some other location?" Priscilla asked. "Do you have to come to my lighthouse?"

"The house where Olivia and her husband lived was torn down years ago," Myrna said. "The cliff is the only place left where the story would make sense."

Priscilla was working on her last bite of muffin, but it occurred to her that the Holtmans had just given her a great reason to suspect one of them of being the Weeping Woman. They knew her story, and they'd never been able to add her to their tour. Maybe they thought if they scared Priscilla away, they could pick up the lighthouse and the story of the Weeping Woman as one of their tour destinations.

"Actually, the story of Olivia and her husband *is* pretty interesting," Ed said.

"I couldn't find much information about them," Priscilla said. "Just that he went to sea and never came back. Eventually Olivia gave up and threw herself off the cliff."

Ed leaned in. "We found some letters written by relatives that cast an interesting spin on the situation."

"Really?" They had Priscilla's attention now. "Can you tell me what you discovered?"

"Of course." Myrna cleared her throat. "A second cousin wrote that the captain had a girlfriend who lived in Boston. His supposed fishing trip the night he went missing was nothing more than a way to escape Olivia. But something went wrong. He disappeared, and so did his boat. He was never seen again."

"Could Olivia have found out about the girlfriend?" Priscilla asked.

"It seems she did. Jeremiah had told his wife he was going to meet his crew at the port in Oak Bluffs, which was just a district of Edgartown back then. When the crew arrived, the boat was already gone, and Captain Hennesey never showed up. His crew was in on the scheme. They were supposed to deliver him to Boston and then make up a story about the captain being swept overboard. Since he never met them that night, there was no way to stick to the plan. In the end, they felt they had to admit the truth to Olivia."

"So the whole Weeping Woman story is false?" Priscilla asked.

Myrna sighed. "No, it's true. Even though she knew he'd lied to her, Olivia kept watch night after night, praying he would come back."

"Maybe he changed his mind and went directly to Boston," Priscilla said.

"No. He never showed up there either. His girlfriend—I can't remember her name right now—never heard from him again. No one did."

"Perhaps Olivia wasn't too forgiving," Priscilla said thoughtfully. "But then why did she stand out on the cliff night after night and cry? Something doesn't add up."

Myrna shrugged. "That's part of the mystery. No one's ever figured it out, but a lot of us have tried."

"I don't suppose you'd allow us to add your property to our tour?" Ed asked, his smile wide. "We'd be happy to give you part of our proceeds, and we wouldn't bother you. We'd simply take the path near the cliff, stop for a few minutes, and then leave. You'd never know we were there."

"For now, I have to say no. Misty Harbor Tours is already coming by every week. I'm not sure I need two different tours going on." Actually, Priscilla planned to increase the number of tours after she finished turning the lighthouse into a museum, but that wasn't something she wanted to share right now.

"What day does the Misty Harbor Tour come by?" Myrna asked.

"Saturdays."

Myrna and Ed looked at each other. "We could plan our tour around the same time," Ed said. "That way you'd only have one interruption every week. One bus comes and goes. Then the other. We'd both be out of your hair in less than an hour."

"I...I don't know. Let me think about it." Priscilla loved the history of the lighthouse. Attaching a ghost story to it felt...cheesy. That was the last thing she wanted to do. She was certain she wouldn't change her mind, but at the same time, making a decision without thinking it through wasn't the way she liked to do things. She really would consider it seriously.

"That's all we can ask," Ed said. "Is there anything else we can help you with?"

"Could I read the letter you referred to?" she asked. "I'm not saying I'd see something you didn't, but I'd love to look at it myself."

"Certainly," Myrna said. "In fact, I think there might be a few more letters that talk about Olivia and the captain. We bought them at the estate sale of a great-great-great nephew who'd inherited them. He had no interest in his ancestors." She took a card from her purse and handed it to Priscilla. "Write your phone number on the back of this. I'll call you as soon as I dig them up. Unfortunately, they're in a box in the basement. It might take me a little while to find it."

"That's fine." Priscilla scribbled her number on the card and handed it back to Myrna. "Why don't you give me another card so I have your number too?"

Myrna reached back into her purse and pulled out another card, which she handed to Priscilla. "Call us anytime. That's my cell phone number, so you should be able to reach us without too much trouble."

"Thank you, Myrna." Priscilla smiled at the woman, who returned it.

Trudy returned to the table and slipped into her chair. Priscilla noticed she stuck her cell phone into her purse. What was that about?

She smiled at the Holtmans. Could these two really be behind what had been happening? It was hard to believe, but for now, Priscilla couldn't risk trusting anyone.

CHAPTER TWELVE

They pulled up in front of the Colonial Inn at the exact same time Joan did. Priscilla waved at her as she exited her car.

The women met at the front door of the restaurant established in a lovely Victorian house. Although many of the flower baskets that usually hung on the huge front porch had been removed to protect them from dropping temperatures, it hadn't affected the building's charm.

Inside, Tilly Snyder, the restaurant's owner, stood behind a lectern near the front door. Priscilla was surprised to see her acting as hostess. She had employees to greet customers and wait tables. Tilly usually liked to float around and talk to customers.

"Why, hello!" she said with a smile. "So nice to see all of you."

Priscilla immediately felt a little intimidated. A force to be reckoned with, the petite owner of the popular inn and restaurant had certain eccentricities. One of them had to do with considering other customers' sensitivities. Having been cleaned off with a sticky roller once in public due to Jake's hair, Priscilla was determined not to endure another humiliation. She now kept a roller in her glove compartment and had cleaned herself off this morning before leaving the house. However, she still found herself brushing her skirt, checking it for dog hair. Thankfully, she didn't find anything. But

Tilly didn't seem to be focused on Priscilla's clothes today. Maybe an inspection wouldn't be forthcoming after all.

As usual, Tilly wore vintage clothes that complemented her restaurant, which she'd decorated with charming antiques. Entering the Colonial Inn was like stepping into the past. The food Tilly served, however, was inventive and *au courant* with the smartest restaurants in larger cities.

Tilly picked up three menus. "Follow me, ladies." She took them into the beautiful dining room. All the tables had lovely white tablecloths and were decorated with silver accessories. She seated them at a table in the corner, which was perfect because it would give them a chance to talk without being overheard.

"You must try our new lobster rolls," Tilly said. "You can have them hot with butter or cold with our handmade mayo. We also have octopus cassoulet today. It's delicious."

Priscilla smiled at her. "Thank you, Tilly. Give us a few minutes to decide." She put her menu down. "Are you short on help today?"

Tilly's smile slipped a bit. "I'm afraid the flu seems to have struck my staff. Hilda is sick, and one of my cooks couldn't make it in." She waved her hand. "But don't worry. I made some calls and have a couple of ex-staff coming in from a café in Vineyard Haven that closed recently." She squared her shoulders. "I'm certain you will be well cared for." Before leaving, she lowered her voice as if sharing an important secret. "I feel I must warn you. We have a customer who smokes a pipe. The stench is overpowering. I had to tell him that he won't be allowed back if he imbibes in this nasty habit before his next visit."

Priscilla bit her lip to keep from giggling. At least she wasn't on the chopping block this time. She felt sorry for the poor pipe smoker but was relieved his pipe had trumped her dog hair.

A man across the room wagged his finger at Tilly, obviously wanting attention. Her eyes narrowed, but she kept a smile pasted on her face. It was clear she wasn't happy about having to serve as a waitress. "What would you ladies like to drink?" she asked, ignoring the man.

The women gave her their orders, and she walked away, stopping at the man's table to see what he wanted.

"Wow. I feel kind of guilty," Trudy said.

"I don't know why," Joan responded. "We're not doing anything wrong. We came to a restaurant that is open because they want customers. Hardly our fault if Tilly's employees don't show up."

"It's not her fault if her servers are sick either." Priscilla frowned. "I hope we don't catch anything."

"I doubt we will," Trudy said. "Tilly is really strict about her employees keeping their hands clean."

Joan grunted. "Well obviously they didn't do a very good job of it."

"You make a good point." Priscilla pulled her purse into her lap. She took out a small container of disinfectant hand gel she always carried with her and set it on the table. "Might be a good idea for us to use this after we handle the menus."

"I agree," Trudy said. "Thanks."

"Well, ladies, I really don't have much to report," Joan said. "I'm sure Trudy told you about our visit to Elmer's. I went by the Art Attack afterward and tried to talk to a couple of the employees, but they didn't know anything about the Weeping Woman painting." She sighed. "I think Aleeta knew what I was up to because she kept watching me. Followed me around the shop. I finally gave up and left."

"What held you up from meeting us at the inn earlier?" Trudy asked.

"I took a chance and checked out some of the art supply houses in town to see if anyone was buying fluorescent blue paint." Joan held up her hand. "Before you tell me I was wasting my time, Trudy, I admit you were right. No one could really help me. I mean, there were small purchases here and there. Nothing major. And nothing that pointed to our Weeping Woman. So I'm afraid our efforts this morning were a bust."

"Don't worry about it," Priscilla said. "Thanks for trying."

As she opened her menu, she noticed a man walking past the dining room. It was the man from the Art Attack. The one who'd been watching her so closely.

She elbowed Trudy.

"Ouch!" Trudy said loudly, causing Priscilla to blush.

"Would you shush?" she said under her breath. "That guy from the showing, the man who kept staring at me? He just walked past the dining room."

"You could have just said that instead of attacking me," Trudy said, rubbing her side as if Priscilla had stuck her with a dinner knife.

"I'm sorry," Priscilla said. "I just got excited. We need to find a way to talk to him."

Trudy sighed. "No we don't. I already know who he is. I wasn't really in the bathroom at Candy's. This thing's been bugging me so I called Sylvia at home."

"What did you tell her?" Priscilla asked, a little horrified. "The last thing I want is to let him know we're interested in him."

"Don't worry." Trudy smiled. "I told her he reminded me of a boy I used to date. She thinks I was trying to find out if it was the same guy."

"Oh great. So you lied."

Trudy sniffed and picked up her menu, staring at the contents. "As a matter of fact, I didn't lie, Priscilla. He really does look like my friend."

"Okay...but it's not him, is it?"

"No, it's not him."

Joan grunted. "If you two are finished going over the ethics of this situation, I'd like to know who he is."

Before Trudy could respond, someone stepped up to the table and asked if he could take their order. Priscilla looked up into Tony's face.

"Tony!" she said. "What are you doing here?"

He gave her the closest thing she'd seen to a smile since she'd met him. "I used to work at Bennie's in Vineyard Haven. It closed a while back, and Miss Tilly called to see if I wanted to fill in some this weekend until her regular staff comes back."

"Are you still going to be able to pass out flyers at two?" Priscilla asked.

"Yeah. I told Miss Tilly I had something planned today I couldn't get out of."

"I hate for you to lose wages..."

"Nah, it's fine. I'm working some tomorrow too."

Priscilla smiled at him. "Okay, I'll pick you up here at two."

"Great. Now, do you ladies know what you want for lunch?"

They gave him their orders. Joan ordered her favorite, the shrimp salad, while Trudy and Priscilla decided to try the lobster rolls. Trudy went with mayonnaise, and Priscilla ordered the butter. She was impressed by Tony's professional attitude. There was no sign of the surly teenager she'd glimpsed this morning.

When he walked away, Priscilla pointed at Trudy. "Okay, so who is that man?"

"You'll be very interested, I think. His name is Norman Whitaker. He thinks your cottage and the lighthouse would make a great bed-and-breakfast."

"A bed-and-breakfast?" Priscilla was dumbfounded. "With just two bedrooms?"

"Yeah. I pulled Candy aside at the bakery and asked her if she knew him. Everyone seems to end up at Candy's. Sure enough, she had a conversation with him. He told Candy the same thing. According to Mr. Whitaker, the covered verandah would be removed and turned into two additional bedrooms. And he also plans to add a couple of small matching cabins to the property."

"He *plans* to add them?" Priscilla took a deep breath to force down the feeling of resentment that rose up inside her. "Where did he get the idea I'd agree to something so ludicrous? He had no business *planning* anything."

"Settle down," Trudy said. "No one can force you to sell your property. Candy said he seems to be the kind of man who likes to make people think he's a big shot. You know, a wheeler and dealer."

"Well, he needs to stop spreading stories like that around. I have no intention of selling."

Trudy smiled. "We know that. Don't worry about him." She swung her gaze around the table. "The bigger question is this. Could he be the person trying to scare you off the island?"

The women were silent for several seconds. It made sense. Maybe they'd finally found their ghost.

CHAPTER THIRTEEN

After lunch, Priscilla took Trudy back to the church to work until her doctor's appointment. Joan wanted to help, but she'd promised an elderly woman who'd been a patient at the medical clinic where she worked as an ultrasound technician that she'd take her to her first chemotherapy treatment. The woman was widowed, and her children lived far away. She was afraid, and Joan wanted to help her any way she could. Trudy reassured her that they had plenty of volunteers and with a plan in place, everything was going well.

After working for a while, Priscilla drove back to the inn. She pulled up in front at two o'clock to find Tony waiting outside. When he opened the car door, she asked him to grab the flyers she'd put in the back seat.

"How do you want to do this?" he asked once he was settled in the passenger seat, the flyers in his lap.

"I'm not sure. What do you think?"

Tony looked surprised by her question, and Priscilla wondered if he wasn't used to being asked for his opinion.

"Well, I guess I'd hit businesses and homes closest to the church and then spread out."

"That sounds like a perfect idea." Priscilla smiled at him. "Should we stay together or split up?"

"Maybe we could stay together but take different sides of the street. That way we won't go to the same places." He smiled shyly at her.

"I love that idea. Let's do it. And when we're done, how about a hamburger at Walt's? Or are you working at the inn tonight?" Walt's was a small restaurant that specialized in burgers. A lot of their business was carryout, but they had some tables too. Priscilla had noticed that a lot of young people liked to hang out there.

Tony's smile widened. "I'm not scheduled until tomorrow. Walt's sounds great. Thanks."

Priscilla drove over to the church. She parked the car, and she and Tony got out and began passing out flyers. Most businesses allowed them to put the flyers on their windows or on their community bulletin boards. At houses, they decided to just stick the flyer in the door and not bother the people inside. Once they finished a street, they went back for the car and then drove up to the next block. After a while, Priscilla found herself getting tired. Tony offered to run back, pick up the car, and bring it to her. That helped a lot. It was almost four when they stopped. They only had about fifty flyers left.

"I'll hand the rest out by myself tomorrow," Tony offered.

Priscilla was only too happy to accept his offer. Even though she loved to walk, her feet hurt, and she was ready to rest.

When they arrived at Walt's, it wasn't very crowded. Most people were just getting off work and picking up food to take home. That made it easy for Priscilla and Tony to get a table. Even though it wasn't haute cuisine, Priscilla enjoyed a great cheeseburger, and

Walt had it down pat. The hamburger was crispy on the outside. It almost looked burned, yet the inside was juicy. Walt also grilled his onions in the hamburger grease and toasted the buns with butter. He used cheddar cheese and made sure it melted just right.

Tony ordered french fries, and Priscilla ordered the onion rings, which were perfectly prepared. As she stared down at her supper, she knew it wasn't the healthiest meal she'd had lately, but boy did it look and smell good.

"So do you need more help at this…church thing?" Tony asked.

Priscilla smiled at him. "We'll take all the help we can get. Your suggestions today were great. Now we're trying to get the booths up. Would you like to help us run one of them the night of the event?"

"I…I can make balloon animals."

"Really? Oh, Tony, that would be wonderful. Kids would love that. Would you be willing to do that for us?"

He took a bite of his cheeseburger and didn't answer for a moment. Priscilla could tell he was struggling a bit.

After he swallowed, he said, "I could do that, I guess."

"That's wonderful. Why don't you let me know the kind of balloons you need, and I'll get them? We'll put up a table for you."

"Sure. I could help set up the booths too."

"We'll be working on them tomorrow and plan to finish up on Monday."

"I go back to school on Tuesday, but I could come on Monday."

"You're not working at the inn?"

He shook his head. "Just tomorrow during lunch. That's it."

"That's great. Is ten in the morning on Monday too early?"

He shook his head. "I'll be there."

Priscilla thanked him again. She really was grateful for his help, but she was also excited about getting him involved at the church and away from the other boys who were such a bad influence.

She took a bite of her hamburger then chewed and swallowed while she tried to come up with something they could talk about. Finally, she said, "So you live with your aunt and uncle?"

He nodded. "My mom and dad died in a car accident last year." He looked away, over Priscilla's shoulder, as if seeing something she couldn't see. His dark brown eyes held the kind of pain no child should have to experience. Priscilla had to blink back tears. She was afraid Tony might react badly to a weepy older woman meddling in his business.

"I'm really sorry, Tony," she said once she had control of herself. "That's horrible."

He swung his gaze back to her, and Priscilla could actually see his emotional shield come up. His expression hardened, and he squared his shoulders. "No one's fault. The road was icy, and a big truck lost control. The driver felt terrible."

"I'm sure he did." Priscilla took a sip of her soft drink before saying, "So what's it like? Living with your aunt and uncle?"

He shrugged. "It's okay. They're nice. They never had kids, so it's hard for them, you know? They don't quite know what to do with me."

"I can understand that. I'm sure they're doing their best."

He nodded. "Yeah, they are. They don't like it when I get in trouble, though. I don't like it either. I never got in trouble before

I came here." His large eyes focused on hers. "I wasn't perfect, you know, but I tried to do the right thing. Then after my folks died..."

When his voice trailed off, he took another bite of his burger. Priscilla struggled with what to say next. She decided to be honest with him.

"My husband passed away about a year ago. At first I was in shock. Then I got angry. First it was with Gary. How could he leave me like that? Then I got mad at God." She smiled at Tony. "But I knew better. God didn't kill Gary. In a perfect world, we'd all live long lives. But it's not a perfect world, and sometimes bad things happen. I can't always explain it, but I know God hates it when we hurt."

Tony didn't say anything, just stared at his plate.

Priscilla took a deep breath and kept going. "You know what? At first I thought my life was over. Then suddenly a surprising door opened, and I moved here. From a farm to a cottage by the sea. With my own lighthouse. Of course, I'd rather be where I was—home with Gary—but a new adventure has begun in my life, and I'm...excited. I know this might sound odd, but I know beyond a shadow of a doubt that Gary wants me to be happy. That he's glad I'm finding a new life. I believe your parents would feel the same way, don't you?"

He kept his head down. Had she said too much? Maybe she'd gotten too personal. Finally, he looked up. When she saw the tears in his eyes, she knew it was okay. She breathed a silent prayer of thanks.

"I know they would want me to be happy," he whispered, swiping his eyes with the back of his hand. "I...I'm gonna try harder with my aunt and uncle. They're great, really. I—"

Priscilla never got to hear the rest of his sentence. The door opened, and four teenagers strode in. One of them noticed Tony and came over to the table.

"What are you doin', Tony?" he said with a sneer on his face. "This your new girlfriend?"

The other boys laughed. They were dressed like any other teenagers from the area. One of them even wore a letterman jacket. But the looks on their faces were meant to display impudence and disdain. Priscilla felt an immediate dislike for them, even though they were just kids. Chastising herself for prejudging them, she pushed away her first reaction and forced a smile.

"Tony helped me pass out some flyers for a Halloween party at Grace Community Church. You guys are welcome to come."

The teens looked shocked that she would address them directly. Then the tallest boy, the one wearing the letter jacket, burst out laughing.

"No thanks, lady. We have other plans for Halloween." He pushed Tony on the shoulder. "Come on, Tony. Or would you rather stay here with your... friend?"

Tony met Priscilla's gaze, but she wasn't sure what she saw in his face. Was it humiliation? Regret? He quickly looked away from her, stood up, and pushed his chair back.

"I've been lookin' for you guys," he said. "About time you showed up. Let's go."

Without saying another word, he left Priscilla sitting there by herself and walked out the door.

CHAPTER FOURTEEN

Priscilla was initially surprised by Tony's behavior, but she understood it. He was embarrassed in front of his friends. Still, it hurt a little. When Rachel was a teenager, she'd had moments of being mortified by her parents, but she'd never walked out on them. Of course, Rachel was their daughter. Tony barely knew Priscilla.

She gathered the remnants of their dinner and was preparing to throw it in the trash when she realized someone was standing next to her table. She looked up to see Gerald. He frowned down at her, his hazel eyes full of concern.

"I was standing in line," he said. "Saw what happened." He grunted. "Don't let it upset you. Those boys are always doing things like that. They don't have any manners."

Priscilla smiled. "It's okay. I'm trying not to take it personally."

"And you shouldn't." He looked down at the table. "Are you getting ready to leave? I was thinking about joining you if you're staying for a while."

"I was going to leave, but I'd rather stay and visit. Frankly, I think I could use the time to calm down a bit."

Gerald put his food and drink on the table and swooped up the trash Priscilla had pushed together. "Let me get rid of that for you." He leaned down. "Walt makes a great lemon milk shake. It isn't on the menu—you have to ask for it—but I guarantee it will make you feel much better. How about it? My treat."

Priscilla's mouth almost dropped open. When she was a girl, there was an ice cream store in Wheatfield that made lemon shakes. Her mother would buy them for her when she needed encouragement or comfort. Gerald's offer made it feel as if her mother were somehow reaching out, trying to console her. She gulped, pushing down a sudden rush of emotion, and said, "That sounds lovely. Thank you, Gerald."

The captain grinned, took the trash, and tossed it in a nearby receptacle. Then he went to the counter and ordered her lemon shake.

For the first time, Priscilla was brave enough to look around the small restaurant to see who had watched her interaction with Tony and his friends. Surprisingly, no one was even looking her way. Either they were too polite, or they were more interested in their own business than they were in hers.

"Here you go." Gerald put the milk shake on the table and handed her a straw. Then he sat down. "Want to tell me what led to that confrontation?"

After she thanked him, removed the paper from her straw, and stuck it into the plastic cover on top of the milk shake, she explained about passing out flyers with Tony. "I thought he needed a friend," she said. "I was told he was involved with a bad crowd, but I had no idea they'd show up here."

"I'm sure he feels awful about treating you that way. Probably ashamed of himself. Peer pressure." He shook his head. "Like drugs to these kids."

Priscilla took a sip of her milk shake while Gerald talked. It tasted so good, she closed her eyes with pleasure.

Gerald chuckled. "Looks like that milk shake agrees with you."

"Oh, it's just wonderful. Reminds me of my childhood. A place in town made lemon milk shakes. Thank you so much, Gerald."

"You're welcome."

"And I think you're right about Tony. Hopefully, he'll contact me later. I'd really like to be his friend."

"I know his aunt and uncle, Marie and Phil Gonzalez. They're good people, trying their best with him. Obviously, he wasn't in good shape when he arrived here, but he'd started to come out of his shell. Then these boys started hanging around."

"Maybe his aunt and uncle need to forbid him to spend time with them."

Gerald sighed. "Easier said than done when they go to his school. They could make it even harder on Tony if Phil and Maria step in."

"It's like they're holding him hostage."

He nodded. "The worst one is Monty Anderson. Tall? Blond?"

"Does he wear a letter jacket?"

"Yeah, that's him. He's on the football team. The school's star quarterback. I think that's another reason the school doesn't crack down on them."

"That's terrible, Gerald. These are children. You can't just allow someone to terrorize a town because they know how to play football."

"I agree." He took a sip of his drink. "But it happens all over the country."

"Well, it shouldn't."

She started to say something else, but her cell phone rang. She opened her purse and pulled it out. The call was from Myrna Holtman. "Gerald, do you mind if I take this call? I won't be long."

"No, of course not."

Priscilla accepted the call as Gerald took his trash to a nearby receptacle. "Hello?"

"Priscilla, this is Myrna Holtman. When I went to look for the letters I talked to you about, surprisingly, I found them almost immediately. I've made copies for you. Can I bring them to your place later today? Say about five thirty?"

"That would be great, Myrna. Thanks."

"Not a problem. I'll see you later."

Priscilla said goodbye and hung up.

Gerald sat down again and smiled at her.

"Sorry about that," Priscilla said. "I hate it when people take phone calls while we're visiting. It's so rude."

"I feel the same way, but I knew you wouldn't answer unless you felt you needed to."

"Yes, you're right. It was Myrna Holtman. I've been waiting for some information she has for me."

Gerald's right eyebrow shot up. "Myrna Holtman? From the ghost tours?"

Priscilla hadn't meant to mention Myrna's name. It had just slipped out. She nodded slowly. "Yes."

"I hope you're not planning to add your place to that silly tour." He frowned at her. "The only ghost I know about in connection to your lighthouse is the Weeping Woman. Is this about her?"

"You know about the Weeping Woman?"

"As a matter of fact, I do. Although not everyone on the island has heard the tale, quite a few of us are aware of it. You know, it really is an odd story. First her husband disappears. Then she does. Most people believe she jumped off that cliff, but others don't. There was an investigation after it happened. The local authorities suspected she didn't commit suicide, but nothing could ever be proven."

"Are there any records from back then?"

He shrugged. "I'm not sure." He searched her face. "May I ask why you're interested?"

She chuckled. "Well, I'm certainly not adding my property to the ghost tour. You don't need to worry about that."

"That's a relief."

Priscilla took a long sip of her milk shake, trying to decide what she should say. Would Gerald think she'd lost her mind if she told him what had happened? She struggled with what to do until she realized she was on the verge of getting a brain freeze. Gerald was a good man, and he knew a lot about the history of the area. Maybe he could help.

She took a deep breath before saying, "Someone is trying to make me think I'm being haunted by the Weeping Woman. I've seen her twice on my property."

Gerald didn't say anything, just looked at her for a moment. Finally, he said, "Why are you doing this? If you're trying to drum up business for your weekly tours, this certainly isn't the way to do it."

CHAPTER FIFTEEN

Priscilla was speechless. At first she wasn't sure she'd heard him right. "I don't understand what you mean."

He scowled at her. "What I mean is that starting up some rumor about a so-called ghost won't bring more attention to the lighthouse or its history. Maybe tourists will like it, but a lot of local people won't."

Priscilla really liked Gerald O'Bannon. Hearing him rebuke her didn't make her angry. It hurt her feelings. Before she could control them, tears jumped into her eyes.

Gerald's expression changed instantly. "Oh, Priscilla. I'm . . . I'm sorry. Of course you wouldn't do anything like that." He reached across the table and grabbed her hand. "Please forgive me."

Having a man hold her hand—any man—made her feel uncomfortable, and she gently withdrew her fingers. "I'm sorry to get so emotional. These last few days have been a little draining. First everything going on at the lighthouse, and now this thing with Tony. I apologize. Just ignore me."

"I'm not going to ignore you." Gerald sighed deeply. "I need to explain my comments."

"No, it's okay. You don't owe me anything."

"I most certainly do owe you an explanation. I was a jerk." He looked past her and stared out the window for a moment as if he needed to gather his thoughts before continuing. "Jeremiah Hennesey is a relation. Several *greats* with the word *uncle* attached." He gave her a small smile. "Please don't think this is somehow personal for me. It's really not. But what you might not know is that Jeremiah was accused of absconding with the town treasury. Supposedly that's why he never returned."

Priscilla's mouth dropped open in surprise. "That certainly isn't the story I heard. Why is this the first time anyone's mentioned this account?"

Gerald shrugged. "My family only found out about it when my aunt started working on our genealogy. When she told my parents, they were very upset. I guess the idea of possibly stirring all that up again made me react the way I did."

"I'm so sorry, Gerald," Priscilla said. "But I don't think this sudden reappearance has anything to do with what Captain Hennesey did or didn't do. I think someone is trying to scare me off the island."

"But why?"

"That's the sixty-four thousand dollar question," she said. "There are several suspects..."

"Suspects? Really."

The look on Gerald's face made her laugh. "Oh my. I don't mean to sound like a police detective."

He grinned. "Well, you'd probably do better than a lot of them." He leaned in closer. "Look, I have the day off. Could you use some help with your...investigation?"

Priscilla nodded. "Actually, I could. I'm meeting Myrna at my place at five thirty. If you're not busy..."

"I'll be there with bells on." He rubbed his chin. "You know, I'm pretty sure I have some old family records that mention what happened. Why don't I look around and see what I can find? I'll bring them with me when I come over."

"That would be fantastic. Thank you. I must tell you, though, that Myrna has a much different story. It will be interesting to see how your information meshes with hers."

"Well, since this comes directly from Captain Jeremiah Hennesey's family, I would suspect my account is much closer to the truth."

"I agree. Hopefully, between the three of us, we can uncover something that will help us figure out who is haunting me. I'm at my wit's end. Having someone show up every night pretending to be a ghost..."

"You know, Priscilla, that's harassment. Have you called the police?"

She shook her head. "I've run the conversation through my head more than once. 'Hello. I'd like to report an irritating ghost.' I just can't do it. Not yet. Not until I have some kind of proof that my visitor is human."

"But to go to these extremes. It sounds dangerous to me."

"I—I hadn't thought about it quite like that."

"Look, I'm glad to help you figure this thing out, but you need to put your personal safety first. If it happens again..."

"I'll call the police."

"Good." Gerald stood. "Let me walk you to your car."

As they left Walt's, Priscilla looked up and down the street, hoping to see Tony, but there was no sign of him. Although it wasn't the most important thing to consider under the circumstances, she wondered if he would actually pass out the rest of the flyers. She'd been so convinced he really wanted to help.

"Here we are," Gerald said when they reached her car.

She unlocked the door, and he pulled it open. "I'll see you at five thirty," he said with a smile.

"Thank you, Gerald."

Priscilla got into her car and had just pulled out of her parking space when she saw Eleanor Gufstead standing on the sidewalk, glaring at her. She'd almost forgotten about Eleanor. Was she following her? Had she seen her with Gerald? Priscilla realized that as she shared her suspicions with Gerald later this evening, she would have to bring up Eleanor. But could she? It would be so embarrassing. The last thing she wanted was to tell Gerald that Eleanor thought Priscilla had feelings for him. Would it ruin their friendship?

She sighed as she drove down the road. This situation was already confusing. Now it was starting to turn messy. And Priscilla didn't like *messy.*

She'd just started to turn toward home when she remembered she was almost out of coffee. With Gerald and Myrna both coming over, she needed to stock up. Instead of heading back to the cottage, she drove to Ortmann's, the local grocery store. As she entered, she waved to Katie Ortmann, who was talking to a customer. It only took a few minutes to find the coffee, check out, and head outside.

She was almost at her car when she heard someone call her name. She turned to see a woman with bright red hair and odd black eyebrows staring at her. Sylvia Peabody. The woman who worked for Elmer McBroom.

"Priscilla?" the woman said as she approached. "I'm Sylvia Peabody. I've never met you, but I saw you at the Art Attack the other night."

"I remember you," Priscilla said. "Nice to see you."

Sylvia smiled, and her odd eyebrows arched. Priscilla wondered if she had learned about applying eyebrow pencil from a clown. Someone really needed to help this poor woman.

"Your cousin Trudy called me this morning and asked about a man I met the other day who is interested in buying your property. He thinks it would make a great bed-and-breakfast."

Priscilla managed to smile. "She told me, but I'm not interested in selling."

"I understand. It's a lovely property. I wouldn't want to sell it either, but this man is so insistent. Perhaps you should talk to him." She reached into her purse and withdrew a card. Without asking, she jabbed it at Priscilla, who took it from her only to avoid a paper cut. "I don't mean to be pushy, but to be honest, he keeps pressuring me to approach you. I want to be able to tell him we've talked so he'll quit bothering me."

Priscilla frowned. "Why would he ask you to talk to me? We don't really know each other."

"I assume it's because I know your cousin Trudy. I could have told him no, but I felt I should warn you about him."

"Warn me? Of what?"

Sylvia hesitated a moment. "He seems much too interested in you and in your beautiful cottage. I'm going to tell him I gave you his card. Maybe he'll back off. But again, he may just turn his attention to you." She sighed. "I apologize if I've done anything to make this more difficult for you. I should have told you about him immediately, but like you said, we don't really know each other."

"It's certainly not your fault, Sylvia. I appreciate the heads-up."

"You're welcome." She smiled then turned and walked away.

Priscilla stared after her. She couldn't fault the woman for approaching her. Maybe she really was trying to help. Priscilla looked down at the card and saw the name *Norman Whitaker.* She stuck the card in her purse. Maybe she should be grateful she had Mr. Whitaker's contact information. After talking to Sylvia, he'd jumped to the top of her suspect list. Knowing how to find him could turn out to be helpful.

She sighed as she hurried to her car. Now she was late. She barely had enough time to drive home, change clothes, start the coffee, and meet Gerald and Myrna.

What a day this was turning out to be. What else would happen before it was over?

CHAPTER SIXTEEN

After taking Jake out, Priscilla barely had time to prepare coffee and put together a plate of her special macaroon cookies before her guests arrived. Thankfully, she'd baked them a couple of days ago. At the time she'd chastised herself for making so many, but now she was grateful she'd gone overboard.

After starting a fire in the fireplace, she jogged to her bedroom. She changed into her dark blue slacks and slid on a green blouse that Gary had said brought out her blue-green eyes. After some light makeup, she felt ready to go.

As she looked in the mirror, she couldn't help staring at her eyebrows. Thankfully, they looked fine. She'd never needed to use eyebrow pencil, but if she did, she'd make sure to remember Sylvia. A cautionary tale, to be sure.

She opened a drawer in the tallboy dresser and pulled out her jewelry box. After taking out a pair of pearl earrings, she put the box back and closed the drawer. When she reached up to put on one of the earrings, the other one fell out of her hand and rolled under the dresser. "Oh phooey," she said loudly. She put in the other earring and then got down on her knees to search for its partner.

The earring was nowhere to be seen. Puzzled, she stood up and moved the dresser. When she got back on her knees, she could see that the earring had fallen into a gap between the floorboards and now lay partway beneath one of the boards. Not sure what to do, she got up again, got a letter opener from the nightstand next to her bed, and then tried to pull the floorboard up. She didn't want to cause any damage, but she couldn't lose that earring. They'd been a gift from Gary on their twenty-fifth wedding anniversary. She had no intention of losing one of them.

To her surprise, the floorboard popped up easily. Priscilla was able to remove the entire piece of wood without affecting the surrounding boards. Underneath, she not only found her earring, she also found a small jewelry box nestled in a hollow someone had dug beneath the floorboard. Someone's hidden treasures? She pulled it out and put it on the floor next to her. After making sure there wasn't anything else under the floor, she slid the piece of wood back into place. Then she got up and pushed the dresser back against the wall.

Priscilla carried the dusty box over to the bed and sat down. When she opened it, she gasped with surprise. There were several fine pieces of jewelry inside, including a brooch that looked like platinum and diamonds, and a bracelet with green stones. Could they be emeralds? And the piece that surprised and delighted her— a ruby ring.

"It must be the ring Gail wanted," she said to herself, taking it out of the box. She slid the box into the drawer of her nightstand, grabbed a ring box from her own jewelry box, and put the ring into it. Then she put it in her purse. She was thrilled to realize she could give Gail the ring she'd wanted so much. Aunt Marjorie must have hidden her special jewels in what she considered a safe place. Then she obviously forgot them.

Priscilla had just finished brushing her teeth when she heard the doorbell ring. She hurried to the door to find Myrna standing there, holding a briefcase. In the short time Priscilla had been home, dark clouds had moved in, and rain threatened. The wind was much colder now too.

She was starting to close the door when Gerald's black SUV pulled up. She waited by the door as he exited his car. He was carrying a box of something, which Priscilla assumed was the information he'd told her about. Maybe she would learn more about the Weeping Woman today. And possibly, with some help, she'd begin to narrow down the suspect pool.

Gerald had just reached the porch when the rain began to pour down. He rushed past Priscilla, bumping her a little.

"I'm so sorry," he said, looking apologetic. He held out the cardboard box in his hands. "I was afraid it would get wet."

"I'm fine, and it looks okay too," she said with a smile. "If it's raining when you leave, I'll find something to put your box in so it will stay dry."

"Thank you so much," he said, a wide smile on his face. "If these pages and diaries were ruined because of my carelessness, I might be kicked out of my family."

Although he followed his statement with a hearty laugh, Priscilla could tell he was serious about keeping his papers in good condition.

He followed her inside to where Myrna waited near the fire-place. Jake sat next to her, gazing up at her with adoration while she stroked his face. Jake was clearly in love.

Priscilla was glad she'd started a fire. The room was warm and toasty, and with the rain and the drop in temperature, the living room felt especially cozy and welcoming.

"Myrna, do you know Gerald O'Bannon?" she asked as Gerald joined them in the living room.

Myrna stood up and shook his hand. "I know of you, Captain, but I'm not sure we've ever met."

Even though Gerald wasn't keen on the local ghost tours, his response was very gracious. "I don't believe we have, but I know of you too. So happy you're willing to help Priscilla with her dilemma." He walked over and patted Jake on the head. Jake's tongue lolled out the side of his mouth. What a character. He was really loving the attention.

It crossed Priscilla's mind that if Myrna was her ghostly visitor, Jake might not be so friendly. Frankly, the more she got to know her, the more Priscilla couldn't believe Myrna was the kind of person to purposely terrorize another human being.

"I'm happy to help if I can." Myrna sat in a chair, and Jake followed her, lying next to her feet. Priscilla and Gerald took seats on the couch as rain began to pound the roof and run down the windows.

"Before we start, can I get you some coffee?" Priscilla said. "I also have some macaroons."

"That would be lovely," Myrna said with a smile. "Thank you."

"Let me help you," Gerald said.

"That would be nice. Thanks."

Gerald followed her into the kitchen, where Priscilla pulled out a tray and set a carafe of coffee on it along with sugar, sweetener, and cream. Then she put the plate of cookies on the tray and grabbed some napkins.

"Those cookies look delicious," Gerald said as he picked up the tray. "After Walt's, I didn't think I'd be hungry again for a while, but I won't be able to turn these down."

"I hope you enjoy them," Priscilla said with a smile.

"If you made them, I'm certain I will."

She followed him as he carried the tray into the living room and put it on the coffee table. A few minutes later, they each had coffee and a cookie. Priscilla noticed that once in a while, Myrna snuck Jake a small bite of her cookie.

"I've told you both about my nightly caller," Priscilla said. "I'm not sure knowing the real story about Jeremiah Hennesey and his wife will give us any answers, but I noticed you both had different accounts of what happened. I'd like to hear what each you has to say and read the documents you've brought. Maybe it will give me some insight." She smiled at Gerald. "Since you're actually related to Captain Hennesey, why don't you start?"

"You're related to Jeremiah Hennesey?" Myrna said, her eyes wide. "I had no idea."

Gerald nodded. "On my mother's side. A great-great—maybe another great—uncle."

"Well, if anyone knows what happened, it should be you."

Gerald nodded. "The story I was told is that in 1854, the town treasury disappeared. For some reason, Jeremiah was accused of the crime. Since he was the owner of a very successful fishing business, most people didn't believe the rumors. However, some decided his disappearance lent credibility to the accusations. He also left his wife behind. Certainly not a relation to be proud of."

Myrna frowned at him. "I'd always heard he took off to be with another woman. In fact, during the research for our ghost tours, we stumbled across these letters. They seem to be from someone in the family." She removed a large envelope from her tote bag then opened it and carefully slid out some papers. She riffled through them and pulled one out. "This was written by a Julia Hennesey to her sister Abigail in October of 1854." She cleared her throat. "'As you have heard, dear sister, our cousin Jeremiah has gone missing. He is purported to have sought solace in the arms of another. He was supposed to sail away three days ago to be with his new love, but he hasn't been seen. Nor has his ship. His crew, who appear to be complicit in this misadventure, say he never showed up in Oaks Bluff the night they were supposed to go to sea. He was to meet with them, and they were to sail with him to Boston, where he would disembark. His crew was to tell Olivia he had been lost overboard, but when they arrived, the ship was not moored in its usual place, and Captain Hennesey failed to appear. Of course, the crew became concerned and had to reveal Jeremiah's deceitful plan. Even though she is aware of his planned betrayal, Olivia is beside herself with grief. I am consumed with concern for her very life.'"

Myrna put the letter down and looked at them. "The next page of this letter is missing, but I have a few other letters that also mention the incident. There isn't any additional information, though. Basically, they just say that Captain Hennesey is missing and that the family is searching extensively for him. Unfortunately, they were never able to locate him. Or the *Lady Olivia*, his boat." She frowned at Gerald. "There's no mention of money missing from the town treasury."

Gerald sighed and picked up the box he'd brought with him. "I don't have any letters, but I found this. My great-aunt Lucy was working on our family genealogy and came across some information about the captain." He nodded toward Myrna. "It's been a bone of contention in my family ever since. Frankly, it doesn't matter to me, but my older relations seem to take it rather personally." He put the box on the table and opened it. First he lifted out a large stack of papers. "These are notes my aunt made while researching our family." He pulled out an old ledger and began thumbing through its pages. Finally, he stopped. "Here," he said, pointing at a page. He picked it up and held it closer to his face.

At that moment, the wind shrieked outside, causing Priscilla to gasp involuntarily. She tried to cover it with a cough while she silently chastised herself for reacting so ridiculously.

"I won't read it word for word because my aunt's train of thought wanders in many different directions. But she says that she uncovered a story about our ancestor, Captain Jeremiah Hennesey. She goes on to explain how he's related to us, and then she writes: 'Supposedly Captain Hennesey absconded with a large sum of money taken from the city treasury. He took off for Boston but never reached his destination. No one knows what happened to the money—or the captain.'

"She also mentions Olivia—that she was so distraught she threw herself off a cliff in Misty Harbor on..." He hesitated for a moment. "*Hmmm*. Hadn't noticed that before," he said softly. He shook his head. "Now don't let this upset you. We all know ghosts aren't real."

"What does it say, Gerald?" Priscilla asked.

He cleared his throat. "She threw herself off a cliff in Misty Harbor on October 31, 1854. Halloween night."

CHAPTER SEVENTEEN

As soon as Gerald finished speaking, lightning cracked outside, causing all three of them to jump. Jake barked loudly, which only added to their consternation. When Priscilla saw the looks on Gerald's and Myrna's faces, she burst out laughing. Seconds later, they both joined her.

Gerald, who was still chuckling, wiped his eyes. "Just goes to show you how susceptible we are."

Myrna grinned at him. "Which is why our tours are so popular. We really don't emphasize the *ghost* part. Instead, we use the stories to educate people about our history. But still... People are always asking us if we've seen ghosts ourselves."

"What do you say?" Gerald asked.

"We try to change the subject. I don't think it would inspire much confidence if we admitted we don't believe in ghosts. And that we've never seen one."

"Maybe Priscilla should go with you," he said. "Seems she's the one who's seen a ghost."

Priscilla shook her head. "Frankly, I'm ready to find out just who my ghost really is." She got up and went to the window. The rain was coming down heavily. If it kept up, maybe the Weeping Woman would stay away tonight. "Looks like it might be a while before the rain lets up." She turned back. "Let's get back to our discussion. Why do we have two stories?"

Gerald shrugged. "I would assume both are true. Captain Hennesey had a girlfriend—and he took the town's money. Maybe he and his lady friend planned to live on it once they were together."

"But he never made it to Boston." Priscilla returned to the couch. "In fact, he didn't even make it to…" She looked over at Myrna.

"Oak Bluffs."

"Right."

"So how could an entire boat disappear? And the captain with it?"

"He must have taken it out earlier," Gerald said. "Maybe he planned to meet his crew, but something happened. It must have gone down. There's no other explanation. If we could only know what the weather was like that night…"

"We can," Myrna said. She grabbed her tote bag again and pulled out her iPhone. "Mildred at the museum. She has a collection of *Farmer's Almanacs*. I'll bet she could find out." She glanced at her watch. "Hopefully, she's still at the museum." Within seconds, she had Mildred on the phone.

"If the boat went down, it couldn't be that far from here," Gerald said softly to Priscilla. "Not if Jeremiah actually planned to meet his crew that night."

"Could it have been a diversion?" Priscilla asked. "You know, like a magic trick. Perhaps he wanted to keep everyone from seeing what he was really up to. While everyone waited for him at Oak Bluffs, he really sailed for Boston without his crew."

"That would make sense, but then why bring his crew in on it in the first place?" Gerald asked. "Wouldn't it have made more sense to keep them in the dark so no one would know about his affair?"

"You're right."

Priscilla was turning this over in her head when Myrna hung up her phone.

"Mildred's going to research the night of October 17, 1854, and call me back. If there was a storm that night, then it's entirely possible the captain's ship went down before he had a chance to put his plan into action."

"But where was he?" Gerald asked. "Wouldn't he normally keep his ship moored at Oak Bluffs?"

Myrna nodded. "That doesn't mean he might not have taken it out himself sometimes, but it certainly is an interesting question. What was he doing before he was supposed to meet his crew?"

Priscilla leaned forward and put her hands on her knees. "I really hate to mention this, but maybe the reason he had the boat out wasn't for his girlfriend. Maybe it had something to do with the money."

The three were silent as they considered that.

"So he takes the money and sails away?" Gerald said thoughtfully. "Leaving behind his friend in Boston and his wife in Tisbury?"

Priscilla snapped her fingers. "Maybe there never was a girlfriend. Could it be that he made that up so everyone would think that's what he was doing instead of stealing money?"

Gerald wagged a finger at her. "Now that makes sense."

Myrna nodded. "He sails somewhere exotic, changes the name of his boat, and lives out the rest of his life in luxury."

"But if there wasn't a girlfriend," Priscilla said, "why not take Olivia with him? I mean, maybe he chose the money over his wife, but unless they had a troubled marriage, wouldn't they have left together?"

Myrna frowned. "Those are great questions. Just how much money did he get away with? If he took it, that is?"

"I'm not sure of the exact amount," Gerald said, "but according to my aunt, it was quite substantial. The fishing and whaling industry was flourishing then, and people were making a lot of money. They were buying property and building homes."

"So it was enough to take care of Jeremiah for a while?"

"I would think so."

"But what does this have to do with your ghost?" Myrna asked.

Priscilla shook her head. "I honestly don't know. I'm just trying to understand the present by looking into the past. You'd be surprised how often they connect."

Myrna glanced at her watch. "I have to leave before long. Ed and I are meeting someone for dinner. We—"

She was interrupted by her phone, which she quickly picked up. "Hello?" After listening for a while, she thanked the caller and hung up. "Well, it seems the weather was fine the night of October 17, 1854. No storms. Calm seas." She frowned as she gazed at Priscilla and Gerald. "I hoped we might find a reason for Captain Hennesey's ship to disappear, but the weather couldn't have been a factor. Sorry."

"Well, at least we can rule it out," Priscilla said.

Myrna sighed. "I'm not sure any of this helped you figure out who's trying to frighten you, but it was certainly interesting. I wish I could stick around to see if the Weeping Woman shows up again tonight." She got up and went to the window. When she pulled back the curtain, they could see that it was still raining, but the sky wasn't as dark, and the rain was much lighter. "Looks like it's clearing up." She turned back to where Priscilla and Gerald sat watching her. "I've really enjoyed this. It was so nice getting to know both of you."

Priscilla stood up. "Thank you so much for sharing your information, Myrna. I really appreciate it."

Myrna handed the letters she'd brought to Priscilla. "These are all copies of the originals. I thought maybe you'd like to keep them."

"That would be wonderful. Thank you again."

"I really hope you catch this person, Priscilla. You're a welcome addition to our community. I hate that one of us would treat you so shamefully."

Priscilla was touched by Myrna's kind comments and gave her a quick hug. "Thank you." She took Myrna's coat from the coat rack and handed it to her then pulled the door open.

Gerald stood up and said goodbye before Myrna slipped out into the rain and jogged to her car. Priscilla closed the door and turned to look at him.

"You know," he said, "Myrna and Ed are at the top of my list for people who might want you to think you're being haunted.

Stirring up a new and exciting ghost story could only help their business."

"I realize that," Priscilla said slowly. "It's certainly been on my mind, but I just can't believe it. She doesn't seem like the type of person to do something like that."

Gerald sat back down on the couch. "I understand what you're saying, but the best con men—and women—know how to look like the last people you'd ever suspect."

"That's true." She bent over and felt the coffee carafe, which was cool. "I'll get us some fresh coffee."

"Can I help?"

"Sure. Why don't you carry the tray back into the kitchen for me?"

"Happy to do it." He grabbed the tray and followed her into the kitchen. "So besides Myrna and Ed, who else do you suspect?"

Priscilla pointed at the counter near the coffeepot, and Gerald set the tray down. "Well, one person stands out above the rest."

"And who is that?"

"His name is Norman Whitaker. Have you met him?"

Gerald shook his head. "The name doesn't sound familiar."

"Seems he's attempted to befriend Sylvia Peabody, trying to get her to introduce him to me, even though she and I didn't even know each other before he came to town. He seems determined to buy my property for some bed-and-breakfast scheme. Sylvia contacted me to let me know what he's been up to and gave me his card."

Gerald snorted. "A bed-and-breakfast? Doesn't this place have two bedrooms? What kind of B&B only has two bedrooms?"

"That's what I said, but supposedly he has plans to expand."

Gerald's eyebrows shot up. "He's already expanding? And he hasn't talked to you?" He leaned against the counter and stared at her. "Why wouldn't this man approach you directly, Priscilla? Why would he go through Sylvia? I don't get it."

As she poured fresh coffee into the carafe and put a few more cookies on the serving plate, she turned Gerald's question over in her head. He was right. Norman Whitaker hadn't tried even once to contact her. It was definitely strange.

CHAPTER EIGHTEEN

Let's put this Norman guy aside for a bit," Gerald said once they were seated again in the living room. This time Priscilla sat on the couch while Gerald took the chair where Myrna had been. "Who else seems as if they might have a reason for you to leave town?"

Priscilla took a sip of coffee, sighed, and then put her cup down. "Unfortunately, it seems there are several people. And then there's Tony and his friends. I doubt they're trying to scare me off the island, but they might think frightening me is funny. I understand they caused some trouble last Halloween. Maybe this is some kind of prank because of the upcoming holiday."

"Yes, they did create a ruckus last year. Besides decorating several houses with toilet paper, some homes were assaulted with eggs, and several children had their candy stolen. Of course, Tony wasn't here when that happened. But everyone is fairly confident Monty and his friends were behind it."

"But why would they put on this elaborate charade?" Priscilla mused. "What would it benefit them?"

"What does throwing toilet paper up in trees do for anyone?" Gerald shook his head. "I'm afraid they do it for the thrill."

"So cheap entertainment?"

"I'm afraid so." Gerald took a sip of his coffee. "Next?"

"Well, I still can't understand how Aleeta Armbruster didn't notice that one of Joan's paintings was gone and the Weeping Woman picture was in its place."

Gerald looked at her in confusion, and Priscilla realized he had no idea what she was talking about. She quickly told him about the exhibit.

"So you saw this painting right before the Weeping Woman showed up on the cliff outside your house?"

"Yes. It seems to be the starting point for my supposed haunting." She shook her head. "Frankly, it was a rather compelling painting. Well done."

"Do you know who painted it?"

"Well, no. Not really." Priscilla launched into the story of the signature and the anagram.

"How in the world did you figure that out?" Gerald asked, looking surprised. "I don't think it would have occurred to me. I would have taken the signature at face value."

"Normally, I would too," Priscilla said slowly. "I can't really explain it, but sometimes my mind just loves puzzles. There was something about the name. And then when Trudy did an Internet search under that name and got nowhere... Well, it didn't seem right. That's when I wondered if it was an anagram."

Gerald leaned forward and clasped his hands together. "I don't like this, Priscilla. *Leave Martha's Vineyard?* That's a little frightening. So someone took the time and trouble to create a painting, put it up in a shop right under the proprietor's nose, and then dress up like a ghost and jump off the edge of a cliff? Doesn't that seem a little unhinged to you?"

"I understand what you're saying, but if whoever this is really wanted to hurt me, Gerald, wouldn't they have done it already? It's not like I'm hard to get to out here."

"Which doesn't make me feel any better." He took a deep breath and let it out slowly.

Priscilla could tell he was worried about her. She appreciated it, but she really didn't feel she was in danger. Someone wanted her to leave town. They didn't appear to want to harm her physically.

"Okay, is that it?" he asked.

She stared at him for a moment, not sure what to say. Bringing up the next name was going to be embarrassing. Finally, she asked, "Do you know a woman named Eleanor Gufstead?"

The color drained from Gerald's face. "Oh no. Why do you mention her?"

"She . . . she confronted me that night at the Art Attack."

Gerald took a deep breath and rolled his eyes. "I'm so sorry. Eleanor was a friend . . . or so I thought. I met her through other friends who invited both of us to dinner one night. Although it was never supposed to be a date, she got a different idea in her head. She seemed nice, and we got along just fine, but I didn't have any interest in her. You know, romantically. But she kept showing up, calling me, asking for another *date*. I finally had a talk with her, tried to explain, but it didn't go well. To be honest, I haven't been sure what to do about it ever since. I've been trying to ignore the situation, hoping she'd come to her senses." He shook his head.

"The last thing I want to do is hurt her feelings, but that may be unavoidable." He looked at Priscilla. "Do you mind if I ask what she said?"

"She just asked where you were. When I said I didn't know, she left. She seemed very upset."

"I'm so sorry," Gerald said.

It was obvious he was upset. "It's all right. Not your fault. But do you think she's the kind of person who would go to extremes to make me—or anyone else—leave town if she thought you were interested in them?"

He frowned and stared into his coffee cup for a moment. Finally, he said, "I'm just not sure, Priscilla. I'd like to say no, but I just don't know her that well. Her actions have certainly taken me by surprise in the past. You're not the first person she's accosted."

"I'm sorry, Gerald. Obviously, the poor woman needs help. What are you going to do?"

"My friends, the ones who invited us for dinner, know her daughter. She lives in Boston. They intend to talk to her, see if she can help her mom. Once I tell them she approached you, my guess is they'll go ahead and reach out to her. I hate to do that, but at this point, it's about the only option we seem to have."

"I hope that will help, but I'm sure it will embarrass Eleanor."

"I agree, but what else can we do?"

Priscilla didn't respond, but she nodded her agreement. Some women felt the need to have a man in their lives. Eleanor appeared to be one of them. Her desperation was heartbreaking.

Gerald drained the rest of his coffee. "It's getting late, and I need to get going," he said. "Unless you'd like me to stay and ghost-watch with you."

Priscilla smiled at him. "It's still raining. If it keeps up, I doubt there'll be a floor show tonight. But thanks." She didn't want him to feel obligated, but truthfully, she didn't want to be alone at night until the ghost was caught. However, the idea of telling anyone she wanted company made her feel weak—and she didn't want to give in to fear.

"I'm going to do a little poking around if that's okay with you," Gerald said as he stood up. "I might not be the detective you are, but maybe I can stumble across something that will help."

"That would be great." She smiled. "You really don't need to bother with this, though. I'm sure you're busy."

"I'm not all that busy right now, and besides, solving a mystery is ... exciting."

Priscilla laughed. "I'm sure I'll feel that way once it's over. Right now? Exciting isn't the word I'd choose."

She smiled as she listened to Gerald's hearty laugh. It was warm and inviting.

"You're right," he said. "I stand corrected."

Priscilla thanked him again and walked him out onto the covered patio. She waved as he drove away then wrapped her arms around herself and shivered in the cold. The rain continued to fall steadily as the night grew chillier. Although Priscilla loved rainy days and nights, she prayed her ghost didn't.

CHAPTER NINETEEN

A few minutes after Gerald left, it started to rain harder again, giving Priscilla even more hope that the night would remain quiet. However, Jake wasn't as happy as she was about the wet weather. Priscilla put on her raincoat, galoshes, and hat. Then she found Jake's leash and finally coaxed him outside. He stayed near the house and did what he needed to do in record time. Then he ran back to the porch so quickly that he almost pulled Priscilla off her feet.

"Settle down, Jake," she commanded. Even though the idea of taking a tumble onto the wet ground wasn't humorous, the look on Jake's face made her giggle. "You're not really the big, brave dog you want everyone to think you are, are you?" she asked him.

When they stepped into the house, she ordered him to stay near the front door while she grabbed a towel to dry him off. When she came back, he'd already shaken himself, sending water droplets everywhere.

"Oh, Jake," she said with a sigh. "I don't suppose you plan to clean this up, do you?"

His doggy grin made it clear she would be handling the mess alone. As she dried him off, he leaned into the towel like it was his salvation. When she was done and told him he could go, he ran over to the rug, dropped down on his back, and began to roll around, trying to dry off even more.

"For goodness' sake. You act like you're going to melt." She grinned at his antics before she carried the towel to the dirty clothes basket. When she came back into the room, he was lying in front of the fire and finally looked content.

"How about some supper?" she asked him.

Food was one of Jake's favorite things, but he just turned his head away and chose to stay right where he was. Obviously being comfortable was more important than his stomach right now.

Priscilla rummaged around in the refrigerator, looking for something to eat. She hadn't finished her cheeseburger at Walt's and was hungry. There were some great leftovers, including a nice helping of beef stew, but she just wasn't in the mood for it. For some reason, she thought about Gary. One of his favorite comfort foods had been grilled cheese sandwiches. Priscilla had butter, cheddar cheese slices, and sourdough bread. Perfect. She also had some slices of ham, but she preferred her grilled cheese with only cheese.

About fifteen minutes later, she sat down in the kitchen with a hot, gooey grilled cheese sandwich, some garlic coleslaw, and a bowl of strawberries. It was a little after eight o'clock, and the sun had gone down. After finishing her meal, Priscilla got up and turned on the radio that sat on her counter. The deejay was reading a weather report for Martha's Vineyard.

"Strong storms are headed your way," he said. "Winds up to sixty miles an hour have been reported. It might be good to remove items from your yard that could blow away. Be sure you have flashlights and anything else you might need if you lose electricity. There will be very heavy rain, and we've got a few flood warnings to tell you about."

Priscilla tuned out the rest of the report, since she wasn't in a floodplain, but she did put her raincoat back on and go out on the porch to tie down her chairs. To her surprise, the rain had stopped. At least for a while.

She was on her way back into the house when she heard a faint noise. Not sure what it was, Priscilla walked down her porch steps and looked around. The cat she'd seen last night came strolling around the side of the house.

"There you are," Priscilla said. "I'm so glad you didn't drown in all this rain."

As the cat rubbed up against her legs, Priscilla reached down to pet him. "You're completely dry," she said, frowning. "How did you manage to stay out of the rain?"

He just sat down and stared up at her.

"Are you hungry? Stay here. I think I have a can of tuna."

She hurried back inside the house, found the tuna, dumped it into a bowl, and went back out on the porch. Thankfully, the cat was still there. She set the bowl down.

"Here you go. I bet you'll like that."

To her surprise, the cat sniffed at the bowl but then turned and walked a few steps away, his tail sticking up almost like a question mark.

"My goodness. You're dry and you're not hungry. I guess some-one really is taking care of you." She reached down to pet him again, and he purred at the attention. "You really are a beautiful cat. I wish I could take you in, but I'm not sure you'd like Jake. I'm happy to introduce you at some point. Who knows? Maybe you'll become friends."

Jake must have overheard her talking to someone on the front porch because he started to bark. The cat immediately ran away, back toward the cliff. Obviously, he wasn't too excited about the idea of meeting her dog. At least Priscilla didn't have to worry about the cat anymore.

She went back inside and located several flashlights and a couple of lanterns that ran on batteries. She was thankful for her fireplace and that there was plenty of wood cut and ready for use.

She'd just put a kettle on the stove when the phone rang. When she picked it up, she heard Joan on the other end.

"I'd planned to come over there tonight," she told Priscilla. "I don't want you to be alone, but the weather is supposed to get pretty bad. I really hate driving when it's raining hard."

"Oh, Joan, thanks, but I'm just fine. I had company all evening. Jake and I are settling down for a cozy night. Besides, I doubt I'll have any unwelcome visitors tonight. Not in this weather."

As if someone were listening, Priscilla heard a clap of thunder. The sound of rain began to slap against the roof.

"I hope you're right," Joan said.

Priscilla could hear the hesitation in her voice. "Really, Joan. I'm just fine. If anything happens, I'll call you, okay?"

"I guess so. I should have started out right away, you know. When the rain let up for a while. I thought I had plenty of time."

"Really, don't worry. I'll call you in the morning."

"All right. Did you say you had company all evening?"

Priscilla sat down at the kitchen table and told Joan about her day. When she got to the part about Tony, Joan interrupted her.

"He did what? Well, that was really rude. What's wrong with him?"

"It's just peer pressure, Joan. I could tell he didn't want to go along with those boys."

"Maybe," she said slowly. "Just be careful, Priscilla. Don't let him manipulate you. I don't trust them. Monty Anderson has done some really awful things. Not only is he a bully, a lot of us suspect he's behind a series of robberies in town."

"Oh, Joan. Robberies? Really? I hate to think about any young person being so confused."

"Confused?" Joan laughed softly. "I just love your heart, Priscilla. I'm afraid Monty isn't that confused. He knows exactly what he's doing."

"What about his parents? What are they like?"

"They're quite wealthy. Privileged—and they know it. Rude. Want their own way. Unfortunately, there are quite a few families like that who live on Martha's Vineyard—or at least spend part of the year here."

"See, Monty just needs some discipline. If he could be taught to respect himself, he would respect others."

"Uh, yeah. You might be right, but at this point, I think you should steer clear of him. And maybe Tony as well."

"I know Tony's a good kid, Joan. I have no doubt about it."

"I hope you're right, but if he shows up again, will you at least let me know?"

"Okay."

At that moment, the wind shrieked outside, and Priscilla heard a click over the phone. Then the lights went off. She called Joan's name several times, but there was no response. The phone was dead. She tried to call her back, but all she could get was a fast busy signal. Then she tried her cell phone but it wasn't working as well. Either the cell tower had been affected, or service was overloaded because of the storm. It was probably the latter. She sighed and put down the phone. Thankfully, with the fireplace going, there was light in the house—and warmth. She'd gone through several power outages at the farm, so this wasn't a new experience for her. Kansas in the spring was full of storms that affected residents—especially those living in the country.

She went into the kitchen and poured some hot coffee into a thermos to keep it warm. As the lightning cracked outside, Jake began to bark and pant. Priscilla and Gary had once owned a dog that hated thunderstorms. Priscilla got Jake's leash, fastened it to his collar so he couldn't run and hide somewhere, talked softly to reassure him, and led him over to the couch, where she settled down with a warm throw, a cup of coffee, and a book. With the light from the battery-powered lamp, she could easily read. Although she was concerned about the food in her refrigerator, she'd learned back on the farm that getting upset about things you couldn't do anything about was a waste of time.

Within a few minutes, Jake seemed much calmer. When he heard thunder, at first he raised his head and looked around, but Priscilla told him everything was okay in a soothing voice. Animals were responsive to the tone their owners set. If you stayed relaxed, they could do the same. Within a short time, Jake was asleep in spite of the thunder outside. Actually, it was turning out to be one of the coziest evenings Priscilla had spent since moving to Martha's Vineyard.

About an hour later, she was starting to get sleepy when the peaceful atmosphere was shattered by the figure of someone walking past the windows outside the cottage.

CHAPTER TWENTY

At first Priscilla tried to tell herself she'd imagined it. But then whoever it was stood in front of a different window. All she could see was a shadow. She eased away from Jake, who looked at her for a moment but then put his head down again. He obviously hadn't noticed anything.

Priscilla walked quietly up to the window and snuck a look through the curtain, but there was no one there. A flash of anger shot through her. She had no intention of giving in to another phantom guest. One was more than enough.

Although it probably wasn't the smartest thing to do, she pulled the front door open and stepped out onto the covered porch. Just as she did, someone ran toward the other side of the verandah.

"Stop!" she called out. "Stop right where you are."

Surprisingly, he halted in his tracks. Her voice had alerted Jake, who began to bark like crazy. Priscilla closed the door behind her so he wouldn't run out and attack the cowering figure at the edge of the porch.

"Turn around," she said. "Who are you?"

The hoodie-covered person twisted slowly around. She was surprised to see Tony's face.

"Tony," she said. "Why are you here?"

He walked slowly toward her. Priscilla's hand went to the door-knob. If something went wrong, she'd open the door and let Jake out. He was protective enough, he would probably chase the boy away. But when she saw Tony's face, her hand dropped. She couldn't believe he meant her any harm.

"I . . . I was worried about you," he said. "I know you live by your-self. Storms out here can get pretty bad. Especially when you're close to the ocean." He looked like a drowned rat, soaked to the skin.

"Stay there," she said. She went inside and put Jake in the bed-room. He wasn't happy about it and barked loudly when she closed the door, but she was afraid he would consider Tony a threat and wanted time to let him calm down. "I'll be right back," she said, trying to reassure him. Then she hurried back to the front door and pulled it open. "Come on in," she said to the wet teenager.

"Thanks." His teeth were chattering so loudly she could hear them. "It's kinda cold out here."

When he stepped inside, water pooled on the floor. "Goodness gracious," she said, sighing. "Stay here. I'll get some towels."

As she hurried to the linen closet, she realized that wasn't going to be enough to get Tony dry. She went into the spare bedroom and pulled out a pair of sweats and a thick sweatshirt that had belonged to Gary. Although she'd gotten rid of most of his clothes, she liked to wear these when she slept. It made her feel close to him. She carried the towels and the clothes into the living room, where Tony stood shivering.

"Here," she said, tossing him a towel. "Dry off the best you can and then take these sweats into the bathroom. After you change, give me your clothes. I'll hang them near the fireplace so we can get them dry."

He didn't say anything, just nodded. After drying his hair and taking his shoes and hoodie off, he went into the bathroom. A few minutes later, he returned with the sweats and sweatshirt on. As he handed Priscilla his wet clothes, she noticed that his feet were bare.

"Oh my goodness. I forgot to get you something for your feet." She pointed at the couch. "Sit down and cover up. I'll get you some socks and then something warm to drink." She hurried to her bedroom, pushed her way past Jake, and pulled a clean pair of thick socks out of a drawer. Hopefully they would fit him. Gary used to tease her about her *giant feet*. "At least you'll never topple over in a big wind," he'd say with a grin. Thinking of him made her ache, but she squared her shoulders and redirected her thoughts. She needed to concentrate on Tony right now.

She grabbed Jake's leash and leaned down so she could see his face. "Now, you listen here," she said. "You're going to be nice to that boy out there. You hear me?"

Jake gave her a sloppy kiss, making her laugh. Together they went back into the living room. Jake didn't bark at Tony. He just stared at him with interest.

"Put these socks on," she said, tossing them to Tony. As he pulled them on, his smile told her they felt good on his chilled feet. "This is Jake," Priscilla said. "Although he hasn't been mine a long time, I truly don't think he'll hurt you."

A wide smile split Tony's face. "I'm sure he won't. I love dogs." He held out his hand, and Priscilla let go of the leash, sending up a short prayer for protection. She needn't have worried. Jake immediately went to Tony and rubbed up against him as the boy ran his hands over the dog's soft head. Instant friends. Priscilla shook her head. Dogs and kids. It was as if they were on a wavelength all their own. When Rachel was little, their dog, Brady, was always so sweet and protective of her. Priscilla never worried about Rachel's safety.

"I have some hot coffee," she said. "Are you hungry?" The way he shrugged, she knew he was. "I can't make you anything hot, but how about a ham and cheese sandwich?"

Tony smiled. "That would be great. I love ham and cheese."

"Good. Mayo or mustard?"

Tony looked confused. "Mustard," he said as if asking that question was totally unnecessary. Priscilla almost laughed. She felt the same way about ham sandwiches, but Gary had always asked for mayo. She'd tried to convert him to mustard through the years, but he'd never wavered.

"Okay. I'll be right back."

She quickly made the sandwich and added some chips to his plate. When she returned, Jake was up on the couch, snuggled next to Tony. It seemed her cozy evening was over. Although she was glad to see Tony, she needed to find out why he'd been skulking around outside.

She waited until he was almost finished eating before asking, "So you came out here to check on me?"

He nodded, chewed, and swallowed. "Yeah, I was worried. You really shouldn't be up here by yourself."

Priscilla laughed. "I'm not alone. As you can see, Jake takes good care of me."

Tony smiled. "Yeah, he's a real killer."

"He really is very protective," she said. "When he knows I'm not worried, he relaxes. He can tell you're someone I trust."

Tony put his sandwich down and frowned at her. "How can you say that after what I did?"

Priscilla shrugged. "I realize it's hard to stand up to your friends."

"They're not friends," he spit out.

"Then why—"

"I guess I was just afraid." He sighed. "I wasn't raised to act like that. My parents would be ashamed of me."

"Oh, Tony. I guarantee you they wouldn't. They'd understand. Look, when we go through really difficult things, it makes us act in ways we wouldn't normally. What we do might not be right, but it's understandable."

He shook his head. "Losing your family is hard."

"I know."

"I...I'm sorry. I really am." His eyes were shiny with tears.

"You don't have to be sorry. No one should apologize for their feelings."

He smiled. "My dad used to say it was okay to have negative feelings, but we shouldn't live our lives by them."

"Your father was a very smart man."

"Yeah, he was. My uncle reminds me of him. I've been trying harder with him and my aunt, I really have. But then those guys come around..."

"You don't have to hang out with them, you know."

"When I first got here, I thought they were nice. They...they wanted to be my friends, and it helped. I didn't feel so lonely. Then they started...doing things. Things I didn't want to be involved in. I tried to break away. But Monty—the tall guy?"

She nodded, urging him to continue.

"He told me they'd ruin my life at school if I didn't stick with them. I was too afraid to say no." He shook his head as he stroked Jake's side. "When they treated you like that today...I mean, they don't even know you."

"No, they don't." She studied him for a moment. "Tony, may I ask about the fight you got into? The one that got you suspended?"

He stared at her for a moment. "Monty was pushing a kid around. Calling him names. The kid is...a little different, you know? Smart. Quiet. Doesn't try to act cool. He used to like school, got good grades, until Monty and the other guys decided to harass him."

"Monty went after him because he likes school?"

He nodded. "Isn't that dumb?"

"Yes, it is. So you were defending this kid?"

"Yeah. His name is Derrick. Lately he's seemed, I don't know, sad. Depressed, you know? It worries me."

Priscilla felt a sense of alarm rise inside of her. "What happened after the fight? I mean, why are you and Monty still friends?"

Tony grunted and rolled his eyes. "I'm being given another chance. I told Monty to leave Derrick alone, though."

Priscilla leaned forward. "Tony, I think you need to talk to someone at your school. I'm worried about Derrick, that he might hurt himself. Do you understand?"

He nodded slowly. "Yeah, I think that's why I got so upset. I knew a guy back in Colorado who killed himself. Derrick reminds me of him. If only I'd been friends with Ben..."

"It might not have made any difference. It's hard to know. But I'm sure Derrick would appreciate having a friend now."

"If I do that, Monty and those other guys will come after me again."

"Are you strong enough for that?" Priscilla asked softly.

She saw a light come into Tony's eyes. "Yeah, I'm strong enough."

"I believe that." She smiled at him. She noticed that the room seemed darker and realized the glow from the lantern was getting low. She grabbed it and stood up. "I need to put new batteries in this. I'll be right back."

Tony nodded.

When she got to the kitchen, Priscilla removed a new package of batteries from a drawer, lit the candle that sat on her kitchen table, and quickly changed them out.

As she headed back into the living room, she took a deep breath, trying to calm her concerns. She couldn't believe Tony had anything to do with the Weeping Woman, but she wasn't so sure about his friends. What if they were behind this? She wanted to know the truth, but she didn't want Tony to get hurt. Right now she was really worried about his safety.

CHAPTER TWENTY-ONE

When she put the lantern on the table, Priscilla asked Tony, "Do your aunt and uncle know where you are?"

He shook his head. "Nah. I told them I was going out with the guys. And I was. But then at the last minute I decided to come here. After I heard the weather report."

"But with this storm, don't you think they're probably worried about you?"

"Yeah, but I can't call them. My cell phone isn't working."

Priscilla nodded. "Mine either." She walked over to the window and looked out. The rain was still coming down, but the wind seemed to have calmed. It looked as if the main part of the storm had moved away from them. "I think I should drive you home. We'll wait until the rain lets up a bit."

"Thanks." He looked down at the sweats he was wearing. "Are my clothes about dry?"

She walked over to the fireplace and checked the jeans and shirt she'd hung over the back of a nearby chair. "Almost. A few more minutes, and they should be fine." She sat down again. "Tony, I need to ask you something. About you and those boys."

He nodded. "Sure."

"Something odd has been happening here on my property. Someone's been trying to scare me. It could be related to Halloween. Is it possible Monty and those other boys are behind it?"

He cocked his head and frowned at her. "If they are, I don't know about it. But you never know with those guys. They're liable to do anything. I can try to find out for you."

"No, that's okay. I don't want you to get in trouble with them."

"How has someone been trying to scare you?"

Priscilla took a sip from her coffee cup. The coffee was cold, but she didn't care. She needed a moment to think. Should she tell him what had been happening? After going back and forth several times, she decided to tell him the truth. If he found out later and realized she'd kept it from him, he might conclude that she didn't trust him.

"I know you haven't been here long," she said slowly, "but have you heard of the Weeping Woman?"

His eyebrows arched in surprise. It was obvious he had no idea what she was talking about. "Weeping Woman? That's a new one on me."

Priscilla quickly went over the highlights of Olivia's story. When she finished, Tony's eyes were as wide as saucers.

"You're telling me you've seen this woman on the cliff?"

"Yes, twice now. I thought she might show up tonight, but with the rain..."

"Look, I wouldn't put anything past those guys," Tony said, his tone serious, "but to be honest, this sounds a little too...complicated for them. I mean, they know how to TP a house or throw eggs at someone's windows, but this is really different. I'm not sure they're creative enough to come up with something like this."

Priscilla could see Tony's point. It did seem a little too sophisticated for them.

"I'd like to see this Weeping Woman," Tony said. "I'm sure I'd know right away if it was them."

"I doubt your aunt and uncle are going to let you come over every night in case my ghost shows up."

Tony laughed. "I think you're right. I can't see that conversation going my way."

Priscilla smiled at him but then got serious. "I really wish you'd cut off your relationship with them. Seems to me Derrick is the one who would make a good friend."

Tony sighed. "My social life would be over, but I think you're right."

"You might not believe this, but I suspect some people at your school would love to see someone stand up to Monty and his crew. You might pick up more friends than you can imagine."

"You don't know what high school is like. It's...it's a battleground."

"Well, it shouldn't be." Priscilla stood up. "I want to help you, but I suspect that if I stick my nose into things, it could actually be worse for you."

He nodded. "You're right. The only way for me to change things is to do it myself. I'm gonna break it off with those guys. But before I do, I'll poke around a little, see what they've been up to. If I find out anything that might help you, I'll let you know." He gave her a tentative smile. "Thanks, Mrs. Grant. For everything."

"You're very welcome," she said, returning his smile. The rain was falling lightly now, and she hadn't heard thunder in a while. "I think I need to get you home now, while I can." She'd barely finished speaking when the lights suddenly came on. "Oh, great!" she said enthusiastically.

Tony pulled his phone out of his pocket and tried it. "Still not working," he said.

"There might be too many people trying to call out right now. The service is overloaded. I'm sure it will clear up before long."

Tony petted Jake a few more times and then gently removed the dog's head from his lap before he stood up. "Can Jake come with us?"

"Of course." Priscilla stopped for a moment, thinking. "Why don't you ask your aunt and uncle if you could do some work for me after school a couple of times a week? I had a lady who helped me with yard work, but she's busy with other things now."

"Sure, I guess so. What kind of stuff would you want me to do?"

"Well, you could remove dead annuals. Plant some new bulbs for me. Thatch the lawn, put down mulch. Fertilize. Weed. I really want to add some color to the yard this spring. The only thing I've found time to do lately is dig a compost pile." She smiled at Jake. "And sometimes Jake needs to be taken out and walked. You could help with him too. Of course, I'd pay you."

"That would be great. I'd really like that."

"Let's get you home before your aunt and uncle decide I'm a bad influence on you."

Tony laughed. "I think you might be the best influence I've had in a long time."

"I'm glad you think that." Priscilla gathered Tony's dry clothes and handed them to him. A few minutes later, he and Jake were ready to go. Jake seemed to have found a new friend.

And Priscilla had too.

CHAPTER TWENTY-TWO

The roads were wet, but it didn't take long to get to Tony's house. When Priscilla turned onto his street, she noticed he'd begun to look nervous.

"Best thing to do is tell the truth," she said softly.

He nodded but didn't respond.

"I need to meet them."

He turned to look at her. "It might be better if you just dropped me off."

Priscilla shook her head. "We never allowed Rachel to spend time with people we didn't know. I'm sure your aunt and uncle feel the same way. I really have to insist."

He was quiet for a moment, but finally he said, "Okay."

He directed her to a small house on the corner. It was light brick with black shutters. The wrought-iron fence was attractive and went perfectly with the house. Window boxes and rosebushes at the corners of the yard made it clear that in the spring, the property would be awash in color.

Tony opened the car door and climbed out. Priscilla did the same after telling Jake to stay. Even before they reached the fence, the front door swung open, and two people stepped out. Tony's aunt and uncle looked like nice people, but it was obvious they were upset.

Tony's uncle walked toward them. He was a tall man, lean and wiry. There was kindness in his eyes, but his face was tight with concern. "Where have you been?" he asked Tony. "We were so worried."

"I'm sorry," Tony said. "I was visiting my friend, Mrs. Grant."

Priscilla held out her hand. Tony's uncle took it, but he didn't look happy. "I'm so sorry you were concerned," she said. "Our phones were down, so we couldn't call you. Tony came over to make sure I was okay during the storm. I live on Misty Harbor, in the cottage with the lighthouse."

"I don't understand," the man said, frowning. He swung his attention to Tony. "You said you were going to be with your friends."

"I know, Uncle Phil. I'm sorry. I decided I didn't want to hang out with them, so I went to check on Mrs. Grant. I was supposed to help her pass out flyers earlier today, but I didn't finish the job. I wanted to explain why."

"He really did try to call you," Priscilla said, "but as I said, we couldn't get through. I wanted to meet you both and let you know what happened."

Tony's uncle hesitated for a moment and then opened the gate. "My name is Phil Gonzalez," he said. "Would you like to come in for a moment? Meet my wife?"

Priscilla nodded. "I would enjoy that, thank you."

As they walked toward the house, the street lamp and the front porch light illuminating their way, Tony was quiet. It was obvious he felt bad about letting his aunt and uncle down.

When they reached the porch, Phil introduced his wife. "This is Maria."

Maria gently shook Priscilla's hand. She was a small woman with dark eyes etched with lines that showed she'd spent a lot of time smiling. "It's nice to meet you," she said. "And you are...?"

"Priscilla Grant. I live in the cottage with the lighthouse on Misty Harbor."

Her expression softened. "I love that lighthouse. It's beautiful. So is your cottage. I'd heard someone had moved in after Marjorie Latham died."

"Yes, I'm her niece."

Phil pushed the door open and gestured for them to step inside. "Why don't we go into the living room?"

Priscilla nodded and followed Maria into a charming room with an overstuffed couch and matching chairs. A fire crackled in the small fireplace.

"Can I get you something to drink?" Maria asked. "Coffee? Tea?"

"Thank you so much, but I'll pass," Priscilla said. "I can't stay long. My dog is waiting in the car."

"I saw him when you pulled up," Phil said. "Tony's been wanting a dog. We told him if he brought his grades up, we'd talk about it."

"That's a great idea," Priscilla said with a smile.

"Is your homework done?" Phil asked Tony.

"No, sir, but I have until Tuesday."

"Why don't you say good night to Mrs. Grant and get a jump on it?"

Tony started to argue, but Priscilla frowned at him. He immediately backed down. "Okay, Uncle Phil." He caught Priscilla's eye. "Maybe you could tell them about the job you offered me. I'd really like to do it."

"I will, Tony," she said. "I'll see you later."

The adults were quiet until Tony was out of sight.

"Please, sit down," Maria said.

Priscilla took a nearby chair. Maria and Phil sat on the couch across from her.

"I'm sorry," Phil said in a low voice. "I don't understand why Tony was at your house. He was supposed to be studying with his friends."

"Frankly, I'm glad he wasn't with them," Maria said. "I don't like those boys."

"Monty Anderson is a football star," Phil said dismissively. "I'm sure he's a good influence on Tony."

"Actually, I don't think he is," Priscilla said. She began to tell them what Tony had been experiencing. The concern in their faces made it clear they cared deeply for the boy.

"He was so angry and hurt when he first got here," Phil said, "but we thought he was coming out of it some. Then these boys decided to get involved in his life."

"Tony doesn't want to go along with them," Priscilla said. "He's a good kid, he really is. My cousin would love to get him involved at her church. They have a very strong youth ministry and several of the kids go to Tony's school. It might help him to make some new friends who could keep him away from Monty and the other boys."

Maria nodded. "That would be wonderful. Our church is small, and almost everyone there is older, like us."

"Thank you for offering," Phil said. "I only hope he'll agree to go. We haven't had a lot of success getting him to do the things we've suggested."

"We never had children of our own," Maria said. "We wanted them, but we weren't able to have any. Frankly, I wonder if we have what it takes."

Priscilla smiled at them. "Please don't think you're failing him. He thinks very highly of you. If you'll just hang in there, I'm confident everything will turn out very well. You obviously love Tony, and he appreciates you. I truly believe if we can just get Monty and his friends out of Tony's life, he'll be okay."

"We'll tell him he can't spend time with them anymore." Phil stared into his wife's eyes. "We have to put our foot down."

Maria looked at Priscilla. "What do you think they'll do if we forbid Tony to see them?"

"I'm not sure what those boys will do, but I don't think you have much of a choice."

Phil sighed. "I'm afraid they'll try to make it harder on him."

"That's possible, but you're in charge here," Priscilla said.

"I'm curious," Phil said. "How do you know Tony?"

Priscilla told them about meeting him at Trudy's church. She decided not to mention her run-in with him at the Art Attack.

"Oh, sure," Maria said. "We knew he was getting counseling. I forgot it was at Grace Community." She frowned. "He's been making rather snide comments about the pastor's advice."

Priscilla nodded. "I think he's just mad that he's being forced to go. To be honest, I think he's listening to Pastor Tim. He runs the youth ministry I was telling you about."

"I pray you're right," Phil said. "I hope he won't resist the idea because he doesn't like being required to attend the sessions."

"I feel pretty positive about it. My cousin Trudy is very convincing." Priscilla chuckled. "She's already got Tony involved somewhat at church. I think he's open to getting more engaged."

"We're really grateful for your help," Maria said.

"It's not a problem. I really like Tony. I hope you don't mind, but I asked him if he'd like to do some yard work for me and help with my dog from time to time."

Maria smiled. "He loves animals. I'm sure he was thrilled." She looked at her husband, and he nodded. "As long as his homework is done, we don't have a problem with that."

"One other thing, I wonder if you might let him help out at a party we're having at the church on Halloween."

"When is that?" Phil asked, looking at his wife.

Maria laughed. "Phil trusts me to remind him of holidays and special days. Like our anniversary."

"It's in November," he said, looking slightly offended.

"I won't ask you the date in front of company," she said, grinning. "Halloween is on Tuesday, Phil."

He took his wife's ribbing good-naturedly. "Sure. I don't see a problem with that."

"If he could just go to the church after school, that would be great. Or do I need to pick him up?"

Maria shook her head. "Let me do that. If you could use another volunteer, I'd love to help."

"Wonderful. We're doing some setup tomorrow and on Monday. Tony offered to help on Monday. I hope that's okay. This got pushed to the last minute, so every pair of hands we can get is greatly appreciated."

"I don't see why he can't help on Monday, but I don't work tomorrow," Phil said. "Why don't the three of us come to the church and help out?"

Priscilla smiled. "Thank you so much. We're meeting at ten in the morning. We told people to bring a sandwich or something for a quick lunch break so we could work into the afternoon." She stood. It was getting late, and she wanted to go home.

Maria and Phil stood up too. "Thank you again, Priscilla. We really appreciate your concern for Tony."

"I'm very happy to know him. He's a nice young man."

Phil walked her to the door and opened it for her. After saying goodbye to the couple, Priscilla hurried to her car. It was still raining. Lightly, but the soaked roadways were already full of water. She drove slowly, hoping she wouldn't get stuck on her way home.

She was happy that things were improving with Tony, but she still had no idea who was trying to drive her away from her home.

CHAPTER TWENTY-THREE

It took Priscilla longer to get back to the cottage than she thought it would. When she pulled up in her driveway, she breathed a sigh of relief.

After getting Jake out of the car, she stood under the porch roof for a bit, gazing out toward the cliff. Nothing. It seemed the Weeping Woman was taking the night off. Jake whined, signaling he was ready for his nightly constitutional.

"Let me change my shoes," she said gently.

She went inside, grabbed her old tennis shoes, threw on her rain coat, and put Jake on his long leash. A few minutes later, they were back. Once again, Jake looked offended, as if somehow Priscilla were responsible for the rain. Although she'd looked toward the cliff several times, she hadn't seen anything unusual. The rain had produced a thick fog so Priscilla wasn't certain she could have seen anything even if the Weeping Woman had stood on the edge of the cliff and danced the cha-cha. Of course, that dance would have been after her time anyway. Priscilla chuckled to herself. "You're starting to lose it," she said out loud.

She dried Jake off with a towel and laughed at his expression. "Sorry, old boy, but this is really out of my control."

After feeding him, she made a cup of chamomile tea and caught up on the latest mystery she was reading. It didn't take long for her to get sleepy. Before going to bed, she checked outside one more time. Still nothing.

"Finally, a peaceful night," she said to Jake. "Let's head to bed."

It had been a long day, and although Priscilla was ready for sleep, she lay in bed for a while, trying to put together a puzzle that seemed to be lacking pieces. What was she missing? Try as she might, she just couldn't figure out who was behind the Weeping Woman—and why.

The next morning when Priscilla got up, she could tell it was going to be one of those days that cried out for a nap. But that wouldn't be happening. She'd kept an eye on the cliff off and on all night, but the Weeping Woman had never appeared. She was relieved, especially as she had other things to worry about today. She had to be at the church at ten. It promised to be a busy day.

She ate a quick breakfast and made a phone call to Gail asking if she could drop Jake off at her house while she worked at the church.

"Of course you can," she said. "Dad would absolutely love it. Believe me, Jake will get more attention than he knows what to do with."

"I don't know. That's a lot of attention. He soaks it up, you know."

"We'll do our best to give him a run for his money."

Priscilla thanked her and hung up. She'd pulled on her coat and was looking for her purse when someone rang the doorbell.

The tour for today had been canceled, so she wasn't expecting company.

She opened the door to find Norman Whitaker standing on her porch. He gave her a wide smile. "Mrs. Grant? I'm Norman Whitaker. So sorry to stop by without calling. I tried to reach you several times last night but couldn't get through."

"Service was down for a while," Priscilla said, trying to ignore a rush of irritation. "It seems to be back up this morning."

"Again, I apologize. I was out this way and decided to take a chance." His smile widened. "I wonder if you could give me just a few minutes? I promise I won't take long. It looks as if you're getting ready to go somewhere?"

"Yes, I am, and I really don't want to be late." She realized she sounded rude, but she didn't know this man and wished he had called before just dropping by. She reminded herself that judging him before actually talking to him wasn't fair. She choked back a sigh of frustration and swung the door open. "I can give you a few minutes."

"Thank you so much. It's very gracious of you."

Guilt and annoyance battled each other for her attention. In the end, guilt landed the fatal punch. "Can I get you a cup of coffee?" she found herself saying.

Norman frowned. "Oh. No thank you. I don't want to be a bother."

"It's no trouble. I just turned off the coffeemaker."

"Then yes. Thank you." He glanced toward her window. "It's still chilly after the rain last night."

"Yes, it is."

He followed her into the kitchen, where she prepared his coffee. Thankfully, he took it black. "Why don't we sit in the living room?" she said.

When they entered the living room, Norman looked around. "This is very nice." He pointed at the painting of Priscilla's lighthouse over the fireplace mantel. "Who painted this? It's quite good."

"Actually, I'm not really sure. My aunt, Marjorie Latham, painted. I assume it's one of hers, but it isn't signed. Kind of a mystery."

"This property has so much history, doesn't it?"

"Yes, it does. Please, have a seat." Priscilla gestured toward the couch, and Norman sat down. He put his coffee cup on the table in front of him.

"I'll get right to the point, Mrs. Grant," he said. "I work for a real estate company in Boston. We're looking for unique places in the New England area for bed-and-breakfasts. I realize you're probably not interested in selling, but I wonder if you'd at least allow me to make an offer for your property."

"It wouldn't do any good, Mr. Whitaker. I have absolutely no intention of selling. You see, my aunt left this property to me. It's been in our family for generations, and I know she wouldn't want it sold. I couldn't possibly go against her wishes."

"I completely understand," he said affably. "This isn't the first time I've been told no for the exact same reason. There are things more important than money. Family is certainly one of them."

Priscilla was struck silent by his response. Not at all what she'd expected. "Th-thank you for understanding," she said finally.

He cocked his head and looked at her through narrowed eyes. "Is there some reason to think I wouldn't understand?"

"No. Not really. I guess I got the wrong impression."

He chuckled. "Let me guess. From Sylvia Peabody? She's a very intense lady."

"Yes, she seems to be." She cleared her throat. "May I ask you a question?"

Norman took a sip of his coffee and then put the cup down. "Of course. Anything."

"This cottage only has two bedrooms. What kind of B&B would it make?"

"Believe it or not, we have some successful B&Bs that only have two bedrooms. But we probably would have found a way to add two or three more bedrooms—without losing the historical features of your lovely cottage, of course."

"No matter how much you tried to keep the look consistent, the value would have been affected," she said, frowning. "Changing historical buildings doesn't help the value. It usually reduces it."

"But turning it into a B&B adds additional value. And of course, the lighthouse will never lose its uniqueness or historical importance. As long as nothing happens to it, that is."

A chill ran down Priscilla's spine. What did he mean by that? "What would happen to it?" she asked slowly.

Norman looked at her as if she'd asked a stupid question. "It needs to be kept up," he said, "so it doesn't deteriorate." He sighed deeply. "You'd be surprised by the number of lighthouses I've seen that weren't well maintained. The outside is falling apart, the inside too. Usually the damage is caused by weather. Unfortunately, some of them have been destroyed by vandalism. Even burned. It's terrible. I hate to see structures so important to our history lost through carelessness or crime."

Priscilla stared closely at him. Was he threatening her? Or was it just an innocent comment? She couldn't be sure. She decided to take a chance.

"Of course, you know about the Weeping Woman?"

Norman shook his head. "I'm sorry? Who?"

Priscilla knew he was at the Art Attack the night the painting of the Weeping Woman was displayed. Could he have missed it?

"The Weeping Woman. Olivia Hennesey. Her husband was the captain of a fishing boat. He disappeared at sea, and Olivia watched for him night after night—right out there on the cliff next to the lighthouse. Then one night she disappeared too. Now she stands on the cliff and cries, still waiting for him to return."

Hoping to see some kind of guilt on his face, she was surprised when he laughed. "What a wonderful story! Just the kind of thing that makes a B&B successful." He pulled his wallet from his pants' pocket and removed a card. "Look, I totally respect your decision not to sell, but I would be remiss if I didn't at least tell you what our company would be willing to pay for your property." He wrote something on the card and handed it to her. "If you should change your mind, please contact me." He stood up. "Thank you so much for your kindness. I know you need to get going, so I won't keep you any longer."

Priscilla got up and followed him to the door. She wanted to ask him point-blank if his comments were an attempt to pressure her, but it was entirely possible they were said in complete innocence. She didn't want to appear unhinged, yet at the same time, neither did she want Norman to think she was frightened of him.

"It was nice meeting you," she said finally. "You don't need to worry about my lighthouse falling into disrepair. I value it greatly and would never allow that to happen. *No one* will vandalize this lighthouse. I can promise you that."

She tried to speak as firmly as she could while meeting his eyes.

He just smiled. "I'm happy to hear that. Well, thank you again." He started to walk away, but then he stopped and turned back. "Of course, a lot of vandalism happens when the owners or curators are away. It's almost impossible to stop it."

With that, he walked to his car, a newer Cadillac. As Priscilla watched him drive away, she wondered if Norman Whitaker was the man behind the Weeping Woman. He certainly had motive, and his last comment had moved him quickly to the top of the list.

CHAPTER TWENTY-FOUR

When Priscilla went back into the house, she stuck the card Norman had given her inside her purse and called for Jake. He'd hung back while Norman was in the house, just watching him from a corner of the living room. Jake didn't warm up to everyone right away. There was clearly something about her visitor that Jake didn't like.

"I think you got this one right, Jake," she said. He came over and leaned up against her. She bent down and stroked his head. "You're going to Gail's for a while. I know you'll be glad to see her and Uncle Hugh."

A few minutes later, they were both tucked into Priscilla's SUV and headed for Gail's house. Although yesterday's storm was evident by the wet roads and a few branches down here and there, all in all, the island seemed to have gotten off pretty well.

When she pulled into Gail's driveway, she was glad to see that everything looked okay. Gail's small house was simple but comfortable. A very happy home. Although Gail had taken on the task of caring for her aging father, she rarely complained. She loved him, and they enjoyed being together. Gail actually had a secret boyfriend, but because they both had aged parents to care for, they kept their relationship on a back burner. Priscilla knew about

Tommy, but she had never mentioned it to anyone per Gail's wishes.

As she was leading Jake from the car, the front door opened, and Gail stepped out, smiling. "Good morning," she called out. She bent down and called to Jake. Priscilla let go of his leash and allowed him to run to her. Jake let Gail pet him for a moment and then hurried inside the house, obviously looking for Uncle Hugh.

"Thanks for letting us watch him," Gail said. "Pop just loves spending time with Jake. I'm sure we'll all get a walk in before you get back."

"I'm so glad you could keep an eye on him. I think I've found a young man who will help when you can't. You know I don't like him to stay alone too long during the day."

Gail nodded. "That's fine, but always put us at the top of the list if you need help. Jake brings some real energy into the house."

"Maybe you should get a dog, Gail."

"I don't know. To be honest, taking care of Pop is about all I can handle right now. We enjoy Jake, but then he goes home and you do the hard work."

Priscilla laughed. "Not sure it's hard, but I understand."

"You said you're working at Trudy's church today?"

Priscilla nodded. "Yeah, for the alternative Halloween party."

"Why don't you sign Pop and me up to help on Tuesday night? It would be great to get him out for a while. He loves kids. Unless you need me to watch Jake, that is."

"We'd love to have you there." Priscilla wanted to give Gail the ring she'd found and tell her about her visit from Norman Whitaker, but she was running late. Presenting her with the ring was special, and she didn't want to rush it. Priscilla decided to tell her about it when she picked up Jake. As far as Norman, she knew Gail would want to talk about it—and there just wasn't time right now.

She leaned over and gave Gail a quick hug. "Thanks. I really appreciate that."

She said goodbye and got back into her SUV. As she drove away, she looked in her rearview mirror and saw Gail waving. Priscilla felt so blessed to have three cousins who had become close friends. She regretted the years they'd spent apart. Of course, there was nothing that could be done about it now. *Look to the future, Priscilla*, she told herself.

When she pulled up to the church, she saw Trudy's car was already there. In fact, quite a few cars were parked near the church's entrance. That made her feel better. They had a lot to do and not a lot of time to do it. The more help, the better.

She got out and hurried inside. She was happy to see the Gonzalez family already working.

Maria saw her and came over. "Thanks for letting us all come. I think doing something together like this will be good for us. Tony seems happy today."

"I guess he'll have to leave to work at the inn later," Priscilla said.

"Actually, Tilly called to tell him he didn't have to work unless he wanted to. She has plenty of help. Tony chose to come here."

"Really? That's wonderful," Priscilla said with a smile. "I'm so glad we have such great volunteers. Hopefully we can give the kids a safe and fun place to go on Halloween."

Maria smiled. "If all the plans your cousin Trudy shared with us work out, this should be one of the best Halloweens we've ever seen on the Vineyard."

"Oh, I hope so. I just wish we'd had more time."

Maria shrugged. "That's the way it goes sometimes. Next year we'll be ready earlier."

Priscilla chuckled. "You're already planning next year?"

Maria put her hand on Priscilla's arm. "We met Pastor Tim. He's wonderful, and Tony really seems to connect to him. I think this might be our new church."

"That's great, Maria. I'm so happy to hear that."

As Maria headed back to the table she and Phil were setting up, Priscilla sighed with relief. If Tony could get involved here and make new friends, he would probably be able to break free of Monty and those other boys.

Trudy, who was talking to a couple Priscilla didn't know, waved her over. "Hi, Priscilla. This is Don Applegate and his wife, Tara. They're in charge of getting supplies and building whatever we need for Tuesday night. Can you explain to them about the different booths you want?"

Priscilla shook hands with each of them. "Sure. Do we have wood to make the booths?"

Don laughed. "I work for a local hardware store. We have enough wood to build a small town. I'm sure we can give you what you want."

"I'll leave you all to it, then," Trudy said before hurrying away to talk to a group on the other side of the church's gym. They looked confused. It wouldn't take her long to get them straightened out and working happily. Trudy had a way with people. She could get them to do almost anything.

Priscilla went over the different booths and attractions they'd had at her church in Wheatfield. When she finished, she asked the Applegates what they thought.

"We can do that," Don said. "I can easily put the attractions together, no problem. We'll need some help painting, though. I don't think Tara can do all of that by herself."

"Let me ask Tony Gonzalez and his aunt and uncle if they want to help paint," Priscilla said.

"That would be super. We can definitely get most of this done today if they can lend a hand."

Priscilla hurried over to the Gonzalez family and explained what Don and Tara needed. "I think I saw some painting smocks somewhere," she said. "They'll help keep your clothes clean."

"We'd be happy to help," Phil said. He pointed down at the old sweatshirt he was wearing. "We figured there might be some painting, so we all wore old clothes. I don't need a smock."

Tony grinned. "I can't see me wearing anything called a *smock*, can you?"

Phil and Maria laughed, and Priscilla joined in. "No, I guess not," she said. "And if I remember right, they might be pink. I'm sure that's another reason you may want to avoid them."

"Let's just all agree that I'll be smockless today."

Everyone laughed again, and Priscilla pointed the Applegates out to the Gonzalezes. They headed over to help them, and

Priscilla joined Trudy, who was instructing someone what to paint on the signs they were working on. She was surprised to see it was Sylvia Peabody.

"Nice to see you again, Sylvia," Priscilla said.

Sylvia smiled at her. "I'm so glad you're doing this. It's really needed. I'm sorry I can't stay long, but I wanted to do what I could to help."

"I really appreciate that. Whatever you can do will be a blessing."

"Let's see what you say after you see my work. Not sure painting signs is my forte."

"I wouldn't worry about it. I'm sure you'll be just as good as anyone else. We're not professional sign painters."

"Just remember you said that when I'm done."

Priscilla grinned at her. "I will. I promise." She swung her attention to Trudy. "When you're done here, can I speak to you for a moment?"

"Sure. You could go to the kitchen and pour us a couple cups of coffee, if you'd like. Oh, and there are doughnuts for everyone in there too."

"Why don't I set up a table in the corner of the gym so people will know there are doughnuts and coffee?" Priscilla asked.

"Perfect." Trudy smiled. "I should have thought of that. See why I need you?"

"Yeah, I'm important. Without me, people might miss out on a doughnut."

"Anything that makes them stay and work is important, Cousin. We need all the help we can get."

Priscilla laughed. "I'll ask Tony to help me set up the tables and carry the doughnuts out here."

Trudy nodded and headed to greet some more arriving volunteers while Priscilla got Tony's attention. When they got to the kitchen, Priscilla was shocked to see all the doughnuts and pastries. Boxes and boxes. They were from Candy's. Wow. Had she donated all of this?

After finding a couple of tables and setting them up in the gym, Tony carried most of the boxes out there. Before long, volunteers were streaming over to grab doughnuts. Priscilla put napkins out and told people there was coffee in the kitchen.

She poured two cups of coffee, put them on a nearby table, and then started looking through the boxes. After selecting a chocolate-covered cruller for herself, she sat down and waited for Trudy. A few minutes later, her cousin came over and joined her.

"Cake doughnut with cherry icing," Trudy said, smiling and holding up her pastry of choice. "Delicious. Got these from Candy last night. Didn't sell yesterday."

"You mean they're all day-old?" Priscilla said. "Wow. Can't tell it. They taste so fresh."

"You know Candy. I suspect some of these were made last night before I came by to pick them up."

"Probably."

"Was there something you wanted to tell me?"

Priscilla nodded. "You'll never guess who came by my house this morning."

"Who?" Trudy asked right before she took a big bite of her doughnut.

Priscilla had just opened her mouth to answer when Trudy's phone rang. Trudy looked at it and frowned. Then she pushed it toward Priscilla and pointed to her full mouth. Priscilla looked down to see that the call was coming from Gail.

"Hi, Gail," she said when she answered. "I'm answering because Trudy's mouth is full of doughnut."

"Priscilla, I've tried at least five times to call you. Don't you have your phone with you?"

Gail sounded upset, which immediately made Priscilla worry. "I'm sorry, Gail. I left my phone in my purse while I've been working at the church." She took a deep breath, trying to stay calm. "Is something wrong? Is Jake okay?"

"Jake's fine, Priscilla. It's the lighthouse. It's on fire!"

CHAPTER TWENTY-FIVE

After shouting out some instructions to the people working in the church gym, Trudy and Priscilla ran outside to Trudy's car. Right before getting in, Priscilla noticed Eleanor Gufstead going into the church. She started to say something to Trudy but was so concerned about the lighthouse, she decided to forget it for now.

Trudy drove so fast, Priscilla found herself holding on to the hand grip above her door. Normally, she would have encouraged her cousin to slow down, but she kept her mouth closed. She wanted to see her lighthouse. Funny how personal it suddenly felt. When she'd first come here, she'd had to remind herself over and over that she owned a beautiful cottage on Martha's Vineyard, along with a real lighthouse. But after a little time, they had become hers—and the idea that she might lose them upset her more than she could have ever imagined.

"There it is!" Trudy hollered as they turned onto the road leading to Priscilla's property.

Thankfully the lighthouse was visible. It still stood proudly guarding the harbor, its walls a slash of white against a blue sky.

As they drove up, Priscilla saw two fire trucks and a couple of police cars. The police were just pulling away as she and Trudy parked near one of the fire trucks. Priscilla thought about going after them, but Trudy grabbed her by the sleeve.

"If they felt they needed to talk to you, they wouldn't be leaving," she said. "You should talk to the fire department. They can tell you what you want to know."

At first Trudy's interference bugged her, but as she thought about it, Priscilla realized her cousin was right. She got out of the car and jogged toward the closest truck. One of the firefighters stood there, watching her as she approached.

"I'm the owner," Priscilla said when she got close to him. She stared at the lighthouse and then swung her gaze at the area around the structure. "Where's the fire?" she asked.

The firefighter, who had removed his helmet, walked over to her. "Everything's okay," he said. "It was just your compost pile. We put it out."

Priscilla shook her head. "I don't understand. My compost pile? How could it catch fire?"

"I suspect it was hit by lightning last night. Because of the rain, the fire smoldered underneath the pile and was finally able to get enough air and dry material to spark a little while ago. It was a small fire. Nothing to worry about." He pointed to where the compost pile had been and said, "You'll probably have to dig another one. Sorry."

"Are you absolutely certain this was caused by lightning?" Priscilla said. "Could someone have purposely started this fire?"

He frowned at her. "Do you have reason to suspect someone of arson?"

"Yes...I mean, no." She shook her head. "I don't know. This is such a shock."

"Ma'am, I'm as sure as I can be that this was accidental." He gestured for her to follow him. When they neared the compost pile, Priscilla noticed the singed earth around it. "You can see where the lightning hit. You'd be surprised at how many calls we get after a thunderstorm. Lightning causes fires. Period. And sometimes during a heavy rain, they smolder. Actually, it's a good thing this happened the way it did. If the ground had been dry, this fire could have grown out of control. Your lighthouse could have been involved."

"I understand," Priscilla said. "Sorry to ask so many questions. I'm just so happy to find out everything is okay." She grabbed Trudy's shoulder and leaned into her, relief making her feel momentarily weak.

He smiled. "You don't need to be sorry. I'm happy it wasn't worse. I believe the fire is completely out, but we'll send someone by later to make sure it doesn't restart."

Priscilla thanked him again as he walked to his truck and got inside. As he pulled away, the other truck followed him.

"Thank God," Priscilla said. "I thought..."

"You thought what?" Trudy asked. "Why did you ask him so many questions? Did you think someone started this on purpose? Is there something you're not telling me?"

Priscilla stepped away from Trudy and locked eyes with her. "That's what I wanted to talk to you about. Norman Whitaker came by this morning. And he...I think he threatened me, Trudy. He said something could happen to the lighthouse."

"What?" Trudy stared at Priscilla with her mouth open. "What do you mean he said something could happen to the lighthouse? Exactly what did he say?"

"Look, let's get in the car and drive back to the church. I'll explain on the way."

Trudy nodded but seemed to hesitate. "Are you sure it's safe? Should we leave the lighthouse unprotected?"

"The guy from the fire department said it was definitely lightning that started this. I believe him."

"I'm sure you're right, but I hate the idea that someone might try to harm this lighthouse."

"I'm sure it's okay for now." Priscilla began walking toward Trudy's car. On the way, her phone began to ring. It was Gail asking about the fire.

"Everything's fine, Gail," she said. "Just a fire that smoldered in my compost pile."

"Well, thank God. When I saw those fire engines headed toward the lighthouse, I was just frantic."

"How did you know for sure the fire was on my property?" Priscilla asked.

"I called the fire department. They asked me to call you."

"Thank you so much. I'm glad you did."

After they hung up, Priscilla climbed into the car. Trudy was already inside. She turned to look at Priscilla. "Okay, spill it. Everything about Norman Whitaker."

As Trudy drove, Priscilla went over Norman's visit that morning, trying to remember everything he'd said.

At one point, Trudy stopped her. "Wait a minute. He actually said it's almost impossible to stop vandalism when the owner of a lighthouse is away?"

Priscilla nodded. "Maybe he didn't mean it as a threat, Trudy. To be honest, I don't know anymore."

"Did it feel like a threat?" she asked.

Priscilla rolled Norman's words over in her head again. "Yeah, it did," she said finally. "Am I sure it was? No. He might have just been telling me that we needed to keep an eye on the lighthouse so vandals won't ever cause problems—like they have with other lighthouses." She sighed. "It's so hard to be sure. Lately, everything everyone says sounds like a veiled threat."

"I see now why you were suspicious about the fire."

"He even mentioned fires, Trudy. That's what frightened me."

Trudy was silent for a while. Finally, she said, "He could be the Weeping Woman."

Priscilla couldn't help laughing. "I'm sorry, it's not funny, but I just got a picture of short, stocky Norman Whitaker in a blue dress with long black hair."

"I didn't mean he's the actual Weeping Woman," she said, shaking her head. "I meant he might be behind the whole thing."

"Well, he showed up in town just about the same time the Weeping Woman made her entrance. You might be right. It makes more sense than anything else."

"It really does. And he has a financial reason for wanting you to sell your property."

"So what do we do now?" Priscilla asked.

"I don't know for sure, but maybe now is the time to contact the police."

"Maybe…"

"You know, being afraid to talk to them because you might be embarrassed isn't a good enough reason to avoid calling them."

Priscilla sighed deeply. "But telling them I'm being haunted by a ghost—and that someone might have started a fire that the fire department is convinced was started by natural causes…"

Trudy pursed her lips. "Actually, I see your point. I wish we had something more concrete. You know, solid evidence that something weird is going on."

"Maybe the police need to stake out my place at night. Then they could see the Weeping Woman for themselves."

Trudy turned to stare at Priscilla. Her gaze lingered so long, Priscilla almost yelled at her to keep her eyes on the road. Riding with Trudy was…well, terrifying didn't quite cover it.

"You know what? You just had a great idea."

"Oh, Trudy. I'm not going to ask the police to stake out a ghost. They'd lock me up."

"I didn't say you should ask them to come out and watch for her. But what if you were able to show her to them? If they were able to see her for themselves?"

Priscilla frowned. "Sorry to be dense, but I'm not getting it."

"We film her, Priscilla!"

"I don't have a video camera. I think my phone will record for a few seconds, but it wouldn't be very clear."

"We have a video camera. A good one. You take it."

"I have no idea how to work it. Do you think Dan would let you come over tonight?"

Trudy sighed. "I'd love to, hon, but tonight's out. Dan asked a colleague from the institute along with his wife over for dinner. It's unusual for him to reach out socially, and I just can't cancel it."

Trudy's husband worked at the Woods Hole Oceanographic Institution studying sea life. A quiet and reserved man, it really was a big step for him to offer an invitation to someone he worked with.

"I understand. Maybe you could just show me how it works?"

"Of course I will. Let's finish up at the church, and then I'll run home and get the camera. If you could get whoever this is on film, I bet the police would pay attention."

"As long as they don't think I'm faking it."

"Look, I trust our police chief, Hank Westin. I'll talk to him with you. We're old friends, and I'm sure he'll listen to the both of us."

"Okay, but first let's see if there are any further *visitations*. If not, we won't have anything to show him—or to talk to him about. What if our ghost doesn't show up again? She knows we're watching for her. Maybe my haunting is over."

"Perhaps. But what about Norman Whitaker? Shouldn't someone be keeping an eye on him?"

Priscilla sighed. "Why? Because he mentioned what happens to abandoned lighthouses? I can't prove he threatened me—or my property. I simply don't have anything on him yet. I think we need something concrete before we approach the police."

Trudy grunted. "Look, I won't contact Hank if you don't want me to. But I'm wondering if we shouldn't get him involved before something else happens."

Priscilla nodded, but she couldn't help wondering just what would have to take place to bring the police into the situation. If someone really was trying to get her to leave Martha's Vineyard, what would their next move be? Would it be more dangerous than a disappearing phantom?

CHAPTER TWENTY-SIX

When Trudy and Priscilla got back to the church, they were immediately surrounded by people wanting to know about the fire. After Priscilla explained that everything was okay and that the fire was contained to the compost heap, the volunteers eventually dispersed and went back to work. Tony lagged behind.

"I'll clean out your compost and make you a new pile," he said.

"Thanks, Tony. That would be really helpful. Why don't you stop by tomorrow afternoon, and we can talk about some of the work I need to have done in the yard? If it's okay with your aunt and uncle, that is."

"I'm sure they won't have a problem with it, but I'll get permission. Should I call you to find out what time to come by?"

Priscilla nodded. "I have a notebook in my coat pocket. Let me write down my number for you."

He followed her to the kitchen, where the women had left their coats, jackets, and purses. She found her coat, tore a blank page out of the notebook, and wrote her numbers on it. Then she handed it to Tony. "The first number is my cell phone. The second is my landline. Between the two of them, you should be able to find me."

"Okay." He stuck the piece of paper in his pocket and started to walk away. Just before he reached the door, he turned back to look at her. "Thanks. I'm really glad I got to know you." Then he walked out the door, letting it close behind him.

After all the stress of the past few days, Tony's simple expression of appreciation touched her heart. In the middle of the storm, God was still working. Still reaching out. Still offering her ways to help people. Priscilla loved Psalm 37:3: "Trust in the Lord and do good; dwell in the land and enjoy safe pasture." No matter what happened around her, all she had to do was trust God to take care of her, and while she waited for His help, it was important to continue to do good. Hopefully, her involvement in Tony's life would turn out to be something positive. Something that would help him become the kind of young man she knew he could be.

Everyone worked the rest of the morning and then broke for lunch. Most people had brought something, but before Trudy and Priscilla had time to go out for lunch, Joan came in with a large picnic basket.

"Trudy told me you were working today. I thought you might like something to eat about now."

"Oh, Joan, how nice of you," Priscilla said. It had been a busy morning, and she was glad she could just sit and relax instead of going out.

They pulled chairs around a table sitting in the corner, and Joan took thick roast beef sandwiches out of the basket, along with homemade potato salad and a plastic bowl full of watermelon.

"This is just perfect," Trudy said. "How thoughtful of you."

"I also brought a container of tea. You ladies serve yourselves while I get it out of the car."

While Joan went outside, Trudy and Priscilla put the sandwiches on the plastic plates Joan had provided. There were also silverware, napkins, and plastic cups in the basket.

"Boy, she thought of everything, didn't she?" Priscilla said.

"She usually does. I wish I was half as organized as Joan."

"Oh, Trudy, you're selling yourself short. Look at all you're accomplishing here. You have to be organized to do something like this." Priscilla waved her arm, gesturing toward all the people gathered together to give the children in Tisbury a special Halloween event. "There aren't a lot of people who could pull an event as big as this together in just a few days."

"Well, maybe. I think my enthusiasm gets projects off the ground, but I'm afraid I need assistance pulling them off. That's why I asked you to help. I knew you could figure out how to do it. And you did! All your creative ideas will make this event a huge success."

Priscilla smiled at her. "Thanks. I'm just copying what someone in Wheatfield did. But I'm still happy I could contribute."

They spooned helpings of potato salad and watermelon onto their plates next to their sandwiches. Priscilla was happy to see Joan coming back with the iced tea. Her mouth was watering. She'd had no idea how hungry she was.

"Trudy, you have paint on your backside," Joan said as she came up behind her.

Trudy jumped up. "Oh no. Is it wet?"

Joan leaned over to check. "No. Dry. Bright yellow. Did you sit in it?"

Trudy nodded. "Tara Applegate said Aleeta Armbruster came by while we were gone. She left several cans of paint for us to use. Someone spilled a little on an old stool, and I accidentally sat on it."

Priscilla couldn't help laughing at her cousin's faux pas. "Oh dear. Well it was nice of her to want to help out."

"Yes, it was. Dan asked if she wanted to stay and help, but she said no. She drank some coffee and watched everyone for a while, though. Then she left."

Priscilla shrugged. "Not everyone has time to work."

As the women ate, Priscilla told Joan about the fire on her property and her visit with Norman Whitaker.

"Wow, that sounds frightening. I'm thankful it wasn't worse." She shook her head and frowned. "I really don't like that man saying the things he did to you. It really concerns me."

Priscilla nodded. "Like I told Trudy, I'm not sure what he meant. It's possible his comments weren't said to intimidate me." She sighed. "I just don't know anymore. I'm starting to suspect everyone."

"By the way," Joan said, "I ran into Gerald earlier. He says he has something important to tell you. He might stop by here later."

She barely got the words out before the door to the church gym swung open, and Gerald walked in. He looked around the room and spotted them sitting at the table. As he strode over to where they sat, Priscilla noticed how nice he looked in khakis and a white shirt. He really was an attractive man. She took a deep breath and scolded herself silently. She had no business thinking about Gerald in any way except as a friend.

"I hope I'm not interrupting," he said when he reached them. "I have something to show you, Priscilla. I'm not sure how it will help your situation, but it's certainly interesting. I think I can tell you what really happened to Olivia Hennesey. And it isn't what you thought."

CHAPTER TWENTY-SEVEN

P lease sit down," Priscilla said, intrigued by Gerald's claim.
He grabbed a chair next to the wall and scooted it up to the table, and then he placed a folder full of papers in front of her.

"Are you hungry?" Priscilla asked. "I'd be happy to share my sandwich with you." Although she'd offered, she really wouldn't be that happy about it. The roast beef was incredible, and she wanted to eat every last bite.

"Thank you," Gerald said graciously, "but I just had lunch. Is it okay if I talk while you eat?"

"It's more than okay," Trudy said. "Please tell us what you've discovered."

Gerald took a deep breath. "It was the money that bothered me. We have two people who disappeared—one who could have been lost at sea, the other who may have taken her own life. But what about the missing money? Where did it go? I began to think that if I could track the money, I might find the truth. So I started wondering just where someone with money might go to start over. And I found my answer."

He opened the folder. "I spent some time in the library. They've transferred all their old microfiche files to their computers, you know, so I started looking through newspapers after October of

1854. And I found something. About two years after Olivia went missing, an engagement announcement pops up in a newspaper in Boston. The woman's name is Odette Harris. She plans to marry a man named Samuel Abbot. Here's a picture of the happy couple."

He pushed an old photograph copied from a newspaper toward them. The resemblance between Olivia Hennesey and Odette Harris was striking. Unfortunately, the picture wasn't very clear.

"I've never seen Olivia," Trudy said.

"I have," Priscilla said slowly, "at the museum. It certainly looks like her. And notice the initials, OH. Quite a coincidence."

Gerald nodded. "I found that very interesting too. So I did some research and found Odette and Samuel Abbot's family."

"Wow," Joan said. "How did you uncover that information?"

"It wasn't very hard. It seems the Abbots were influential in Boston society. Checking through family genealogical records was simple. Eventually, I found a William Manford Abbot who still lives in Boston. With a middle name like that, he was easy to find."

"Did you contact him?"

Gerald nodded. "I certainly did. What I heard from him convinced me he's a descendant of the woman we know as Olivia Hennesey."

Priscilla frowned at him. "And how could you know that?"

"Because Bill told me that his aunt, who's been trying to put together a family tree, was stumped when it came to Odette Harris. There were no relatives. No life before she came to Boston in 1854."

"Oh, Gerald." Priscilla went back to the picture in the newspaper. "It must be her."

"Here are some other articles about Odette." He pulled out more copies he'd made at the library. There were announcements of social events, births of children—and finally, Odette's obituary. Every single photo matched the picture Priscilla had seen in Mildred's book at the museum.

Trudy sighed. "So Olivia survived and moved to Boston, where she started a new life."

Gerald nodded. "This is pure conjecture, but here's what I think." He cleared his throat. "I'm trying to be careful because I don't want to jump to conclusions, but with everything else we know, I think the captain took the money and was planning to join his girlfriend in Boston. Somehow Olivia found out about it, got the money, and..."

"Got rid of her husband?" Priscilla couldn't keep a note of dismay from her voice. She hated to think Olivia was a killer. It wasn't that she liked Olivia—she had no idea what kind of a person she really was—but the idea of a wife murdering her husband was heartbreaking. How could love turn to that kind of hate?

"Or maybe he really did have an accident at sea and Olivia found the money. Instead of turning it in, she decided to start life over. Took the money, went to Boston, and made a new life for herself."

"Odd that the captain's girlfriend also lived in Boston," Trudy said. "Wouldn't the two women run into each other?"

Gerald smiled. "The 1800s weren't like today. I doubt his girlfriend ever saw a picture of Olivia. Back then, social media consisted of local newspapers that rarely made it to other areas of the country. If Olivia changed her name, the girlfriend would never know she was Jeremiah's wife."

Trudy nodded. "I guess that's right."

Priscilla gathered the papers together and put them back in the folder then handed it to Gerald.

"No, you keep it," he said. "I did this for you. I don't really have any use for it." He took a deep breath and let it out slowly. "Not sure what it has to do with whoever is trying to frighten you, but at least you have more information about Olivia than you did."

"I certainly do." Priscilla noticed the time. "We've got to get back to work, but I can't thank you enough for all the effort you put into this."

"Happy to do it." He hesitated a moment. "I guess I'll see you tomorrow. I wonder if you might like to have lunch after church. To...to talk more about Olivia and everything that's been going on."

"Okay," she agreed. "That sounds nice. I'll see you then."

Gerald said goodbye and left.

"So, lunch with Gerald?" Trudy said, giving Priscilla a mischievous half-smile.

"Don't be silly. He's just interested in the Weeping Woman. You're getting carried away."

"I agree," Joan said, frowning at Trudy. "Hush up."

Although Trudy looked somewhat offended, she clamped her lips together and made a motion of turning a lock.

Priscilla rolled her eyes and prepared to get back to work. She really did appreciate Gerald's efforts, but this information only added to the mystery. Was Olivia Hennesey a murderer? Or was she a grief-stricken wife who took advantage of her husband's crime and started life over again in Boston? Maybe Priscilla would never have the answer to those questions, but at least she knew Olivia hadn't ended her life yards away from Priscilla's home.

And that brought her a measure of peace.

CHAPTER TWENTY-EIGHT

A little after four o'clock, Priscilla surveyed the work that had been done at the church. They were in great shape. The booths were up, and every volunteer spot had been filled. There would be a cake walk, face painting, balloon animals, a fishing booth, a bean bag toss, and several other fun games for children and families. With all the donations of toys and candy, they were stocked and ready for Halloween night. The only things left were supplies that needed to be picked up. Priscilla wrote up a list and divided it between several people who offered to do some shopping.

"I think we've got it under control," she told Trudy.

"I do too. I'll call Pastor Billings and let him know."

"Monday we can come back and add the rest of the supplies to the booths, including any remaining toys and candy. Then on Tuesday we'll need all the baked goods, and the guys serving food can get set up."

Two of the church's members ran a small café in Vineyard Haven. They'd offered to provide a fried chicken dinner for everyone who came to the event. They'd put on several meals for the church, and the pastor recommended them highly.

"Sounds great. I think our event will be a huge success."

"I do too. Let's just hope we have a good turnout."

Trudy cocked her head toward Tony and his aunt and uncle, who were sharing something funny. It was so nice to hear Tony laugh. "I think you've done something great there too," she said.

"How's Tony getting on with your youth pastor?"

"Tim says he feels they're making progress. He's spoken to some of the other kids in the youth group. They're more than willing to step in and provide Tony with some positive friendships at school."

"That's such good news. I just pray Monty and his crew will back off and give Tony some space."

Trudy smiled. "I feel good about the outcome, but let's keep praying for him. Now, if you'll wait here a bit, I'll go home and grab my video camera."

"All right, but to be honest, I'm so tired that I'm not sure I feel like trying to film my spooky blue friend."

Trudy shrugged. "It's up to you, but we need to catch this person. What if this keeps up, Priscilla? How long are you willing to put up with it?"

"Okay. I know you're right. I'll do my best to get something on film."

"Good. I'll hurry. I know you want to get home."

"And I need to pick up Jake."

Trudy left, and Priscilla said goodbye to all the volunteers as they walked out. Tony came up to her as his aunt and uncle were heading for the door.

"Do you still want me to come over tomorrow to work on your compost heap?"

"If it's okay with your aunt and uncle, that would be great. I could also show you what else needs to be done. There's nothing that has to be tackled right away. Your schoolwork comes first."

"Okay. Thanks again for the job. I enjoy working with plants and stuff. And it will give me something to do."

"You know, I understand the youth group here is pretty active. Might be a good idea to check it out."

Tony nodded slowly. "I will. To be honest, I'm a little shy. I think that's why I followed after Monty and those guys so much. They approached me first, and I really wanted friends. I learned a lesson from that. Being alone isn't the worst thing there is."

Priscilla smiled at him. "No, it's not. Trust me, you'll make friends, Tony. You're a great kid. And you might be surprised at school. I'll bet a lot of the other kids dislike Monty and his followers. Once you stop hanging around with them, it might make others feel more comfortable talking to you."

"Do you think so?"

"I really do. Something like that happened to my daughter, Rachel, once. Right before high school started, her best friend moved away. A group of girls attached themselves to Rachel, but they were mean. You know, liked to pick on other people?"

"Bullies."

"Exactly. Rachel was afraid to walk away because then they'd come after her. But when she finally made the break, she gained all kinds of friends—good friends—who realized Rachel wasn't like those other girls. She's still close with most of them."

Tony smiled. "Thanks. That's encouraging." Phil called for Tony, and he waved at his uncle. "I'd better go. Thanks again, Mrs. Grant."

"You're welcome. If your aunt and uncle give you permission, why don't you come by around two tomorrow?"

"Sounds good."

Priscilla smiled as Tony hurried over to his aunt and uncle. She was so relieved he was doing better.

After checking the room and making sure everything was secure, Priscilla went to the kitchen to get her purse and her jacket. Once she had them, she walked back into the gym, sat down, and gazed around at all the work they had done. They still needed some signs, but everything looked really good. She noticed the sign Sylvia had made, and it wasn't half bad. Priscilla was glad to see Sylvia show up and help. Obviously, her first opinion of the woman had been wrong. That was what came from jumping to conclusions.

About ten minutes later, Trudy ran into the gym. "Here you go," she said. She handed a leather case to Priscilla. "I'm running late. Have to get dinner ready for Dan's friend. I wrote the instructions on a sheet of paper and stuck it in there. You shouldn't have any problems. It's an older video camera, but it should do the trick."

"Thanks, Trudy. I'll do my best to get something on here. Can't believe I'm hoping my ghost will show up tonight."

"If it helps us to catch her, it's worth it." She gave Priscilla a hug. "Thanks again for today. I'll call you tonight after our company leaves. Hopefully, you'll have something to show me."

"Hopefully." Priscilla got up and walked Trudy to the front door. "We need to lock this, don't we?" she asked.

"Yep. Just turn this button and close the door. It will lock behind you."

Priscilla followed Trudy's instructions and checked the door after she pulled it closed. Sure enough, it was locked.

She waved at Trudy as she drove away and then ran to her car, but before she could leave, another car drove into the parking lot and parked next to her. Joan got out. She jogged up to Priscilla's window. "You won't believe what just happened," she said.

"What in the world, Joan?" Priscilla said. "You look like you've just seen a ghost."

"You're exactly right," she said, keeping her voice low and leaning in the window. "I just saw the Weeping Woman."

"What are you talking about?"

Joan looked around as if making sure no one else could hear her. "The painting. I just saw it. I know where it is."

CHAPTER TWENTY-NINE

Take a deep breath and tell me exactly what happened," Priscilla said.

"I went to the Art Attack to get my paintings. Aleeta was busy talking to some other exhibitors, but I heard her tell them that everything from the show was in the storeroom. The door to the storeroom was open, so I went inside, thinking I could save her the trouble by getting my paintings myself. As I was looking through the canvases stacked and leaning against the wall, I found *The Weeping Woman*. The same painting we saw that night, Priscilla. I almost took it, but when I heard someone coming, I put it back and ran to another part of the room. I actually found my paintings there and was pulling them out when Aleeta came up beside me." She gulped and shook her head. "I hope she didn't see how nervous I was. I tried to act perfectly normal. I didn't want her to know I'd seen the other painting."

"Did she seem suspicious?" Priscilla asked.

Joan hesitated a moment, her forehead wrinkled in thought. Finally she said, "I don't think so. She did look over toward the other pile of pictures, but I tried to act as if I had no idea there were any other paintings. She helped me get my paintings out to my car, and I hurried out of there as fast as I could so I could tell you about it."

"So she lied. She does know about *The Weeping Woman*," Priscilla said slowly.

"Oh yes. She definitely knows about the painting. You should have seen her eyes flicking over to that other stack of artwork. I'm so glad I put everything back the way I'd found it."

"So Aleeta must be the one behind all of this."

"But why?" Joan said. "Why would it benefit her to get you out of the Vineyard? It doesn't make any sense."

"No, it doesn't. But it's time to insist on the truth." Priscilla glanced at her watch. "Do you think Aleeta's shop is still open?"

"Probably. For a little while longer anyway. What are you going to do?"

"I'm going over there to confront her."

"If you're going, I'm going with you."

Priscilla didn't argue. Right then, she welcomed the company. By the time they reached the Art Attack, Priscilla was starting to doubt they'd drawn the right conclusion. But regardless, Aleeta had lied about the painting. Confronting her might not be comfortable, but it had to be done. Priscilla was thankful Joan was with her, not only for moral support, but because she would be a witness to whatever Aleeta said.

When they walked into the Art Attack, they found Aleeta standing behind the front counter. She looked surprised to see them but quickly pasted an artificial smile on her face.

"Hello, ladies. What can I do for you today?"

As Priscilla tried to find a way to frame her questions, Joan jumped right in.

"You can tell us why you lied about the painting of the Weeping Woman."

The fake smile slipped off Aleeta's face like a fried egg on a Teflon pan. "I don't understand what you mean. I've told you there was no painting of Olivia Hennesey in this showing."

"That's not true, Aleeta," Joan said. "I saw it with my own eyes when I was here earlier to pick up my paintings."

"You're mistaken." Aleeta sniffed. "I must ask you ladies to leave. You're accusing me of something I haven't done, and I won't continue to contend with you."

"But we'll be happy to contend with you," Priscilla said, her temper flaring. "My cousin isn't crazy. If she says she saw the painting, then she did."

"Why don't you go into the back room and look yourself?" Aleeta said. "If you find the painting, show me. Maybe I missed it. It's possible, I guess."

Priscilla was certain Aleeta was still trying to hide the truth. She nodded at Joan, who headed toward a door at the back of the shop. Priscilla followed her into a large storage room.

"The painting was right over here," Joan said. She walked over to a stack of canvases and began to slowly go through them while Priscilla watched.

Aleeta stood near the door, her arms folded across her chest, her face locked into a scowl. "I told you there's no painting of Olivia Hennesey," she said in a low voice.

Finally, Joan stopped and turned around. "It's gone," she said. "She removed it after I left."

"I didn't do any such thing." Aleeta pointed toward the front door. "I insist you get out of my store. I've tried to be accommodating, but I don't like being accused of lying."

Priscilla stomped up to Aleeta. "You might think you're going to get away with this, but you won't. Joan saw *The Weeping Woman* today, and I'm sure others saw it as well. I think it's time to bring the police into this situation. Let's see what kind of stories you come up with for them."

With that, she and Joan headed outside. But before she walked out the front door of the shop, Priscilla looked back. Aleeta's expression had gone from indignation to terror. She was clearly afraid of something. But what?

As they stood outside on the boardwalk, Priscilla told Joan about the look on Aleeta's face. "She's scared. That makes me think she's working with someone, but not because she wants to. Because she feels she has no choice."

"Maybe we should go back and try to reason with her," Joan said. "Perhaps if we promise to protect her..."

"But we can't do that, since we have no idea what she's really done."

Joan was silent for a moment. "Yes, you're right," she said finally.

"So now what?" Priscilla asked. "I told her we were going to the police."

"Then let's go."

Priscilla hesitated. "I don't know..."

"I know you want to deliver the *ghost* to the police, but we can't do that," Joan said emphatically. "All we can do is tell Hank what we know and ask him to look into it further. I can't believe you're still afraid you don't have enough evidence."

"That's not it," Priscilla replied. "It was Aleeta. She really was frightened. What if what we do next causes her some kind of pain—or distress? I think I'd like to talk to her once more before we talk to Chief Westin."

"Seriously, Priscilla," Joan said, "I think it's wise to get Hank involved. Maybe if Aleeta is scared enough, she'll finally tell the truth."

"Give me a chance to talk to her one-on-one. If I can't get her to open up, we'll do it your way. Agreed?"

Although it was clear Joan wasn't sure she was doing the right thing, she nodded. "I guess," she said with a sigh.

"Will the Art Attack be open tomorrow?"

"Yes. Shorter hours, though. Ten to four."

"I'll come by after church and talk to her."

"I don't know. Maybe you should do it now. If you give her time, she might get rid of the painting for good."

"I know that's a risk, but I feel like she needs some time to think. Right now she's too upset." She shrugged. "Of course, I could be mistaken, but I think this is the wrong time to approach her."

Joan shook her head. "I'm really starting to worry. I know your ghostly visitor didn't show up last night, but you just said that Aleeta looked frightened. That tells me there's something to be afraid of. You need to make sure whatever it is doesn't come after you."

Although she tried to dismiss Joan's concern, Priscilla couldn't help but wonder if she was right.

She gave Joan a hug and drove her back to her car. After they said goodbye, she headed home. On the way, she stopped by Walt's and got a cheeseburger and onion rings. Although she'd intended to wait until she got home to eat, she found herself sneaking into the sack and plucking out onion rings while she drove. They were so good.

By the time she got to Gail's, half the onion rings were already gone. Before she got out of the car, Priscilla put the bag from Walt's in the glove box. She had no intention of fighting Jake for her cheeseburger. Although she wanted to tell Gail about Aleeta, she decided to put it off for a while. She was certain Gail would also insist she call the police. Besides, she wanted to give Gail the ruby ring and didn't want anything else to overshadow the moment.

As she got out of the car, the front door opened and Gail waved at her. Priscilla grabbed her purse and walked through the door.

"So how was my furry friend today?" she asked as she stepped into Gail's cozy living room.

Gail put her finger to her mouth, indicating that Priscilla should be quiet. It only took a quick look around to figure out why. Uncle Hugh was sound asleep in his recliner, Jake cuddled up next to him. They both snored lightly.

"I took several pictures with my phone," Gail whispered. "I'll e-mail them to you."

"Please do. That's just precious. Jake really loves your dad."

"Pop is crazy about him too." Gail pointed toward the kitchen. "Let's go in there, okay?"

Priscilla nodded and crept quietly into the kitchen. She sat down at Gail's table and sighed. "What a day. Between all the work at the church and the fire, I'm beat."

"Hopefully, you'll have a quiet night."

"Well, Trudy hopes it won't be that quiet. She's loaning me her video camera so I can film the Weeping Woman. That way the police won't think I'm nuts."

"Oh, Priscilla. Why would the police think that?"

"Well, let's see. 'Hey, Chief Westin, the ghost of a woman who disappeared in 1854 is haunting me almost every night. Could you come and take a look, please?'"

Gail frowned. "Okay. When you put it that way, it does sound a little nuts."

"Gee, ya think?"

"I could get away for a while tonight if you need me. I don't want to leave Pop alone too long, but..."

Priscilla waved her comment away. "You stay home and take care of your father. I'll be fine. I'm convinced the Weeping Woman isn't interested in hurting me. She just wants to scare me. She's done a pretty good job of that so far."

"Well, I'm grateful the fire today was just an accident. If it had been arson..."

"Yeah, that would have changed things quite a bit. Frankly, I almost wish it were. I'd feel better about calling Chief Westin. I would love to catch whoever's doing this and bring their reign of terror to an end."

"I understand," Gail said with a smile. "Do you have time for a cup of tea before you go?"

Priscilla shook her head. "Thanks, but I need to get home. I've got a cheeseburger in the car, and I'd like to eat it while it's still somewhat warm."

"Okay. Come with me. I'll wake up Pop."

Priscilla grabbed Gail's arm as she started to walk past. "Before you do that, I have something for you. I found a small jewelry box hidden under the floor in the cottage. I assume it was a hiding place Marjorie either forgot about or didn't have time to reveal before she passed away. There was something inside I think you'll want."

She reached into her purse to take out the small box with the ruby ring.

It was gone!

CHAPTER THIRTY

Priscilla, is something wrong?" Gail asked.

"I—I can't find it." Priscilla pulled her purse wide open and dumped everything out on the table. She picked through each and every item, but the box wasn't there. Her fingers closed on the card that Norman Whitaker had given her. She hadn't even looked at it, and she wasn't interested in it right then. She slid it into an inside pocket in her purse. Had she done the same thing with the box? She quickly checked every single hiding place inside and outside her purse. No box.

"Oh, Gail. I can't believe it." She tried to blink away the tears that filled her eyes. She'd lost Gail's ring.

"What is it?" Gail asked, her face full of concern. "It can't be as bad as that."

"Yes, it is. I found your ring. Your ruby ring. And now it's gone."

The color drained from Gail's face. "I don't understand. You said you found a jewelry box under the floor?"

"I stumbled across a loose floorboard in the bedroom under the dresser when my earring fell off. There was a small jewelry box under the floor with several things inside. One of them was a ruby ring. I put it in a ring box and stuck it in my purse. Now it's not there."

"Maybe it fell out. Check your car."

Priscilla shook her head. "I keep my purse zipped shut. The box was here earlier when I dropped Jake off. I never opened my purse again. Even at the..."

"At the church?"

Priscilla nodded.

"You said you bought a cheeseburger at Walt's. Could it have fallen out then? Or what about when you called me after the fire?"

"No. I had some cash in my pocket. I paid with that. And my phone was in an outside pocket of my purse. I'm certain I never opened my purse at all." She thought for a moment. "I'm going to call Trudy. I think someone may have taken the ring at the church." She grabbed her phone and quickly punched in Trudy's number. It took a while for her to answer.

"Trudy, I'm so sorry to bother you," she said quickly, "but I think my purse was robbed while we were at the church."

Trudy's loud sigh came across the line. "I'm sure you're right. I've gotten six other calls from women who are missing cash and jewelry from their purses."

Priscilla quickly checked her wallet. She'd stuck forty dollars in it the other day. It was gone. "My cash is missing too," she told Trudy.

"What else did they take?" Trudy asked.

"Oh, Trudy. I found Aunt Marjorie's ruby ring. I was going to give it to Gail. If only I'd taken the time to give it to her this morning."

"You found the ruby ring?" There was a long silence from the other end of the phone. Priscilla completely understood it. The joy of finding the ring was dashed now, since it was missing again.

"So someone went into the kitchen," Priscilla said, "and rifled through our purses. Any idea who did it?"

"Oh, Priscilla. You're not going to like this. A couple people think it was Tony."

"That's ridiculous. Tony would never take anything from us."

"Well, he was in the kitchen for a while. Remember he helped us carry out the doughnuts."

Priscilla shook her head. "He didn't do this. I'm sure of it."

"I certainly hope you're right. I called the police. Pastor Billings is going to meet them at the church, but I'm going to run down there too. Just in case they have any questions for someone who was actually there today."

"Do you need me to drive back?"

"No, I don't think so. Not unless you noticed anyone in the kitchen who shouldn't have been there."

"Tony and I went into the kitchen just before lunch to get something out of my coat pocket. But I was with him the whole time, and he left the room before I did. That's the last time I was near the kitchen. I'm sorry."

"That's all right. If you think of something, just call me."

"Okay, but what about your dinner party?"

"I'm all set. If I have to leave for a while, they won't miss me. They'll be talking about things that float around in the ocean. Getting out for a while will be a blessing."

"This is just awful. I can't believe someone is pointing their finger at Tony. He was doing so well today. I'm afraid this will just send him backward." A thought suddenly occurred to her. "Hey, could you call Pastor Tim and let him know what's going on? Maybe he could help Tony through this if he's actually accused."

"That's a great idea, Priscilla. I'll do that now. I'll call you later and let you know what happened."

"Thanks, Trudy."

Priscilla hung up and slid her phone back into her purse. "Oh, Gail. I just can't believe it. We had such a nice day with everyone working together. Tony was happy. Now this."

"Don't give up yet, Priscilla. Maybe they'll find the real thief. Don't assume the worst yet."

"You're right." She met Gail's eyes. "I'm so sorry about the ring. I was so excited to give it to you, and now it's gone. If only I'd given it to you when I dropped Jake off this morning. That's what happens when you get in a hurry."

Gail put her hand on Priscilla's arm. "Don't you realize that I already have the greatest treasure Marjorie could have ever given me? I have you. The ring will never be as important to me as you are."

Whether it was the sweetness of Gail's reassurance, the stress of the thefts, the Weeping Woman, her worries about Tony, or all of it combined, Priscilla couldn't stop the tears that slid down her face. Gail put her arms around her.

"It will be okay, Priscilla. I promise. You just hang in there."

When Gail let her go, Priscilla wiped her face with the back of her hand. "You know, that's the really strange part of this Weeping Woman thing. Someone really thinks this will scare me away. They absolutely don't know me. I would never run away from what I've found here. This is my life now. You're my family."

"You're right," Gail said. "I hadn't thought of it before, but whoever it is really *doesn't* know you, do they? So it's got to be someone far removed from you." She shrugged. "I guess that doesn't help much, but at least you can cross out friends and close acquaintances."

"Actually, no one I suspect is close to me, but any insight I can gain is helpful. At this point, I need all the help I can get."

"No clear suspects?"

"Still the same ones, but I'm not gaining any ground with them." Priscilla frowned. "I know it's not Tony, and if his friends were involved, he'd have told me. I truly believe that."

"He might not have told you, but he probably would have confronted them."

Priscilla looked at her. "Why wouldn't he tell me?"

Gail laughed. "Young people these days don't like to *snitch*."

"Wow. I hope he wouldn't go to them. I don't trust them. Especially that Monty Anderson."

"I'm sorry, Priscilla. I didn't mean to put something in your head. I really don't think it's the boys. I can't see any of them putting on a dress and wailing on the cliff. Definitely not cool."

Although the situation wasn't actually funny, Priscilla had to laugh. The idea of Monty in a dress was humorous. She suspected it wouldn't do much for his reputation. Her laugh woke up Uncle Hugh, who mumbled something and opened his eyes. Jake jumped down from the recliner and came over to her, wagging his tail. She bent down to pet him.

"Looks like you've been having a great time," she said, smiling.

"He went outside not long before he and Pop took their nap," Gail said.

"I'll walk him when I get home. Thanks."

Uncle Hugh got up from his recliner and smiled at Priscilla. "Good to see you," he said. "And thanks for bringing over your friend. We had a good time together."

"I'm sure he had a great time too," Priscilla said. "Anytime you want to come over and spend some time with him, you're welcome."

"Well, thank you, Priscilla. I'm not gettin' around too well these days, but I might be able to do that."

Gail brought over Jake's leash and the tote bag with his food and toys. Priscilla thanked Gail again and headed to the car with Jake.

When they got home, she nuked her cheeseburger a bit. It still tasted good. After sharing a few bites with Jake, she snapped his leash on his collar and they stepped outside to a chilly October evening. The sun hadn't gone down yet, but it wouldn't be long. Priscilla decided to descend the long wooden steps that led to the beach. She wanted to walk along the water and listen to it lap against the shore. The sound always soothed her.

As they walked, she noticed someone else coming toward them. A woman—followed by a black-and-white cat. She realized suddenly it was the same cat that had been hanging around. Priscilla tightened her grip on Jake's leash, not sure how he would react. Surprisingly, the cat ran up and stopped right in front of Jake. They touched noses, and Jake's tail wagged with enthusiasm.

"Oreo loves dogs," the woman said as she approached.

"Sylvia?" Priscilla said. "Is that you?"

Sylvia Peabody strode up to where Oreo and Jake stood checking each other out. "I live up the road a ways and like to walk along the beach when I can."

"So Oreo is your cat?"

Sylvia shook her head. "He's a stray. Not sure where he came from. I tried to find his owners, but I couldn't. I feed him. Make sure he's okay." She stepped a little closer to Priscilla. "Actually, I wanted to talk to you about him. As you might know, I'm moving. My house has been sold, and I plan to leave as soon as I finish packing. I'm worried about Oreo. I'd take him with me, but I can't. Not where I'm going. Do you think you could look after him? Make sure he has food?"

"Of course, but I'd like to see if I can find someone to take him in permanently. I think that would be better for him."

"I agree. I tried to find him a forever home, but I wasn't successful. Maybe you'd have more luck." Sylvia knelt down, and Oreo ran over to her, rubbing up against her thigh. It certainly gave Priscilla a different view of the woman. She might seem rather caustic in her other dealings, but her love for Oreo was real and touching. It made Sylvia seem softer. Friendlier.

"I'll have some cat food left over before I leave. If it's okay, I'll bring it by your place."

"Certainly. And don't worry about Oreo. I'll do my best to look after him."

"Thank you, Priscilla. That means more than I can say."

As Sylvia stood up, Priscilla asked, "Where are you moving?"

"California. My mother lives there. She needs some assistance, and I intend to provide it. She's allergic to cats. That's why I can't take him."

"She's blessed to have a daughter who cares so much for her."

Sylvia smiled. "I'm the fortunate one. She's a great mother."

The sun slipped behind the horizon, and the golden beam from the lighthouse suddenly split through the dark and lit up the sea like fire.

"Beautiful," Sylvia said softly. "I never get tired of that."

"Me either."

Sylvia took a deep breath and pulled her sweater closer. "Well, I'd better get going. It was nice to talk to you, Priscilla. I can't tell you how much better I feel, knowing you'll keep an eye on Oreo."

"I'm glad."

Priscilla watched as Sylvia walked away down the beach. Instead of following her, Oreo stayed next to Jake. Priscilla smiled at him. "Well, I know why you turned your nose up at my tuna. Regardless, you're welcome to come by and visit anytime."

She tugged on Jake's leash and headed back to the stairs leading up the cliff. Oreo trotted behind them, but when they reached the top, Priscilla turned around to see that he had disappeared. She looked for him, but he was nowhere to be found.

Just like the Weeping Woman, Oreo had completely vanished.

CHAPTER THIRTY-ONE

When she got back to the cottage, Priscilla brought Jake inside. Still concerned about Oreo, she opened a can of tuna and put it outside on the porch with a bowl of water. Maybe he would be drawn to it this time.

After reading Trudy's instructions for the video camera, Priscilla sat in a chair by one of the front windows, not only keeping an eye on the cliff but also watching for Oreo. She finally grabbed a book and began to read, glancing outside every few sentences.

About ten after seven, the phone rang, and Priscilla answered it.

"Hey, Priscilla, it's Trudy. Chief Westin just left the church. He's going to look into the thefts."

"What about Tony? Did anyone mention him?"

"Unfortunately, yes. A couple of the volunteers contacted the chief and told him they suspected Tony. I took Hank aside and told him about Tony—what he'd been through, how he was trying to get away from those other boys. I also told him you and I trusted Tony and that we never saw him anywhere near those purses."

"I hope he listened."

"He did. He said he'll treat Tony just like anyone else who was on the scene during the robberies. And he'll be careful not to make it seem as if he's a suspect."

Priscilla breathed a deep sigh of relief. "That's wonderful news, Trudy. I'm so glad. Does the chief have any leads?"

"No, not yet. Too early. People lost a lot of cash, and several of the women had removed their jewelry because they were going to be painting and using glue. Maria Gonzalez was one of them. She took off her wedding rings, and they were stolen."

"But that proves it wasn't Tony," Priscilla said quickly. "He would never steal from Maria."

"You and I know that, but I'm not sure everyone will feel that way. They might think he knew his aunt's rings were in her purse and took advantage of that knowledge."

Although Priscilla hated to admit it, she could see Trudy's point. The brief flash of euphoria she'd felt vanished.

As if realizing it, Trudy said, "Don't worry, Priscilla. Hank won't arrest anyone unless he's sure. We're a long way from that now. Oh, I called Pastor Tim. He's feeling really positive about the path Tony is on. We need to keep praying. God is certainly listening."

"That makes this almost bearable," Priscilla said. "I want that ruby ring back, Trudy. I'm going to believe it will be returned. I can't accept that it was finally found only to disappear again. That just can't be."

"I'm praying the same thing. I have a good feeling about it."

Although she didn't say anything, Priscilla recognized that Trudy usually had a *good feeling* about everything. Probably one of the reasons she was always upbeat and happy. Something Priscilla envied and wanted to emulate.

"Thanks for calling me. I hope your dinner party wasn't ruined."

Trudy laughed. "The food was ready. I put it out before I left, they ate while I was gone, and I don't think they even missed me. They're talking about single-celled amoeboids, and I'm talking to you. Couldn't work out much better than that. After I hang up, I'm going to try to look interested without nodding off." She sighed. "I know this stuff is fascinating to Dan, but I can only listen so long without my mind shutting down. I try, though, for him. I would never want him to think I don't believe he's the smartest man in the whole world."

Priscilla laughed. "You're a good wife, Trudy."

"I'm trying."

Priscilla said goodbye and hung up.

The sound of a vehicle came from outside, accompanied by headlights sweeping across her front porch. Priscilla got up and looked out the window. She was shocked to see a bus with the words *West Tisbury Ghost Tours* painted on the side. The bus stopped, and someone got out. They went to the side of the bus and pulled the door open then helped several people climb out.

When Priscilla looked closer, she recognized Ed Holtman. Then she saw Myrna walk around the other side of the bus and start talking to the people gathered in a small circle. What in the world was going on?

Under usual circumstances, Priscilla might have waited until they left and called the Holtmans later. She tried to avoid confrontation whenever possible. But with everything that had been going on, something inside her rose up. Was it indignation or simply irritation? She wasn't sure, but she grabbed her coat and strode quickly toward the parked vehicle.

When Myrna saw her, her expression turned sheepish. She grabbed the arm of a female tourist standing near her and started leading her back to the bus, waving the others back as well.

"Myrna Holtman!" Priscilla called out as she approached the group. "What are you doing? Why are you here?"

Ed ran over to his wife, who was busy pushing their clients into the vehicle. He said something to Myrna then took over herding the tourists away from danger.

Myrna took a few tentative steps toward Priscilla. "I'm sorry, Priscilla," she said. "It's just that…well, the Weeping Woman is the talk of the town. They begged to see the cliff where she was seen. We have no intention of coming near your cottage—or the lighthouse."

"That may be true, but you're still on my property. You should have asked my permission, not just taken it upon yourself to trample all over my land."

Myrna looked away for a moment. "You're right," she said in a low voice. "I guess telling myself you wouldn't mind was deceitful. We'll leave right away."

"I have to wonder if you're behind the Weeping Woman appearances. Maybe you thought it would help your business. Why else would you ignore my feelings and come up here anyway?"

Myrna's eyes grew large. "That's not true, Priscilla. I—we would never do anything like that."

"But you would do this?" Priscilla shook her head. "You need to leave. Now."

"Of course. I'm truly sorry."

Myrna went back to Ed, who looked distressed. Then they climbed back into their bus and slowly drove away. Their taillights weren't even out of sight before Priscilla began to feel awful about the way she'd talked to Myrna. It was true. They hadn't come near the house. There really wasn't any harm done.

As she walked back to the cottage, she said out loud, "Well, Lord, I really blew it this time, didn't I? That poor woman didn't deserve that. I could have allowed them to finish their stop and talked to the Holtmans later with a little compassion. I'm sorry, and I'll apologize to them. Please forgive me."

Feeling convicted, she went back inside and sat down. Her purse lay next to the couch, and she suddenly remembered the card Norman Whitaker had given her. She still hadn't looked at it. She fumbled through her purse and finally pulled it out. When she turned it over, she gasped. The amount of the offer he'd written on the back was at least twice what the property was worth. Why was he willing to pay this much? And even more important, what was he willing to do to secure her property?

Priscilla got out her notebook and began writing down new evidence and new questions. She wrote down the names of the various suspects and what she'd discovered about them.

Tony Gonzalez. Don't believe he had anything to do with it.

Monty Anderson, Teddy Martin, and Jason Atwater. Not sure about them, but I think if they were behind it, Tony would know and he'd tell me.

Aleeta Armbruster. She knew about the painting. She's been lying—hiding something. What? Is she the mastermind or just an accomplice? She could have painted The Weeping Woman. *Seems frightened. But of what? I intend to talk to her more.*

Priscilla underlined the last entry. Besides the way Aleeta had acted earlier, she was tall and willowy. Just like the Weeping Woman.

Ed and Myrna Holtman, West Tisbury Ghost Tours. Motive? They want to add my lighthouse to their tour. Tonight they even came onto my property without permission. But would anyone really go to all this trouble just to add one more stop to a tour that's already popular as is? Doesn't really make sense. They even helped me learn more about Olivia Hennesey.

As she made the notes about Myrna, Priscilla realized something. Myrna and Ed certainly knew a lot about Olivia and her husband. They could pull off the Weeping Woman story because of all the background information they had. Myrna didn't look like the tall, thin Weeping Woman, but she certainly could be paying someone to act the part. Their little stunt tonight moved them up the list.

Priscilla went back and added to the entry about the Holtmans: *They have the knowledge to pull off the Weeping Woman.*

Her next note mentioned the person who was still number one on her list.

Norman Whitaker. Wants to buy my property for much more than it's worth. Why? Is there something about the land or the lighthouse I don't know? I find Mr. Whitaker very suspicious. Of course, he's not the Weeping Woman, but he certainly could pay someone to play Olivia.

Mr. Whitaker is a stranger and doesn't know what the lighthouse means to me or my family. He might think that I will sell to him because I'm afraid.

After thinking about it for a moment, Priscilla drew a big star in front of Norman's name. Maybe he really had threatened her, and maybe that was who Aleeta was afraid of.

She moved on to the next entry.

Eleanor Gufstead. Likes Gerald. This seems like a rather intricate plot for someone to create just to chase a man. She does seem a little strange, though. Maybe off mentally? Does that mean she might actually go to these lengths? She was at the Art Attack Wednesday night and could have exchanged the paintings.

After thinking about it, Priscilla added an additional note and underlined it.

All of these suspects were at the art gallery and could have manipulated the paintings.

Priscilla stared at the list. Six suspects. Six individuals or groups who were at the art gallery when the painting of the Weeping Woman was displayed. Was she any closer to an answer than she was when she first started asking questions?

When the clock struck eight, she knew it was getting close to the time the Weeping Woman might emerge. Just as she was thinking about grabbing Trudy's camera and going out onto the porch, she heard a car pull up. Priscilla opened the front door and saw Gerald getting out of his Coast Guard vehicle. Although she was always glad to see him, Priscilla wished he'd called first.

She was tired and didn't feel like entertaining anyone at this late hour.

As if he'd read her mind, he only walked up to the edge of the porch. "I don't want to bother you, Priscilla, but I'm going to swing by here in the evenings for a couple of hours until we find out who's behind your *visitations*. I was afraid you'd hear the car and worry about who was hanging around."

"I . . . I don't understand."

"Until you're ready to contact the police, I'm going to patrol. I don't like the idea of you being here alone with whoever has gone to these elaborate lengths to frighten you. What if they decide to take this even further?" He shook his head. "Nope. Not gonna allow it." He waved at her. "You go on back inside. Don't mind me. And if anything happens after I leave, you call me right away, okay?"

Priscilla was so surprised, she could only choke out, "Thank you."

Gerald got back into his SUV and drove toward the cliff. Priscilla could hardly believe he cared enough to keep an eye on her. It actually made her a little emotional. Life had changed so much when she lost Gary. One thing that she hadn't expected: her protector was gone. Gary had always made her feel safe. If she felt threatened or afraid, he was there. For Gerald to take her safety personally meant more than she could say. He was a good friend, and she really appreciated it.

As she closed the door, she took a deep, cleansing breath. A cup of tea, a little reading time, and then bed. Tonight she wouldn't be watching for the Weeping Woman after all. With Gerald out there, she'd never show up. Even though Trudy wanted to get whoever was playing Olivia Hennesey on video, Priscilla was thrilled she could lie down and sleep without thinking about what was happening on the cliff.

And it felt great.

CHAPTER THIRTY-TWO

When the alarm went off the next morning, Priscilla rolled over on her back and stared at the ceiling for a few minutes before getting out of bed. She'd looked forward to a peaceful night's sleep, but instead she'd dreamt she was chasing a woman in blue through an old house that had all kinds of rooms and hallways. Every time Priscilla neared the woman and was about to grab her, she'd laugh and run around a corner.

Today she would talk to Aleeta alone. Hopefully, when she was finished, she'd be one step closer to finding the truth about the Weeping Woman.

Priscilla finally got out of bed, turned on the coffee maker, changed clothes, brushed her hair, and got Jake's leash. When she opened her front door, something fell to the floor. A folded piece of paper. She picked it up and opened it. It was from Gerald.

Everything quiet tonight. Hope you had a peaceful evening.

Gerald

Priscilla smiled and refolded the note. She stuck it in the pocket of her skirt and took Jake outside. It was a brisk morning, and she wished she'd grabbed her thicker jacket instead of the sweater she'd thrown over her shoulders. For some reason, Jake seemed to be taking his sweet time this morning.

"Hurry up, Jake," she said, trying to scold him lightly without making him feel he was doing something wrong. As they walked near the cliff, something ran right in front of her. Without meaning to, she let loose a high-pitched squeal. But when she looked down, she realized it was only Oreo, who had come to say hello to his new friend, Jake. The two touched noses, and Jake's tail wagged so furiously that Priscilla was surprised it didn't fall off.

"You two are so funny," she said with a smile. "Where did you come from, Oreo?" She would almost swear he was living with someone. Well fed, clean, and he seemed happy. Still, living outside had its own set of challenges. Down through the years, Priscilla had seen too many feral cats living around the farm—many of them abandoned by owners who didn't want them anymore and thought dumping them in the country was okay. It wasn't. Predators, cars, and contact with animals with rabies or other diseases could shorten the lives of cats living without owners to care for them. She was determined Oreo wouldn't be one of them. Either she'd take him in herself, or she'd find someone who would. For now, since Sylvia was caring for him, she decided to wait until Sylvia moved to California. Whatever she was doing seemed to be working wonderfully.

Finally, she and Jake headed back to the house. She thought Oreo might follow them, but he didn't. Once again he leaped over the cliff and disappeared. Back at the cottage, she checked the can of tuna she'd set out the night before. The tuna was gone, so at least she was pretty certain he'd eaten.

Priscilla was on her way to church when she remembered that she'd told Gerald they could have lunch today. She couldn't believe she'd forgotten. Lunch with him sounded nice, and she began to look forward to it.

As she pulled up into the parking lot of Faith Fellowship, she waved at Bruce Gore, the church's choir director. Then she greeted Cheryl Finnegan, who ran the children's ministry.

"Winter's on the way," Cheryl said, referencing the cold front that had moved in overnight.

"Yes, it is," Priscilla agreed.

As she went inside the church, she immediately noticed Eleanor Gufstead leaning against the wall in the foyer. Priscilla greeted her with a nod and went into the sanctuary. She'd just sat down in a pew when Gerald slid in next to her.

"Everything was quiet last night," he said in a low voice. "I think your ghost has hit the road. Too many people looking for her now."

Something occurred to Priscilla for the first time. "You've never seen her, have you? How do you know I'm not delusional?"

Gerald's soft, full laugh made her feel warm inside. "First of all, I don't think you're the kind of person who is *delusional*. Secondly, you'd have to have the power to make your cousins see the same thing. You may be an extraordinary woman, but I'm afraid that's a little too much even for you."

Although she had to laugh at his attempt at humor, her cheeks grew warm when he called her extraordinary. *He didn't mean anything by it, Priscilla*, she chided herself. *Don't be silly.*

"I noticed Eleanor when I came in. How are things going with her?" she asked.

"Actually, I think we're good," Gerald said. "My friends spoke with her daughter, and she called her mother. Eleanor came to me after the phone call and apologized. She's just very lonely and realizes she went too far. We've agreed to be friends. I feel much better about it, and I believe she does too."

"I'm so glad." Priscilla intended to pray for Eleanor. If anyone could understand what it felt like to be lonely, it was Priscilla. But she'd decided to go on with life, whereas Eleanor's life had stopped when her husband died. Maybe now she could move forward.

The choir was wonderful, and the sermon was excellent. Pastor Rona reminded them that faith without works was dead. That if faith didn't produce compassion and a desire to help those in need, it was useless. Priscilla was reminded of Myrna and her failure to show the tour guide a little grace. She decided to call Myrna later today and apologize.

When church was over, she walked out to the parking lot with Gerald. "I have an errand to run after lunch," she told him, "so why don't we both take our cars?"

Gerald suggested the Colonial Inn, and Priscilla agreed. It didn't matter that she'd just been there. The food was great, and it was open on Sunday. When they went in, Priscilla noticed they seemed fully staffed. She was thankful not only for Tilly's sake, but also because it meant Tony would be able to concentrate on Priscilla's yard work.

She and Gerald were immediately seated at a booth near a window, a spot usually reserved for Gerald, who was a friend of Tilly's.

Once they ordered and had been served their drinks, Priscilla tried to let go of the things she'd had on her mind. Gerald was a good friend, and he deserved her full attention.

"Are you okay?" he asked as she sipped her iced tea.

She hadn't planned to share all that had been going on. She opened her mouth to say, "Fine. Just a lot happening," but instead, everything came pouring out. It was like an underwater spring had been unplugged and the water was going everywhere. When she finally stopped talking, Gerald looked somewhat shell-shocked.

"I'm sorry, Gerald," she said immediately. "I don't know where all of that came from. I shouldn't have dumped everything on you."

"Nonsense," he said, cutting off her protestations. "Obviously you needed to talk." He shook his head. "So Aleeta Armbruster knows more than she's saying? That's the first person you've caught in an out-and-out lie, isn't it?"

"Yes. That's why I'm going by her shop after lunch. I want to give her a chance to tell me the truth. She's definitely afraid of something. You should have seen her face." Priscilla sighed. "Between Aleeta and the burglaries, my head is spinning. I'm not quite sure where to focus my attention."

"I understand," he said. "You know, the theft at the church isn't the first burglary we've had in Tisbury. There have been quite a few of them. Did Mildred ever tell you about the gold cross that went missing from the museum?"

"Yes, she did. Hard to believe someone would take something with so much historical significance to the Vineyard." She frowned at Gerald. "This area doesn't seem as if it would be home to a group of thieves."

"There are thieves everywhere, Priscilla." He grunted. "A lot of us believe there's a connection between the thefts. They all seem to occur at public places or events where people gather. So far, no one's been able to solve them—or stop them. I know our police chief is about at his wit's end."

"Well, I hope they find this person soon."

"I do too. I'm so sorry about your aunt's ring. To find it and then lose it like that..."

"I really hope it's found. I'm praying it will be."

"I'll pray the same way."

Priscilla smiled at him. "Thank you, Gerald."

"You're welcome. You know, last night while I was driving around your property, I remembered playing on the beach when I was a boy. Right below the lighthouse. In fact, it was a very popular place for children on Martha's Vineyard."

"Really? Kids played there? Do you mean they swam?"

He shook his head. "Sure, we swam some, but the main attraction was the caves in the rocks along the seacoast. We loved to play in them. Unfortunately, they became unstable and were eventually filled in. It's too bad. We had great fun. We'd pretend to be pirates storing our bounty inside where the law couldn't find it. One of my favorite caves was right below your cliff. Where the Weeping Woman has been appearing." He laughed. "Maybe she's taken up residence in that old cave."

"I doubt it, if it's filled up. Of course, if she's really a ghost, she could slip in and out without any problem."

"Yeah, that would be the only way to get inside now. The city was afraid the sea wall was going to collapse due to the instability of the caves. Thankfully, they caught it just in time."

"I'm glad no one was hurt before the problem was solved."

"Me too. Especially since I might have been one of the victims." He nodded at her. "Of course, protecting your seawall is another part of that project. If it had collapsed, your beautiful view would have been seriously affected, as well as the stability of your lighthouse."

"You're right."

"I hope I didn't throw a kink into your plans last night," Gerald said. "My presence might have kept your visitor at bay. I realized later that perhaps you wanted her to show up so you could catch her."

"Heavens no. The truth is I'd rather she never come back. Last night I felt so much safer."

"I'm glad. Are you focusing on Aleeta now, or do you have anyone else still on your list of suspects?"

Priscilla reached into her purse and took out her notebook. "I've ruled out Tony and his friends."

"I agree. How about the Holtmans?"

Priscilla sighed and told him about their visit the night before. "I'm ashamed of the way I reacted," she said. "I think they were just trying to appease their customers without invading my privacy. It seems the story of the Weeping Woman is being circulated in town. I should have made allowances for them. At least this one time."

Gerald shrugged. "At the same time, it's your property—and you told them you didn't want them bringing their tour by your place. They were in the wrong, Priscilla. You weren't."

"I realize that, but I have the responsibility to treat people with kindness and compassion. I certainly failed yesterday."

Gerald grinned. "So the nice lady can bite, huh?"

Priscilla laughed. "If she's pushed to her breaking point, yes. I'm not always so mild-mannered."

"I think that just makes you more interesting."

"I'm not sure Ed and Myrna would agree with that."

The waitress, Hilda, brought their food to the table. After she left, Gerald steered the conversation back to Priscilla's plan to talk to Aleeta Armbruster. "You should be careful. I mean, she's obviously guilty of something. Guilty people can be defensive." He put his fork down and stared at her. "Although I won't tell anyone about Aleeta, I must insist that you let me come with you. Please don't be offended, but I don't believe I could relax knowing you might be in some kind of danger."

Frankly, Priscilla was grateful for the company. She wasn't sure she wanted to be alone with Aleeta. "Thank you. I might need you to wait out in the car, though. I want her to relax. Give her a chance to come clean without feeling threatened."

Gerald, who was enjoying his seared pecan-crusted ahi tuna, nodded his agreement. "Not a problem. I hope she decides to be honest with you."

"Me too."

Tilly walked up to their table. "How are your crab cakes, Priscilla?"

"They're wonderful. The best I've ever had."

"Good. If you two need anything else, just let us know. I'm glad you're here today." She winked at Gerald and walked away.

Priscilla wondered what the wink meant. Tilly didn't seem like the kind of person who winked at people. Of course, she and Gerald were longtime friends, so maybe it made sense. But still. What exactly was she winking at?

CHAPTER THIRTY-THREE

Priscilla and Gerald finished their lunch and declined dessert. Priscilla was pleasantly full. Adding dessert would have made her uncomfortable.

"It's a little after one o'clock," Gerald said. "Are you ready?"

"Yes and no." Priscilla sighed. "Even though I told off Myrna Holtman yesterday, I really don't like confrontation. I want Aleeta to trust me, but after our confrontation yesterday, I have serious doubts I can make amends. What if she doesn't confide in me?"

"You can't force her to be candid with you. All you can do is try. And if you can't get the truth from her, you plan to talk to Hank Westin?"

Priscilla nodded. "I don't think my cousins will let me change my mind. They're pretty determined to bring in the police. They're concerned for my safety."

"Do you think the thefts at the church are connected to your Weeping Woman?"

"I'd really prefer that you not call her *my* Weeping Woman."

Gerald chuckled. "Sorry. I see your point."

"I don't know. I mean, how does someone dressing up like the Weeping Woman tie into a simple burglary?"

Gerald pointed at the notebook Priscilla was putting back into her purse. "Anyone on your list at the church yesterday?"

She thought for a moment. "Yes, a few, but no one I'd suspect of stealing."

He frowned. "Probably unrelated. I can't see any reason they'd be connected. I guess it's just an odd coincidence."

After paying the bill, Gerald and Priscilla left the restaurant and went outside. It was cloudy, and the sky was growing dark.

"We're supposed to have rain again today," he said, "but I think we have enough time to talk to Aleeta and then get home before it starts. I think we'll stay dry." He looked down at her, and his expression became concerned. "Are you all right?"

"I'm fine. Just…I don't know. Do you ever feel as if you're missing something that's right in front of you, but you're not sure what it is?"

"Actually, I do. It's happened more than once. I've learned to pay attention when that happens. It could be important."

"I feel that way, but I don't know why."

"Best to turn it over to God and let Him show you. There's only so much we can figure out with these little minds of ours."

Priscilla smiled at him. "Now that's the truth." She glanced at her watch. "I guess we better get to the shop."

"Let's take my car. I'll bring you back to get yours when we're done."

"Sure," she agreed. "That sounds fine." She knew she sounded distracted, but alarm bells were going off in her head. She wished she could discern their message.

Gerald held the car door open, and she got in. It only took a few minutes to drive to the Art Attack. Although autumn could be busy on the Vineyard, Sundays were usually quieter because some of the shops were closed. They had no problem finding a parking spot in front of Aleeta's store.

When Priscilla went to the front door, she was surprised to find it locked. She peered into the window, but the lights were off. No one was there.

"I thought this was open on Sundays," Gerald said behind her. He'd gotten out of the car after he'd seen her trying the door.

"It's supposed to be." She pointed to a schedule painted on the door. "Look. Sundays 10:00 a.m. until 4:00 p.m."

"Well, there's not much you can do," he said.

"I guess not."

Gerald pointed to a coffee shop across the street. "Look, let's get some coffee. We have time. We can wait a bit to see if Aleeta comes in."

Although Priscilla had her doubts that the shop owner was going to show up, the threat of telling Chief Westin about her the next day made Priscilla decide to wait a bit.

"Okay." She looked up at Gerald. "You certainly don't need to wait with me. Why don't you go home?"

He shrugged. "And do what? Sit around? This is much more interesting."

The twinkle in his eyes made her smile. "All right. I guess we can give it a little time."

They left his car where it was and walked across the street. The coffee shop wasn't busy, so it didn't take long to get a couple of cappuccinos and grab a small table near the front window. The coffee hit the spot.

"So what's your guess about Aleeta?" Gerald asked. "Why do you think she put that painting up? I can't see how she would benefit from you moving away."

"I don't think she's behind the Weeping Woman," Priscilla said, "but I believe she knows who is. To be honest, my gut tells me Aleeta is being blackmailed."

Gerald's eyebrows shot up. "How did you come to that conclusion?"

Priscilla took another sip of her coffee and then set the large ceramic cup down in front of her. "Look, as you said, there's no reason in the world for her to want me out of town. So why put up the painting? Why lie about it? Why try to hide it later? It's clear she did it for someone else. And that person has to be behind the Weeping Woman. And why would Aleeta become involved in something that could hurt her reputation?"

"Because she fears something worse."

"Exactly. Nothing else makes sense."

Gerald seemed to study her for a moment. "You have an analytical mind. A way of taking facts and putting them into order so they make sense. Not everyone can do that."

Priscilla felt herself blush. "I love puzzles and crosswords. And I think running a farm helped. Organization was key—as was the ability to prioritize."

"I'm sure that's true, but I also believe you have a natural gift."

Priscilla looked away, pleased but embarrassed by Gerald's kind comments. "Thank you. Right now I'd love to use my *gift* to find the Weeping Woman and catch the person who stole from our volunteers on Friday." She sighed. "So far my analytical mind hasn't helped much."

"It will."

She looked at her watch and then the still-empty art gallery across the street. "I'd better head home. I'm supposed to meet Tony at two o'clock. He's going to do some yard work for me."

Gerald looked up at the sky. "You may get rained out."

"Well, maybe I can at least take Jake out before it starts. He hates going out in the rain."

Gerald drove her back to the restaurant, where he let her out next to her car.

"Thanks for listening," Priscilla told him. "I'm sure you're getting tired of hearing about all my problems."

He smiled at her. "Don't be silly. My ears are ready to listen anytime."

She waved at him as he drove away and then got into her car and headed back to the cottage. By the time she got home, it was a few minutes after two. Priscilla hated being late and hoped Tony wouldn't be upset.

When she pulled up, she saw him sitting on her porch, his bicycle leaning against the side of the house. She quickly parked the car and got out.

"I'm so sorry," she said as she hurried toward the cottage. "Hope you weren't waiting long."

He smiled. "I just got here. Didn't know you were late."

"Good." She unlocked the front door, and Jake was there, waiting. When he saw Tony, he immediately jumped up on him. "Jake, get down," Priscilla said.

"It's okay," Tony said. "I don't mind at all."

Priscilla laughed. "All right, but if you change your mind, just tell him to sit. He'll do it."

"Okay." Tony knelt down next to Jake, who began to lick his face.

"I'll get you something to drink. You must be thirsty after that long bike ride."

"I ride my bike all the time," he said. "It's really not a big deal."

She gestured toward him. "Have a seat at the kitchen table. I'll get us some lemonade, and we'll talk about the yard."

He came in and sat down while Priscilla put ice and lemonade in two glasses. She put one of the glasses in front of him.

"Thanks," he said. He took a big drink. "Wow. That's good. Doesn't taste like lemonade from the store."

"It's not. I made it myself. My husband used to love my lemonade after working on the farm." Although it snuck up on her, she couldn't keep a note of sadness out of her voice.

"I'm sorry about your husband," Tony said softly. "I can tell you miss him."

"Yes, I do. And I know you miss your folks." She put the pitcher back in the refrigerator. "I think it's one of the reasons we're friends. We understand each other."

Tony stared at his glass for a moment. "I think you're right."

She sat down across from him. "Tony, if you ever need to talk…"

"Thanks. I appreciate that. I have been talking to Pastor Tim. He's really helping me."

"I'm so glad. He seems like a great guy."

Tony nodded. "He is." He frowned. "Aunt Maria said some people got robbed at the church yesterday. Her wedding rings were stolen. Do you know about it?"

"I'm afraid so. Seems someone took things from several of the women's purses."

Tony's eyebrows shot up. "Wow. Did they steal very much?"

"Unfortunately, yes." She searched his face. "Any chance you saw anyone back there? Someone who shouldn't have been near the purses?"

Tony was silent for a moment, his forehead wrinkled in thought. "I don't think so. Just some of the women, but I didn't think much about it. I mean, I figured they were getting something out of their purses. The only time I was back there was when we brought the doughnuts out to the main room and when you and I went in there to get your notebook. After that, I might have noticed a few women going back there, but I can't remember who. I can't think of anything that seemed out of line."

Priscilla nodded. "You know, you just made a good point. I hadn't thought about it quite like that, but the thief was probably a woman. If a man had been rifling through purses, people might have thought it was odd." She smiled at Tony. "That's a great help, Tony. Thank you."

The boy looked pleased at Priscilla's praise. It was clear to her he'd had nothing to do with the thefts. She prayed silently that he would never find out some people suspected him.

"I'll tell you what," Priscilla said when they had finished their lemonade. "Why don't we take Jake for a walk, and I'll show you what needs to be done in the yard? It might rain soon, so we should probably get moving."

"Sounds good." Tony looked down next to his chair, where Jake sat looking up at him. Tony had been stroking his head ever since he'd sat down. "Can I hold the leash?"

Priscilla laughed. "Of course. He's pretty strong. You'll probably be able to handle him even better than I can."

"So sometimes you might want me to come over and take him out when you're gone for a while?"

"Yes, if you're interested." She saw his eyes light up at the thought. "I'll give you a key to the cottage and let you know when I need you to stop by." The truth was, she usually didn't need help with Jake. Normally, her time away from the cottage was brief, and if she needed to be gone for several hours, one of her cousins was happy to help out. But Priscilla knew Tony liked Jake, and she felt it would be good for them to spend time together.

She mentioned a price per hour for helping with Jake and the yard, and Tony grinned. "That would be great. Thanks."

Priscilla stood up, got the leash, and handed it to Tony. While he put the leash on Jake, she went to her purse, took an extra key to the front door off her key ring, and gave it to Tony, who put it in his pocket.

"I'll put it on a special key ring when I get home," he said. "I won't lose it or anything. I promise."

"I know you won't. I trust you."

He pulled on his jacket, and she grabbed her coat. When they stepped outside, Tony and Jake took off. Jake's tail stuck straight up with excitement, and Tony's laughter rang out as they sprinted ahead of her. She couldn't help but giggle at the two boys—one human and one canine—who both loved to run. Something she really couldn't do much of with Jake. Maybe for a little while, but not with the enthusiasm Tony possessed.

When she finally caught up to them, they were near the cliff. "Why don't we walk along the beach?" she said. "Jake loves it. We'll check out the yard when we come back."

"That would be awesome," Tony said.

They took the steps that led down the side of the cliff. When they reached the beach, Priscilla pulled her coat even tighter. It was always chillier near the water. She walked behind Tony and Jake, watching the water lap the shore.

Suddenly Jake spotted a seagull and pulled on the leash. Tony and Jake took off, sprinting toward the hapless bird, who decided it was a good time to fly away. As she laughed at their antics, Priscilla happened to look down and spotted something lying on the ground near the water.

She reached down and picked up a small, dark blue bag, wet and covered with sand. She slowly pulled the top of the bag open, and several pieces of jewelry fell into her palm. Among them,

Marjorie's ruby ring. Shocked, she stared at the pieces for a moment, but then she put them back in the bag and looked up the shore at Tony and Jake.

Had the bag fallen out of Tony's pocket? Was it possible he really was the person who had robbed the volunteers at Grace Community Church?

CHAPTER THIRTY-FOUR

Priscilla quickly stuffed the bag into her coat pocket. She needed to think. At that moment she felt sick to her stomach. As Tony and Jake turned around to come back to where she stood, she heard someone call her name. She turned around to see Chief Westin and one of his officers walking toward her.

"Mrs. Grant?" he said. "We need to talk."

What was he doing here? She wondered if Gerald or one of her cousins had decided to call the police instead of allowing her to wait and contact them when she was ready.

"What can I do for you, Chief?" she said as he approached.

The chief pointed toward Tony, who came up next to them. "I'm sorry, but someone has filed a complaint against Tony Gonzalez. Says she saw him getting into the purses in the church's kitchen yesterday." He looked at Tony. "I need to take you to the station, young man, and ask you some questions."

The color drained from Tony's face, and he looked at Priscilla. "I didn't do it."

She took Jake's leash from his hand. "It will be all right," she said. "I'm sure it's a mistake."

"I wouldn't be so sure, Mrs. Grant," the chief said. "Our witness is convinced it was him."

"And who is your witness?" Priscilla asked.

"Sorry. She asked me not to reveal her identity." Westin shook his head. "Look, I'm not going to charge the boy on the word of one person. I'll talk to him. If there's no other evidence, I'll let him go home until we can find something more substantial."

"If Tony had been rifling through purses, don't you think more than one person would have noticed?" Priscilla insisted, despite the jewelry bag in her pocket. "Although the purses were in the kitchen, we could easily see into the room through the pass-through. I don't see how in the world he could have gotten away with it. Your thief has to be a woman. It's the only thing that makes sense. No one would think anything about a woman getting into a purse. They'd assume it was hers."

The chief nodded. "Actually, I had the same thought." He studied Tony for a moment. "Look, son, to be honest, I sincerely doubt you're the one who did this, but I have to follow up this report. I don't have a choice. That's why I want you to come down to the station and talk to me. See if we can straighten this out."

"I...I understand, I guess," Tony said. "But I'm not a thief. Besides, my aunt was one of the people who was robbed. I would never steal from my aunt. Never."

"And I have no reason not to believe that. Why don't you just come with me? We'll call your aunt and uncle when we get to the station."

Priscilla patted Tony's arm. "You go with the chief. I'll get your bicycle and meet you downtown. Everything will be all right."

Tony nodded slowly and followed the chief up the steps. He looked so small next to the tall law enforcement officer. Priscilla stood on the beach with Jake's leash in her hand. The bag in her pocket felt as if it weighed a ton. She should have turned it over to Chief Westin, but she just couldn't.

"He's not guilty, Jake," she said softly.

Jake whined as if he understood her. They walked up the steps and went back to the cottage, Priscilla praying that God would show her what to do next.

Once she was inside, she slipped the bag of jewelry into the back of a drawer in her kitchen and loaded Tony's bike in the back of her SUV. By the time she got to the station, Maria and Phil's car was already there. When Priscilla went inside, she found them waiting outside the chief's office door.

"Oh, Priscilla," Maria said, "I just can't believe it. Tony isn't a thief. I'm sure of it."

"But maybe losing his parents did something to him," Phil said, his face twisted with worry. "How can we be sure he didn't do this?"

"I don't believe for a minute he's behind it," Priscilla said. "Besides, if he wanted to steal from you, he's had plenty of time to do it. Has he ever taken anything?"

Maria and Phil shook their heads.

"Then he wouldn't start now, in public. Besides, how could he go through all those purses and not be spotted? It's impossible." She explained her theory about a woman being behind the crime.

"You know, I believe you're right," Maria said. "I had to get into my purse several times because I have a cold, and my medicine and cough drops were in my purse."

"Exactly." Priscilla frowned at Maria. "Did you notice any particular woman in the kitchen more than the others?"

Tony's aunt was silent as she considered the question. Finally, she said, "You know, there was one woman who was back there several times. At the time, I didn't think much about it, but now . . . well, it does seem a little odd."

"Who was it?"

Maria looked at her husband. "What was her name, Phil? I know we met her. Was it . . . Alice?"

Phil shook his head. "Sorry, I'm not sure who you're talking about."

Maria looked a little embarrassed and lowered her voice. "She has very strange eyebrows."

"Sylvia?" Priscilla interjected. "Sylvia Peabody?"

Maria snapped her fingers. "Yes. That's it. Sylvia Peabody."

Priscilla was surprised—and disappointed. Sylvia certainly didn't seem like someone who would steal money and jewelry from other women. Still, it would be foolish to ignore this information. "I'll tell the chief about it," she told Maria. "Maybe he can talk to her."

"Please don't tell her we accused her. Frankly, I visited the kitchen as much as she did. If you're looking for someone suspicious, you could wonder about me."

Priscilla smiled. "Never crossed my mind. Don't think it would occur to anyone else either."

Even as she said it, she prayed she was right. What if someone decided Tony and Maria were in it together? She couldn't even begin to comprehend the damage it could cause to Tony and his family.

Priscilla was trying to think of something encouraging to say to Maria and Phil when the door to the chief's office finally opened, and he came out with Tony.

He nodded to Maria and Phil. "You can take him home. Sorry for having to question him, but I had to follow up on a tip given by a citizen. Hope you understand."

"So you know he's not guilty?" Maria asked.

"I'm not saying that, but there's no real evidence against him. I can't arrest someone because they were in the vicinity of a crime. I'd have to arrest several people, including you, Mrs. Gonzalez. At the moment, Tony isn't under suspicion. Now, you all need to take off. I have an investigation to conduct."

"Chief Westin, may I speak to you for a moment?" Priscilla asked.

"Is it important?"

"It might be."

The chief sighed again. "All right. Come into my office."

Priscilla turned to Maria and Phil. "Tony's bike is in the back of my SUV. It's not locked."

"Thank you, Priscilla," Maria said. She turned to Tony. "Let's go home, okay?"

Tony didn't move. His gaze was fixed on Priscilla. "I didn't take that stuff." It was obvious he wanted her to believe him.

She smiled. "I told you that I believe you. Trust me, okay? Now go home. We'll reschedule the tour of my yard for a later date."

"Do you want your key back?" The uncertainty in his eyes almost broke Priscilla's heart.

"Of course not. Why would I?"

Thankfully, the tension on his face eased some. "Thank you."

"There's nothing to thank me for. Wait until I show you all the yard work I need you to do. You may wish you'd never met me."

Although it was meant to add some lightheartedness to the situation, Tony didn't smile. "That will never happen," he said quietly before he turned and followed Maria and Phil out of the station.

"You've really established a relationship with that young man," the chief said as he ushered Priscilla into his office.

"It's not hard. He's a fine young man."

"I agree."

Priscilla almost sighed with relief. "So you think he's innocent too?"

The chief plopped down in an old leather chair behind his ancient desk. His large frame made the chair creak almost as if it were in pain. He removed his hat and ran his hand through his thick brown hair before putting it back on. "I don't have the luxury of *thinking* someone's innocent. I have to assume they are until I can prove otherwise. That applies to Tony too." He moved a stack of papers over to the one place on his desk that was clear. "Now, what can I do for you?"

"Someone told me they saw a woman in the kitchen several times on Saturday. Seemed a little unusual."

"Who told you this?"

Priscilla shrugged. "Sorry. I can't reveal her identity."

The chief's right eyebrow shot up. "Oh, I see. What's good for the goose..."

She leaned forward in her chair. "Look, Chief. I don't want to play games with you. I just want you to find out who really did this. Clear Tony's name." She took a deep breath and let it out slowly, trying to calm her ragged nerves. "Maria says this person was in the kitchen quite a bit. And before you ask why Maria was in the kitchen herself, she was getting medicine and cough drops because of her cold."

"And who was this woman?"

"Her name is Sylvia Peabody. She works for Elmer McBroom. Do you know her?"

The chief nodded. "Elmer's been around a long time. He's my insurance agent. Nice old guy. And I know Sylvia too. Also knew her late mother before she moved away."

"Do you think she's capable of stealing?"

The chief shrugged. "Frankly, I have no idea. But I find this information interesting. Especially since Sylvia is the person who pointed the finger at Tony."

Surprised, Priscilla said, "Sylvia said she saw him getting into the purses?"

"I shouldn't have told you that much," the chief said gruffly. "Let's just leave it there, okay? I don't want to be rude, but I've really got to get back to work."

After thanking the chief for speaking with her, Priscilla left. All the way home, she went over the information the chief had given her. So Sylvia had accused Tony? Yet Priscilla was certain he was innocent. Did that mean Sylvia was the thief? To be honest, she was shocked. Working for a respected businessman. A longtime pillar of the community. Maybe Sylvia had decided to rob a few people before she left town? Although that made a kind of sick sense, no one just suddenly decided to become a thief out of the blue. Something wasn't adding up.

When Priscilla got home, she went inside, made a cup of coffee, and got the jewelry bag she'd found out of the drawer. It was still a wet mess. She grabbed a napkin and lay the bag on it, hoping to soak up some of the water. As she stared at it, she realized that when she'd found it, it was almost covered with sand. That meant there was no way for it to have just fallen out of Tony's pocket. It had been there for a while. Long enough for the waves to wash sand over the top of it.

She opened the bag and removed the jewelry. There was a set of wedding rings. Priscilla picked them up and noticed an inscription on the inside of the wedding band. It read: *Maria—mi amor por siempre.* Although Priscilla's high school Spanish was a little rusty, she was pretty sure that translated to *my love forever.* It didn't take any great deductive reasoning to conclude these were Maria's wedding rings. Priscilla carefully removed Marjorie's ruby ring, a beautiful white gold engagement ring, two more wedding rings, and a silver bracelet.

After looking them over, she put all the jewelry back in the bag. She'd turn it in to the chief as soon as she could, but she wanted some time to think about everything. Besides the theft, there was Aleeta's lie about the painting, the appearance and disappearance of the Weeping Woman, and now trying to figure out why Sylvia Peabody had accused Tony of the burglary at the church. All of these situations swirled around in her head. Were they connected? In the end, it didn't seem as if the theft of the jewelry had anything to do with Olivia Hennesey. But why had she found the bag on the beach near her property? That certainly seemed like an odd coincidence.

Priscilla sipped her coffee and wondered if she should call her cousins and let them know what was going on. She heated up a bowl of broccoli and cheese soup but only ate half of it.

As if he knew something was wrong, Jake lay quietly at her feet, his head resting on his paws. After supper they went for a brief walk but not down to the beach.

As they were heading back to the cottage, Gerald drove up. He rolled down his window. "Just on patrol," he said. "You doing okay?"

She knew she should tell him about Tony, but she was tired and just wanted to go home and get some sleep. She'd tell him tomorrow. "I'm fine. Walking Jake before we turn in for the night."

"Looks like the rain missed us. You should make it back without getting wet."

That feeling was back. The sense that she was missing something. She stared at Gerald as if the answer was written on his face, and suddenly something else he'd said clicked in her head, along with something she'd heard in Chief Westin's office.

In a matter of seconds, all the pieces of the puzzle fell into place.

"Are you sure you're all right, Priscilla?" Gerald said. "You look strange."

All she could say was, "The cat was dry, Gerald! The cat was dry!"

CHAPTER THIRTY-FIVE

Gerald drove Priscilla and Jake back to the cottage so she could put Jake inside. He wasn't happy about it, but she didn't need to be tripping over him right now.

Gerald drove her back to the edge of the cliff, and they both hurried down the stairs to the beach.

She watched as Gerald began to climb up the cliff. He didn't seem to have any trouble finding places to step or rocks he could grab to pull himself up. After a short climb, he turned around and gestured to her. Grateful she had on sensible flat shoes, Priscilla followed the path he'd just taken and joined him on a large jutting rock.

"Look here," he said. "This looks like rock, but it isn't. It's some kind of painted tarp, designed to blend in to the cliff wall."

He pulled the tarp back to reveal the entrance to a cave. After securing the tarp so it would stay open, he took her hand and pulled her inside. Almost immediately, they were greeted by a soft meow. Priscilla looked down to see Oreo staring up at her. He'd been lying on a pet bed with a pan of water and a bowl of food next to it.

She reached down to pet him. "Oh, Oreo. It never occurred to me you'd bring me the answer to my mystery." As if he understood her, he purred loudly.

"I'm confused," Gerald said. "What does this cat have to do with anything?"

"The other night when it rained so hard, Oreo came by right after it stopped. He was perfectly dry. I didn't think about it much when it happened, but how could a homeless cat stay dry through a drenching thunderstorm?"

"He had a place to hide out."

"Then when you told me about the caves..."

"You figured out he was hiding inside a cave?" Gerald looked confused. "I guess it's interesting, but what does that have to do with the Weeping Woman?" Even as he said the words, a look of realization washed across his features. "This is how she disappeared. Down the cliff wall, into the cave."

"Yes. But there's more. I found something on the beach." She told him about finding the bag of jewelry. "At first, I was afraid it had fallen out of Tony's pocket, but then I realized it had been there for a while. Long enough to be almost covered by sand."

Gerald grunted. "I don't understand. How did it get there?"

"Only one way. The person pretending to be Olivia Hennesey also robbed the purses at the church. Your story about playing in the caves and pretending to hide your *bounty* made me realize the connection." Priscilla walked over to a large chest pushed up against the cave wall. When she opened it, she found it full of money and other items, including a long dress painted with blue fluorescent paint. Next to it was a black wig and a pale mask with black patches taped over the eyeholes. They looked as if they'd been cut from some kind of hosiery. That explained Trudy's insistence that the Weeping Woman had black holes for eyes.

Priscilla carefully picked up a particular item and showed it to Gerald. It was the cross Mildred had described that had been stolen from the museum. "I'm sure a lot of the items stolen from town down through the years are here." She leaned in and noticed something that really did surprise her. "Oh my."

"I guess I should have left town earlier." The voice came from the front of the cave. Priscilla stood up and turned to face Sylvia Peabody, who held a gun in her hand and was pointing it right at them.

"You might have made it," Priscilla said. She gestured toward the trunk. "Seems like you've been at this for a long time."

Sylvia snorted. "Years and years and years. Stealing from my boss in small amounts he wouldn't miss. Taking things from people who don't need them. All in anticipation of my escape from this horrible island."

"Some people think Martha's Vineyard is a wonderful place to live."

"Sure, if you have money," Sylvia snarled. "But not for the rest of us who have to struggle for every penny."

"You have a good job, Sylvia," Gerald said. "Why are you struggling?"

"If living in a little house and never really seeing the world is your dream, I guess this is a great life."

"But that's not what you want, is it, Sylvia?" Priscilla said.

"No. I planned to leave Tuesday for someplace tropical. I guess today will have to do. Sorry not to mention where I'm going. Just in case you two survive this."

"But why put your ill-gotten gain in a cave?" Gerald asked. "Where someone could easily find it?"

"Let me try to answer that, Sylvia," Priscilla said softly. "You had this hidden in your house, but when you put your house on the market, you needed to move it, right?"

Sylvia shrugged. "Right. I remembered the caves, searched until I found this one. It was sealed but not filled like the others. A few hours of digging gave me access. I felt pretty confident about it—and then you moved into the cottage." She glared at Priscilla as if she'd come to Martha's Vineyard just to ruin her plans.

"So you decided to scare me off. That way I wouldn't see you going in and out of the cave and get suspicious."

"Yeah, but instead of leaving, you started blabbing to everyone and their dog about the Weeping Woman." Sylvia glared at her. "I have to ask how you knew. I mean, about the cave. About me."

Priscilla smiled. "A lot of things. Oreo, for one. The other night it rained, but he was dry. He had to have found a place to get out of the rain. Then Gerald told me about the caves. It suddenly occurred to me that if there used to be a cave in the cliff right outside my house, it would be the perfect place for the Weeping Woman to go when she *disappeared.* From there it all fell into place. Chief Westin mentioned your *late* mother, so I knew you weren't going away to take care of her like you told me. And I also knew you were lying about Tony. You had to be the thief. I found a bag of jewelry you dropped on the beach. Why was it there? Because the Weeping Woman and the thief from the church were the same person. One by one, the clues pointed to only one person. You."

Priscilla prayed that Sylvia wouldn't hear the small sound behind her and quickly said, "Did Aleeta paint the Weeping Woman?"

Sylvia nodded. "Yes. I've been impersonating the Weeping Woman for a couple of months now, two or three nights a week, trying to scare you out of your house. But I had no way of knowing when you'd be looking at the cliff. So I decided I needed to get your attention. Aleeta was more than willing to cooperate. I know about a couple of pieces she sold that she claimed were painted by a famous New England artist, J. Alden Weir. She made a lot of money from them."

"But they were fakes?" Gerald said.

"Right. She needed the money to save her shop. I'd promised not to tell, but when I needed help chasing you out of town, I threatened to go to the police if she wouldn't do what I asked. She painted *The Weeping Woman* and then made sure you saw it. I was standing by, ready to make Olivia Hennesey come to life. If I'd actually met you before putting my plan into action, I would have realized you're not the kind of person to be frightened away by a ghost. I finally decided I had to give up the charade and leave while I still could." She shrugged. "Live and learn, I guess."

"I take that as a compliment," Priscilla said with a smile. "Is there anything else we need to know?"

"I don't think so. I intend to remove my money and leave you two trapped in this cave." She shook her gun at them. "I won't shoot you unless I have to."

"But you're willing to let us die in here?"

"I'm just going to tie you up. I'm pretty sure you won't get loose right away. That should give me time to get to my destination. Of course, in the end, whether you live or die will be up to you."

"Actually, it will be up to me," a man's voice said behind her.

Sylvia swung around to face Chief Westin, who stood at the cave's entrance with two other officers. Their guns were drawn.

"Put the gun down, Sylvia," the chief said. "There's no way out for you."

For a moment, it seemed as if Sylvia would ignore him and try one last desperate attempt to get away. But after glancing at the three armed officers who had her in their sights, she slowly lowered the gun. The chief stepped up and took it from her hand. Then he pushed her toward one of his officers. "Cuff her, April," he said. He walked over to where Gerald and Priscilla stood.

"Good thing you called me on the way here," he said, "but I have a few questions. Seems as if I should have heard from you a little sooner. Before things went this far."

Priscilla smiled at him. "It's a long story, Chief, and I know my cousins would agree with you. But at least you were here when it was important."

Gerald and Priscilla watched as Sylvia was led out of the cave in handcuffs. At first it seemed as if Oreo would follow them, but instead he stayed near his bed and stared up at Priscilla.

"You two need to leave now," the chief said gruffly. "This is a crime scene. We'll need to process it."

"Chief, I have a feeling you've actually got two crime scenes," Priscilla said.

Westin frowned. "What are you talking about?"

"Come over here." She led him and Gerald over to the trunk and pointed at something lying on top of its contents. "See that large sapphire ring?"

"Yeah."

"I've seen it before. It belonged to Jeremiah Hennesey." She pointed at an area of the cave where there was a large hole. "I'm pretty sure Sylvia buried this trunk when she moved it in here so no one would accidentally discover it. Then she dug it up because she was getting ready to leave town. My guess is that somewhere in that hole you'll also find the remains of Captain Jeremiah Hennesey, minus one sapphire ring."

"What do you mean?" Gerald asked.

"Looks to me like Captain Hennesey never left the Vineyard. I think Olivia took the money he stole, killed him, and buried him here."

"And left that valuable ring behind?"

"How could she take it?" she replied. "Too many people knew it belonged to her husband. There was even a picture in the newspaper of the captain wearing the ring. Even though she was going to Boston, it was too big a risk. Not many men wore large blue sapphire rings. Taking it with her was just too dangerous. She had no choice but to leave it with him. She started a new life while Jeremiah and his ring remained in this cave for all these years."

Chief Westin shook his head. "I don't usually get everything handed to me on a silver platter like this. We'll have to make sure all your information checks out, but I think the Weeping Woman has finally retired, and a lot of people are going to be happy to get some of their stolen property returned."

"And I'm sure Elmer McBroom will be thrilled to get his money back."

The chief nodded. "He's wanted to retire for a while, but he didn't think he could afford it. He had no idea Sylvia was stealing from him all this time. Now he can retire in style."

"By the way, Chief," Priscilla said, "I have a small bag with some of the jewelry from the robbery at my house. I'll turn it over to you right away. I found it on the beach after Sylvia dropped it."

The chief clucked his tongue. "Should I ask why you didn't notify me immediately when you found it?"

Priscilla gave him a sheepish smile. "You could ask..."

He sighed. "Just bring it to me as soon as you can."

"I will. Thanks, Chief."

Gerald took Priscilla's arm and started to lead her out of the cave, but she pulled back. "Wait a minute." She knelt down and scooped Oreo up in her arms. "We need to take care of this little hero. After all, he's the one who really solved this mystery."

Gerald laughed. "I don't think that's true, but you're right about one thing. He definitely needs to be rewarded." He picked up the pet bed and the bowls. "No matter what else she did, Sylvia was kind to this little guy."

"Yes, she was. Most people who do wrong things aren't completely bad. Sylvia loved Oreo, and he loved her too. In the end, he kept her from doing something horribly wrong. I hope one day she'll realize how much he helped her."

They stepped out of the cave and slowly made their way back down to the beach.

"So what will you do with Oreo?" Gerald asked. "Are you taking him home?"

Priscilla shook her head. "I don't think so. I know a museum director who needs a friend, and I think Oreo would make the perfect companion."

"I think that sounds like a good plan," he said. "I like happy endings."

"I do too," she said softly as Oreo rubbed his head on her chin and purred.

CHAPTER THIRTY-SIX

I think it's a great success, don't you?" Trudy said, looking around the gym packed with little trick-or-treaters and their parents. She and Priscilla were taking a much-needed break after helping run the beanbag toss and giving out candy.

"I really do. We're certainly putting all our volunteers to work."

Priscilla smiled at the extra help that had come in at the last minute. Trudy, who accurately predicted they might have a larger attendance than expected, had gotten on the phone and called in the troops. Joan, Gail, and Uncle Hugh were painting little faces. Uncle Hugh was having a great time, and the kids loved him.

Tony and his new friend Derrick were making balloon animals while Phil and Maria ran the cake walk. Gerald had volunteered for the fishing booth. When the kids threw their line over the top of the display painted with water and fish, he would attach prizes to the little plastic hook on their line. When he tugged on the line, the children would squeal and pull in their catch. Frankly, Gerald seemed to be having as much fun as they were.

Although no one expected any further thefts from the kitchen, Pastor Tim had elected to stand guard. A few of the young people sat with him in the kitchen and talked while they ate cookies and drank punch.

"So Sylvia is in jail?" Trudy asked.

Priscilla nodded. "I really feel sorry for her."

"I don't." Trudy made a noise of disgust. "She robbed that poor Elmer McBroom for years. And what about everything else she took?"

"I know. Thankfully, everything will be returned after the trial. I'm so happy that Gail will finally have Aunt Marjorie's ring."

"I am too. That ring means a lot to her." Trudy shook her head. "I'm surprised we didn't find the hiding spot. We cleaned that place from top to bottom before you moved in."

"It wasn't easy to see."

Trudy put her arm around Priscilla. "Nonsense. We just weren't sleuthy enough."

"Sleuthy? I'm not sure that's a word."

"I'm declaring it a Priscilla Latham Grant word. You are the sleuthiest person I've ever known." Trudy squeezed Priscilla's shoulders before withdrawing her arm.

"Well, thank you. I accept your new word."

"You'd better. So what happens next? Not to Sylvia—I know she's going away for a long time. But all the other people involved one way or another in this thing."

"Well, Aleeta had to contact the person she sold those fake paintings to. She promised to return their money. They haven't decided if they'll file charges against her or not. As far as Jeremiah and Olivia are concerned, the police found old remains inside the cave. I'm certain they belong to the captain."

"You really think Olivia killed him?"

Priscilla shrugged. "We may never know. Remember that his ship went missing. Maybe he drowned and Olivia buried his body in the cave before she left with the money he took. Either she stood on that cliff night after night, putting on a show so people would think she killed herself and not look for her when she left town—or she really was grieving. Either way, she needed people to believe she was dead so she could start a new life."

"You know what? I'm glad we'll never have the answer. I'm going to believe they planned to leave together, but Jeremiah died accidentally, and Olivia grieved so much that she buried him and left the Vineyard."

Priscilla smiled and nodded. It was a better story than what she suspected was true. Trudy had conveniently forgotten Jeremiah's girlfriend. She imagined the truth was much darker. It was more likely that Olivia had killed Jeremiah, taken the money, and hidden his boat so she could use it to sail to Boston. When she arrived, she probably ditched it or sank it so no one would ever know what really happened. But there was no one left to prosecute and no reason to contact the family. A dead end on their genealogy chart was a lot more palatable than telling them their ancestor was a murderer.

"I called Myrna Holtman and apologized," Priscilla said. "She was very gracious."

"I hope you didn't tell her you'd allow them to include the Weeping Woman in their tour."

"Well…"

"Priscilla! Really!"

"Relax. Only on the Saturday before Halloween. One time a year. I can deal with that."

Trudy sighed and shook her head.

Priscilla knew Trudy didn't agree with her decision, but that was okay with her. She didn't need everyone to see things her way. Right or wrong, she'd bridged the gap with Myrna and felt much better about it.

"Did you ever find out why Norman Whitaker offered you so much for your property?" Trudy asked.

"He really believes it's worth that much. Maybe it is. I don't really know." Priscilla shrugged. "We live on the Vineyard. Tourists might be willing to pay a high price for what we take for granted."

"Maybe so, but I can't believe *you're* taking it for granted yet."

Priscilla shook her head. "Oh, believe me, I'm not. I love it here."

"Even with all the weird things you've been through?"

"Yeah. Even with that."

"I'm assuming Sylvia decided to point the finger of suspicion at Norman as a way to keep you from looking too closely at her," Trudy said.

"Not just Norman. She also tried to divert attention to Tony. Thankfully, she didn't get away with it. She was hoping to keep us looking in the wrong direction so she could make her getaway."

"I bet Mildred was thrilled to get that cross back." Trudy looked around the gym. "By the way, I thought she was going to help tonight. I haven't seen her."

Priscilla grinned. "She's babysitting. Jake and Oreo are having a playdate. I asked her to watch Jake when she called to say she wasn't coming. According to her, Oreo needs more time to acclimate to her place before she leaves him alone. She was happy to have Jake come over, since he and Oreo are such great friends."

"Oh, come on. That cat isn't nervous about anything."

Priscilla nodded. "I think his owner is the one with the nerves, although Oreo may have a problem dealing with his new name."

"Which is?"

"Hiacoomes."

"You're kidding."

Priscilla shook her head and laughed. "I'm not."

"That was a stroke of genius. Putting Mildred and Oreo—sorry—Hiacoomes together."

"It really wasn't that much of a stretch. Mildred mentioned losing her cat the other day. I could tell she really missed her."

Trudy searched Priscilla's face. "Admit it. You were kind of hoping she'd refuse to take Oreo in, and you'd be forced to take him home with you."

"I don't know," she said slowly. "I would have loved to have him, but to be honest, Jake and I are still finding our way. I don't think he needs the competition right now."

"You're probably right." Trudy looked at her watch. "Another hour, and we're out of here. How about stopping by Candy's before we go home?"

Priscilla snorted. "We're drowning in candy, cake, and cookies, and you want to go to Candy's?"

"Yeah."

Priscilla sighed. "Okay."

Both women burst out laughing.

Joan came up to them, pulled over a chair, and plopped down. "Wow. I'm tired. Gail and I were talking. How about going to Candy's after this is over?"

As Priscilla and Trudy shrieked with laughter, Joan looked at them like they'd finally lost their minds.

AUTHOR LETTER

Dear Reader,

It was so much fun to write *Maiden of the Mist*—my very first "ghost story"! I love our setting in Martha's Vineyard. The New England area is a beautiful part of our country, one that I am particularly drawn to, but this is the first time I've had a chance to use it as a setting in a book. I also adore lighthouses. (Who doesn't?) If I close my eyes, I can see myself living in Priscilla's cottage and watching her incredible lighthouse send its welcoming beam through the night whether the skies are clear or stormy. What a comfort it must have been to sailors on rough seas trying to find their way home!

In *Maiden of the Mist*, Priscilla not only had a mystery to solve, but she also met a young man who faced tragedy. I hope readers enjoyed finding out the truth about the legend of the Weeping Woman and were also touched by Tony's story and Priscilla's stubborn commitment to believe in him.

So, welcome back to Misty Harbor and our wonderful series! I pray you've enjoyed your visit!

Nancy Mehl

ABOUT THE AUTHOR

Nancy Mehl is a best-selling, award-winning author who lives in Missouri with her husband, Norman, and her Puggle, Watson. She's authored almost thirty books. Besides working on Mysteries of Martha's Vineyard, she is currently writing a new series for Bethany House Publishers based on the US Marshals. The first book, *Fatal Frost*, in her Defenders of Justice series released in November 2016. The second book, *Dark Deception*, hit store shelves in June 2017. Book three, *Blind Betrayal*, will be released in the spring of 2018.

All of Nancy's novels have an added touch—something for your spirit as well as your soul. "I welcome the opportunity to share my faith through my writing," Nancy says. "God is number one in my life. I wouldn't be writing at all if I didn't believe that this is what He's called me to do. I hope everyone who reads my books will walk away with the most important message I can give them: God is good, and He loves you more than you can imagine. He has a good plan for your life, and there is nothing you can't overcome with His help."

Readers can learn more about Nancy through her website: nancymehl.com. She is part of The Suspense Sisters at suspensesisters .blogspot.com, along with several other popular suspense authors. She is also very active on Facebook.

AN ARMCHAIR TOUR OF
MARTHA'S VINEYARD

Special Events of Martha's Vineyard

In *Maiden of the Mist*, I highlighted an October event in Martha's Vineyard, Fall for the Arts, a month-long celebration of the depth and diversity of the island's arts and culture. Visitors can stroll through unique shops and stores displaying some of the best and most creative work done by island artists.

There are quite a few special events in Martha's Vineyard throughout the year, including Built on Stilts, a dance festival that takes place in August. Participants come not only from the island, but also from major dance companies in New York and Boston as well as several other cities. Other events include Shakespeare in the Park, presented by the Vineyard Playhouse; the Native American Artisans Festival in July; the Sail Martha's Vineyard regatta; Grand Illumination, a magical evening at the gingerbread cottages; and the Martha's Vineyard Wind Festival, which includes kite-fliers in friendly competition with one another in categories like highest-flying and best wind sculpture.

Martha's Vineyard is not only a lovely place to visit because of its incredible beauty, but there are events for everyone's taste! To learn more, visit: http://www.mvy.com/arts-culture/festivals.aspx

SOMETHING DELICIOUS FROM
OUR SEASIDE FRIENDS

Priscilla's Easy Coconut Macaroons

⅔ cup all-purpose flour

5½ cups flaked coconut

¼ teaspoon salt

1 (14-ounce) can sweetened
   condensed milk

2 teaspoons vanilla extract

Preheat oven to 350 degrees. Line cookie sheets with parchment paper or aluminum foil.

In a large bowl, stir together the flour, coconut, and salt. Add the sweetened condensed milk and vanilla and combine, by hand, until well blended. Use an ice cream scoop to drop dough onto the prepared cookie sheets. Cookies should be about golf-ball size.

Bake for twelve to fifteen minutes, until coconut is toasted.

Read on for a sneak peek of another exciting book
in the series Mysteries of Martha's Vineyard!

Making Waves
by Tricia Goyer & Cara Putman

A salty breeze wafted through Priscilla's open car window as she drove through the storybook village of Vineyard Haven. It was warmer today than it had been the last couple of weeks. November had blown in with a chilling fury, and Priscilla was thankful for the sun and the respite from the frigid temperatures. November had also brought sad memories: grief over Gary's death, thoughts of their last anniversary, and even further back memories of her last visit to Martha's Vineyard with her mother. That last Thanksgiving, when she was only eight years old, had brought about a dispute that had kept her from the island for fifty years—a feud between her mother and aunt that she didn't completely understand, but which time had chipped away at like the waves against a rocky outcropping.

Trying to push those gray thoughts from her mind, Priscilla hummed "Boogie Woogie Bugle Boy" and waved her finger to the beat as she pulled up in front of the East Shore Historical Museum. With a smile she parked, rolled up her window, and then got out and moved to the other side of the car to grab the bags of paper goods she had set on the passenger seat. She pushed the passenger door shut with her foot and shifted her bags as she walked up the sidewalk to the small museum.

When Mildred Pearson had asked for help setting up for the one hundredth birthday celebration for one of the town's special citizens, Priscilla had quickly agreed. It felt good to know her friend was willing to ask her for help, and Priscilla looked forward to meeting the honored guest.

Residents of Martha's Vineyard considered Deanie Spangler, a World War II veteran, something of a local hero after she received the Congressional Gold Medal from the president almost a decade ago. Now it was time to honor this woman with a party to celebrate her milestone birthday. To get in the mood, Priscilla had listened to classic songs from World War II, and the catchy melodies wouldn't leave her thoughts. *He had a boogie style that no one else could play...* Her finger continued to shake as she moved to the building, and it amazed her that Deanie had actually played an important part in the history Priscilla had only read about.

The museum building was a sunny yellow Queen Anne Victorian tucked slightly off the road. Priscilla smiled as she noted the small Happy Birthday banner that ruffled in the breeze from its post at the top of the porch. She climbed the wide, pale gray steps and crossed the old-fashioned porch to the front door of the converted house. The door opened as she shifted the bags again so she could twist the knob.

The moment she entered, she saw Mildred wore her gray hair up in its normal twist and was dressed in a nice pair of navy slacks paired with a cashmere sweater set in a lovely coral. Mildred was one of the few women who could make Priscilla feel petite. "There you are. I was beginning to worry."

Priscilla held up the bags. "I have everything you asked for." She glanced at her watch. "And I'm not even a minute later than I told you I'd arrive." Mildred was such a stickler for punctuality. Priscilla had learned to arrive a few minutes early to any appointment with her friend. She entered the museum then turned to Mildred. "You look nice."

"Once in a while it's appropriate not to wear period clothes." Mildred turned and walked briskly toward the reception area. "I have several tables set up over here. I also have a few chairs, but we need to organize them. Deanie will need a chair, and we'll want to have a few rows for her friends."

"How about setting them up as conversation groups? There's not a formal program, is there?"

"No, it's supposed to be informal, so we can try groups as long as they fit in the space."

Priscilla set the bags on the table Mildred indicated and then started pulling out the tablecloths. It only took a moment to cover the tables. Then the women worked together to arrange the plates, cups, and utensils.

Mildred indicated the first table. "We'll have the cake and punch bowl there. Then that table will have the basket for cards and any small gifts people bring."

Priscilla nodded as she scattered a fall-colored confetti of reds, oranges, and yellows across the table. "It will be nice."

"I hope so." Mildred sighed and cocked a hip against a table. "Deanie's family has been part of our community for generations. She's earned an evening of celebration, but the family insisted on keeping it small."

"I imagine many of her friends are gone."

"True." Mildred stepped from the table and headed to the small kitchen. "Did I tell you she's donating her Congressional Gold Medal as well as her WASP uniform and paraphernalia to the museum? We're going to set up a permanent display."

"That's exciting. Why did she receive the medal again?"

"Here, let me show you." Mildred set a pitcher of water on the food table then led Priscilla to a display table Priscilla hadn't noticed. "She received the award for her years of service as a Woman's Air Force Service Pilot. Until she was honored in 2009, many of us didn't know she'd served as a WASP."

"She was a pilot?"

Mildred nodded. "I've heard that Deanie's first flights before the war were shuttle flights from the mainland to the island and taking the occasional visitor up for an aerial tour. Then a letter showed up inviting her to apply for a new division of female pilots. I guess it was hard back then to find enough people with the required minimum flight hours, so they started asking women."

"I've always thought that would have been a fascinating way to serve."

"You'd never know all that she's accomplished by talking to Deanie, but I agree. She downplays that she did anything special, but I think that's a characteristic of her generation." Mildred slipped off a velvet cloth covering the display case. Inside was a shelf with a letter that looked like the invitation to apply for the special group. Next to it was a scrapbook, and below that a uniform and hat were arranged. And next to the uniform and hat was a shining gold medal, larger than a silver dollar. On it was an image of three pilots in the foreground in flight uniforms walking toward their aircraft, the letters WASP at the top. Tears pricked Priscilla's eyes. The display represented a woman's life, a woman's sacrifice, and finally a woman's honor.

"The other side of the medal features the three types of aircraft flown by the WASPs: trainers, fighters, and bombers. Deanie told me specifically which types of aircraft they were, but I've forgotten. I'm sure she'll tell you if you ask." Mildred tilted her head and looked at the display case with pride. "I have a special tray for the medal. The case is designed to let us slip everything easily from the back. Deanie wanted those attending tonight to have the opportunity to see it up close."

Priscilla ran her fingers along the edge of the display. Her father-in-law had been a World War II veteran, but he never wanted to talk about it. Gary had told her Clifford had experienced so many painful things that sharing them was the same as reliving them. "It's exciting she's willing to share her medal with everyone like that. What a true gift."

"Yes." Mildred winked. "You'll have to ask her about how she received it. And who she received it from."

Priscilla smiled, knowing it wouldn't be hard to have a conversation with Deanie, especially since she'd been honored by the president. Priscilla had so many questions about what Deanie had done and seen during the war.

Mildred glanced at her watch. "The guests will start arriving anytime. Will you watch the table for me during the party? I don't want anyone sticking their fingers in the cake or getting too close to the medal." Mildred cocked an eyebrow. "They can look, but let's make sure they don't touch."

"Absolutely." Priscilla took another look at the display then settled the velvet cloth back in place. "Anything else you need me to do right now?"

"Just turn on the music. I have a Glenn Miller CD ready to go. I figured that will be something Deanie will enjoy. Then if you could check out front and see if our guest of honor has arrived, I'd appreciate it."

"Sure." Priscilla stopped near the desk and turned on the music. Soon the strains of big band tunes filled the space, and she headed toward the front windows. Her eyes widened as she looked out.

"Mildred," she called. "Are you sure it's a secret? Because something's got the attention of the town." Several cars had joined hers, and others were pulling into the lot. "How many people did you say we expected?" All down the street there seemed to be a long line of arriving vehicles.

They aren't all coming here, are they?

"Twenty or thirty guests."

"I think you need to revise that number." Priscilla did a quick count as people exited their cars. She recognized one of the guests immediately. An older woman wearing pink with tight gray curls was being helped from a car into a wheelchair. "It looks like Deanie's here, and from what I can see from the people parking, we've already exceeded thirty people, and more cars are arriving."

"Oh my." Mildred hurried to the window and stood next to Priscilla. Her mouth dropped open when she saw the full parking lot with people streaming in from all directions.

Priscilla also noticed a man with a camera hanging around his neck and a notebook in hand. Had the media arrived?

"Oh dear. Even the newspaper is here," Mildred mumbled under her breath, confirming Priscilla's guess. "The family wanted it to be a small event."

Priscilla placed a hand to her cheek. "Who else knew?"

"I don't know. I mentioned it to Jedd Patterson, the local reporter who's making his way inside. I asked him to mention the new display in an article next week, but I made sure he knew today's birthday celebration was a private event." Mildred sighed. "I specifically told him not to let the word out yet. The last thing I wanted was to overwhelm Deanie with a large crowd—she is a hundred years old after all."

"Maybe we can send away the uninvited guests?" Priscilla watched as the first group came through the door.

"Good idea." Mildred stepped outside, with Priscilla right behind her, and raised her hands. "I'm sorry. Did you each receive an invitation to this event? It's a private, family affair."

A tall man with salt-and-pepper hair shook his head. "That's not what I heard."

"Me either," said the stocky woman next to him.

"I'm sorry there's been a miscommunication, but I really must insist you leave." Mildred took advantage of every inch of height she had.

Joan Abernathy, Priscilla's cousin, slowed where she was on the sidewalk. "Are you sure? There are so many of us here to celebrate. Deanie is considered a sweet friend by so many on the island."

"I really must insist." Mildred stiffened her posture, and Priscilla imagined she was ready to defend the right and wrong of the party.

Just then a tall young man in his midthirties worked his way up the sidewalk, pushing Deanie in a wheelchair. His jacket was exquisitely tailored and layered over a cable wool sweater, the perfect relaxed yet formal Martha's Vineyard fall look. Add in his loafers and pressed khakis, and he looked stiff next to the hot pink bling that Deanie wore.

"Are all these people here for me? How wonderful!" Deanie Spangler was a sparrow of a woman as she sat in the wheelchair. Her posture was still straight, but her skin was fragile as tracing paper stretching across slim limbs. Her blue eyes sparkled beneath her cap of snow-white hair. "I love a good party."

Priscilla glanced at the man pushing the wheelchair. "Would you like everyone to stay?"

The woman of honor nodded before the younger man could say a word. "I've always loved a big celebration. The more the merrier! I've attended some amazing shindigs during my time, but rarely was the party for me." She clapped her hands with delight.

Her smile lit her face from within, stretching the hot pink lipstick where it had slid into the wrinkles around her mouth.

Mildred looked around. "Well then, let's have them stay." She placed a hand on Priscilla's arm as she leaned toward her. "Even though it's warmer today, too bad it's still too cold to keep the party outside." She sighed as she glanced toward the kitchen. "And pray we have enough cake and punch. Maybe not everyone will want some."

The crowd of people continued to stream through the door and chat with each other, but one voice rose above them all.

"Let's get me out of this wheelchair and to a place where I can enjoy everyone." Deanie's words were stated with a regal air, but Priscilla noted the fun behind them.

Priscilla nodded toward the door. "Maybe we could station you near the door but away from the cold air. Then you could say hello to everyone as they arrive."

"That's perfect, dear." Deanie turned to the man pushing her. "Andrew, I'd like that to happen."

"All right, Aunt Deanie, but I think you might be more comfortable if you stayed in the chair."

"Shows how rarely you've ridden in one of these contraptions!" Deanie reached up and patted his hand. "You take good care of me, Andy, but I insist. I will not spend the evening in this chair."

Mildred leaned close to Priscilla's ear. "That's her great-nephew Andrew Wright. Deanie doesn't have any children, but thankfully Andrew has always been there for her. He lives near the retirement home where she lives and helped plan the party." Then, offering a smile that Priscilla knew was forced, Mildred turned to the pair. "Then let's get you settled. And oh, what a lovely surprise all these extra guests are!"

With commanding steps, Mildred guided Andrew to park the wheelchair in a corner near the parlor entrance. Together they helped Deanie toward a more comfortable padded chair that Priscilla had grabbed from the elegant parlor. Once Deanie was settled, Mildred turned back to Priscilla. "If you could stay near Deanie and also try to keep an eye on the display table, I'd appreciate it. I'm going to see if I can figure out how to cut the cake to make it go further."

"Sure." Priscilla wouldn't mind the chance to talk with Deanie, but it only took minutes before the elderly woman was surrounded by well-wishers. She slipped away every few minutes to check the table and then eased back to see if the guest of honor needed anything.

Deanie allowed each well-wisher to shake her birdlike hands or kiss her wrinkled cheeks. Delight brightened her eyes as person after person wished her a happy birthday and conversed with her. Most of the visitors were from town, and they made it clear Deanie was well loved. Others seemed to have heard about the event as they had enjoyed their days—visitors who'd come to Martha's Vineyard to catch the last of the brilliant fall colors. They mostly wanted to see what the fuss was about but were delighted to be introduced to a woman who played such an important part in United States history.

Mildred stepped in front of her desk and clapped her hands. Priscilla gave a shrill whistle, and the voices stilled.

"Thank you to everyone for coming." Mildred smiled at
assemblage. "It's a delight to have you here as we honor Dea
Spangler."

Priscilla slipped into the small kitchen to get the lighter,
then she lit the ten candles clustered around Deanie's name o
large sheet cake.

Deanie clapped her hands in delight. "Is all that for me?

"Let's sing 'Happy Birthday,' and then our guest of hon
make a wish," Mildred instructed.

"And blow out the candles." Deanie tittered as she edged
closer, her great-nephew keeping a close eye on her, looking ready
to launch forward to grab her if needed.

Priscilla stepped toward her. "Let me help you."

A moment later, as everyone sang the classic birthday song,
Deanie stood, leaning on Priscilla and Andrew, her grin revealing
perfect dentures. As soon as the song ended, she shuffled to the
table and then blew out the candles in two attempts. Everyone
applauded, and she took a small bow before sitting again.

Mildred waved for the crowd's attention. "Feel free to grab
cake and punch and continue to say hello to Deanie. After a bit,
we'll unveil a surprise."

People strolled by the still-covered display case without slow-
ing, eager to get their cake and punch. As the bowl of sugary drink
disappeared, Priscilla filled it with more punch. She kept an eye on
the supplies and nibbled her bottom lip as she wondered if the cake
and punch would last for everyone. One by one, people stopped to
say a word to Deanie and then took their places in the line.

mix well First 2 ingredents
then add t. of Baking soda ·
leave on 15 min b4 rinsing
with w. kewarm water

Instead of overwhelming her, the crowd imparted energy to Deanie. The longer they chatted, the more she perked up and glowed. Finally, thirty minutes later than planned, Mildred regained the crowd's attention. Andrew had wandered off from his great-aunt, and Priscilla tried to keep a closer eye on Deanie.

"It's time for a presentation the museum is thrilled about." Mildred stepped through the crowd and stopped in front of the covered display.

"And it's one I'm delighted to make." Deanie gestured toward Priscilla. "Will you help me stand?"

"Of course." After Deanie was standing, Priscilla helped her to the display case, still looking for Andrew. He was nowhere to be seen.

Mildred beamed at the centenarian. "Please remove the cloth."

Deanie grinned. "With pleasure." She tugged off the velvet cover.

Then her eyes widened, and she gasped and clutched her chest. The color drained from the older woman's face, and Priscilla wrapped her arms around Deanie's waist as her knees gave out. It took every ounce of strength Priscilla had to keep Deanie from tumbling to the floor.

A NOTE FROM THE EDITORS

We hope you enjoyed Mysteries of Martha's Vineyard, published by the Books and Inspirational Media Division of Guideposts, a nonprofit organization that touches millions of lives every day through products and services that inspire, encourage, help you grow in your faith, and celebrate God's love.

Thank you for making a difference with your purchase of this book, which helps fund our many outreach programs to military personnel, prisons, hospitals, nursing homes, and educational institutions.

We also create many useful and uplifting online resources. Visit Guideposts.org to read true stories of hope and inspiration, access OurPrayer network, sign up for free newsletters, download free e-books, join our Facebook community, and follow our stimulating blogs.

To learn about other Guideposts publications, including the best-selling devotional *Daily Guideposts*, go to Guideposts.org/Shop, call (800) 932-2145, or write to Guideposts, PO Box 5815, Harlan, Iowa 51593.

Sign up for the
Guideposts Fiction Newsletter
and stay up-to-date on the books you love!

You'll get sneak peeks of new releases, recommendations from other Guideposts readers, and special offers just for you . . .
and it's FREE!

Just go to Guideposts.org/Newsletters today to sign up.

Guideposts®   Visit Guideposts.org/Shop
or call (800) 932-2145

Find more inspiring fiction in these best-loved Guideposts series!

Mysteries of Martha's Vineyard

Come to the shores of this quaint and historic island and dig into a cozy mystery. When a recent widow inherits a lighthouse just off the coast of Massachusetts, she finds exciting adventures, new friends, and renewed hope.

Tearoom Mysteries

Mix one stately Victorian home, a charming lakeside town in Maine, and two adventurous cousins with a passion for tea and hospitality. Add a large scoop of intriguing mystery and sprinkle generously with faith, family, and friends, and you have the recipe for Tearoom Mysteries.

Sugarcreek Amish Mysteries

Be intrigued by the suspense and joyful "aha!" moments in these delightful stories. Each book in the series brings together two women of vastly different backgrounds and traditions, who realize there's much more to the "simple life" than meets the eye.

Mysteries of Silver Peak

Escape to the historic mining town of Silver Peak, Colorado, and discover how one woman's love of antiques helps her solve mysteries buried deep in the town's checkered past.

Patchwork Mysteries

Discover that life's little mysteries often have a common thread in a series where every novel contains an intriguing whodunit centered around a quilt located in a beautiful New England town.

To learn more about these books, visit Guideposts.org/Shop